COL
OSS
US

COLOSSUS

A NOVEL

ROSS BARKAN

Arcade Publishing • New York

Arcade Publishing books may be purchased in bulk at special discounts for sales promotion, corporate gifts, fund-raising, or educational purposes. Special editions can also be created to specifications. For details, contact the Special Sales Department, Arcade Publishing, 307 Fifth Avenue, 4th Floor, New York, NY 10016 or arcade@skyhorsepublishing.com.

Arcade Publishing® is a registered trademark of Skyhorse Publishing, Inc.®, a Delaware corporation.

Visit our website at www.arcadepub.com.

First Edition

10 9 8 7 6 5 4 3 2 1

Library of Congress Cataloging-in-Publication Data
is available on file.

Jacket design by David Ter-Avanesyan

Print ISBN: 978-1-64821-177-5
Ebook ISBN: 978-1-64821-178-2

Printed in the United States of America

For Debbie

All we really want is to get to the point where the past can explain nothing about us and we can get on with life.

—Richard Ford, *The Sportswriter*

PART I

1

I sit and watch. This is what I do.

There goes Big Landry Shocker, lifting us off. I can listen to Big Landry for hours, his cumulus-gray mustache flapping, a little Fu Manchu sag on the ends. He's purpling now, really feeling it, and I steeple my fingers and wait. He speaks in two or three-minute clips, and it's the stamina that grates or impresses, depending on what station of life you've slid into, what's got you by the throat.

"Moses said to Pharaoh, let my people go, but he didn't stop there. No he did not!"

Big Landry has always done the reading. He reads almost as much as me, and with a desperation to please that can, ultimately, soothe to varying degrees, as his reddened, nubby finger stabs at the pages.

"We think this is a world of freedom, freedom, freedom. We all want the messages to be for us. They're not just for us. There's a word you have to follow. You have to *read*. Moses wasn't talking about freedom, the freedom to do *whatever it is you want*. Here's what he said: 'Thus saith the lord God of Israel, Let my people go, that they may hold a feast unto me in the wilderness.' Feast *unto me in the wilderness*. Think on that. God was not telling Moses and Aaron to do whatever it is you like to do, to run free. It was about worship of Him. It was about the hard work of prayer. That's right."

Big Landry exhales. He's satisfied, so I'm satisfied. Big Landry is a locus of gravity, if never a neutral force than performing, like gravity, all possible outcomes. There is malevolence in Big Landry, who built Big Landry's Furniture Palace from scratch—or a very generous business loan from a cousin who was an executive at First County thirty years ago—and advertises his wares with enormous and wildly colorful signage on the southbound side of 127. It is an American malevolence, and I can appreciate that—he is capable, more than anyone else at Trinity, of raw destabilization, a stray comment mucking an afternoon, a sidewinding initiative at Men's Group that turns the whole batch sour. It is this malevolence, more than his money, that truly intimidates. But he is capable of great love too, like a henchman of Santa, and he can be a whirl of hugs and kisses at Christmastime, for adults and children alike.

"Pharaoh would not let them worship. Pharaoh said no. Pharaoh sought control. We all have personal Pharaohs. We all have the spirit of Pharaoh hovering over our life."

"Ah yes, Landry, I think I understand," replies Gregg Eggles, who surely does not. Gregg, one of my favorites, is an earnest Navy veteran and father of three, two boys and a girl, with an ex-wife he doesn't see much of anymore. He is here with Tamara, his new wife, who is seven years younger than he is and only on her first marriage—therefore operating at a distinct disadvantage. I've said this to her more than a few times. Gregg drives a semi and makes good money, but he's on the road for large, painful chunks of the year. Tamara, then, comes to church alone, and sits quietly as the boys talk up a storm about Christ.

Next week, I am going to sell a nice cabin up north to Gregg.

"For alcoholics, the pharaoh is the love of drink—the addiction. For drug addicts, Pharaoh is begging them for one more taste, one more hit. For adulterers, more adultery," Big Landry charges on, as if Gregg never spoke at all.

I know Gregg admires Big Landry, just as Tamara admires Big Landry's money and hopes, one day, Gregg can come into some of his own. It is almost plausible. Driving a semi is good money now, the robots haven't come for the gig as promised, and if Gregg sticks with it another year, he will be into the six figures. Around here, in Pine Haven, that makes you rich. He could even get into property management. After the pandemic, real estate became the golem awoken from its long slumber. What a time, even with the surging rates. For decades, housing here was practically Japanese, hardly appreciating at all, little grandmothers moldering in three-bedrooms that had only tacked on $5,000 in value in twenty years, if that. The recession knocked the prices back hard, and it took the oddity of a worldwide plague to kick them up to levels I had, in my business, longed for quietly, not quite begging on the level of prayer but, to be frank, coming rather close. Now it's May, cabin season, and Gregg is sure he's found the place for Tamara, tucked into Six Lakes. Gregg is sure because I'm sure. He's sold on it, just on the virtual tour, and I plan to take him up next week to close the deal.

"It's not easy to conquer our sins," says Gertrude Breckenridge. "God doesn't make it easy. He wants, I think, for us to struggle."

That's my cue. I stifle a smile—it's always hard to keep from smiling here—and take a final survey of my group before I speak. It's Sunday, nearing 10:45, and we're in the home stretch of our morning meeting before services begin. I won't lie and say this is my favorite part of the job, huddling with our twenty to twenty-five most dedicated parishioners to wrangle over particulars of the Old Testament as Big Landry insists on treating his elementary insights as pathbreaking profundities, but I do enjoy bundling it all. That's partially my role, to be a mediator and a master of agglomeration, summing up sensibly what was said and adding my fine-tuned insights.

I'm sitting up straighter now, my gaze firm, and my lips open slowly, making my practiced "o." Sometimes, in moments like these, I wonder if I'm too unlike them, too far apart—but then I remember we're all here together, at Trinity, and I'm collecting a commission. I've committed to them that I would grow their flock and, indeed, I have.

"Struggle, yes, Gertrude raises an excellent point," I begin. I feel the warmth of her agreement, my acknowledgment of her, and the way this has flattered her sensibilities. There's a rising action in the long, wood-lined room, little curlicues of heat hanging invisibly above us all. Rich sunlight slashes through the awning windows, leaving half of us, including Gertrude and I, in cool shadow. I catch it in my periphery, a watercolor painting of floating hydrangeas ninety degrees from where I sit, hung there by the pastor who preceded me, the late Abraham Whitson. I consider when it would be appropriate to replace it. I have ideas for this meeting room, some of them grand, and I have to weigh how much I can do without upsetting the balance of old and young, those with fond memories of Pastor Whitson, who preached here through three presidential administrations, and those who know nothing of him, only as a face on a gilded plaque and the recipient of a proclamation from the old Republican governor. "Jesus intended us to *struggle*."

I sigh, as if this is a surprise, or unwelcome news I now must deliver. Big Landry is on board. And if Big Landry is on board, there's the thirty percent of Trinity that may matter most, those who land at the upper third of Pine Haven's, Sebastian's, and Orchard's varied and highly stratified income brackets. Here's a bit of honesty, before I go on: when I got to Trinity, it was a poor church. Or a *poorer* church, I should say. It struggled against Good Shepherd, Orchard Church of God, St. Anne's, West Superior Christian, United Methodist, Nazarene, or even Four Square, which I'm fairly certain is a cult run out of a clapboard house near Pine Haven's city limit. We were beating the Mormons, but that was about it and not much to brag about since Mormonism has long been on the decline in the area, mirroring the downslope of the Tigers and Pistons. We were not poor in spirit, but we were lacking in funds. Funds for upkeep, funds to pay a pastor—more importantly, though, funds that parishioners could theoretically command.

The potential for funds matters almost as much as the funds themselves. It matters because potential is the same as perception, and perception rapidly hardens into reality when you're dealing with town folk. What you appear as is what you are, and if you aren't careful, this appearance will never change. It will become a kind of feudalism, binding you into place for generations, and cursing your descendants.

I was determined, when I got to Trinity, to not let that happen. And that meant coming to Big Landry personally, laying my hat on the counter of his office at the furniture palace, and making my pitch, little stars in my eyes. If word got out Big Landry was ready for the word of God as it should be, all would follow.

"Christianity is not easy. When you sign up to walk with Jesus, you accept the burden of that knowledge, that wonder. You accept and understand what it is to struggle and suffer. Consider the martyrdom, the bloodshed. The followers of Jesus were mocked, ridiculed, spat on, and slaughtered. It was not enough to be kind. Kindness is not deliverance. Kindness is not enough."

I draw in breath for a pleasurable, if grave, affect. I can feel Gertrude's gaze on me and Big Landry's wandering eye ranging between Gertrude and myself. His wife died a decade ago and he never remarried, pledging to carry on her memory to his grave. This, I can understand—it's not as if I'd ever want to replace my own family—and I can admire his dedication, if I ever decide it's genuine. But this has yet to happen, knowing Big Landry's appetites, and understanding what a man born around the midcentury mark may agitate for, even with a belly long poured over the belt buckle and eyes gone half-astral.

"In a life like this one, struggles are here to test you. You do not reach eternity without struggle. Consider Paul, whom I will talk about later today, when we're with the congregation. Paul persecuted Christians. He knew what it was to harbor evil in his heart, to attack those who have walked God's path. Paul was made blind when the light of Jesus came upon him. A struggle and suffering for faith—consider what you are willing to do, what you will sacrifice."

I don't want to make it seem like I only want Big Landrys or even Greggs in my church—men with $2,300 lawnmowers or, in Big Landry's case, two separate cabins up north. I keep in mind diversity of income, the brackets and bands, the need for some mixing here. Pine Haven, which I can talk about until I'm big and blue in the face, is a miniaturized America, absent the racial component, though more Hispanics, Sikhs, and even Chinese move in every year, thanks to the college's influence and the perpetual need, among the Arby's and Jimmy John's and McDonald's and Wendy's and Burger Kings and Subways of the land, for deeply cheap and willing labor. Here in Pine Haven, you'll find men with nearly a million in IRAs living within two miles of men with missing front teeth, frozen drainpipes, and lice the size of ladybugs.

We've got, among our little Sunday Bible study cohort, members of several distinct classes. Gertrude, who lives with Harry out on the Breckenridge homestead, is of midrange farmer stock, earning just enough from a receptionist job at the college for the annual vacation to Orlando. Titus Shimski, who sits three souls over from Gregg Eggles, was in the Marines, and once watched three of his buddies get blown sky-high when an IED went off near Fallujah, barely sparing him. He's worked his way up at Walmart and I'm proud of him—PTSD is a demon like you wouldn't quite believe—and he'll offer his own quirky interpretations of scripture when he works up the courage. And there's Bob Saddlebrook and his wife, Ann, one of three Anns in the church, who retired from driving a tow truck not too long ago. Bob, who has a bit of institutional memory I'd like to pick at more when I get a chance, is a taciturn man with an egg-shaped forehead and cobalt-blue eyes. He sat through decades of Abraham Whitson sermons. To be honest, Bob is someone I'd fear I'd offend if the watercolor of the hydrangeas is ever moved. Right now, he's wedged next to Adrian and Jessica Mueller, who are the proud parents of eight children, five of whom are currently sequestered with two of mine across the hall in Sunday school. Adrian is a project manager for a Christian nonprofit, Beacon International, and banks a comfortable $125,000 a year while working remotely from the Toledo HQ. Jessica, a homemaker, occupies the first floor while Adrian manages a computer station and home office in his finished basement. Their four-bed, four-bath is a real beauty, like a great white wedding cake staring out onto the roadway and I'm proud to say I sold it to them, winning Adrian over with the crown moldings and the concrete and tile in-ground pool. And anchored at table's end, as always, is an inveterate member of our prayer circle, jovial Brendan Hannon, who is a VP of logistics at Everest & Rulopaugh, the luxury pontoon boat manufacturer. His wife, one of the Anns, is a paralegal at the personal injury law firm in town, Ricketts Bites Back. Their logo is a pit bull, the idea being that they'll fight for your money like a violent, depraved yard animal.

A good church, I've found, has its planetary qualities, small bodies orbiting large ones, mysterious forces tugging at them all from the cloudy beyond. This isn't a church for much astronomy and I think I'd come down pretty hard if we ever drifted too far in that direction, but outer space is always useful for an internal metaphor. Matter and antimatter—what is it, really, that draws us here or there, that leads to the formation of such intricate hierarchies, that allows, ultimately, for so many people to place their faith in *me*? God and his Son above us all, and I'm here, to the best of my ability, as His intermediary for them. Even Big Landry couldn't bring himself to *really* preach. The answer to all of this, obviously, is God. God created matter and antimatter, dark and light. God created right and wrong.

"Consider how we live today, how we are always seeking the easy answer, the easy solution; modernity demands that our existence be eased as much as possible. To find enlightenment, all you do is sit back and wait. Or maybe pay. False prophets abound because it has never been easier to be false. Even the Apostles, in their infinite wisdom, would find the 2020s bewildering. At the swipe of a finger, all your problems can be solved. It's an age of magic, of little crystals and astrological signs and manifestations. Instead of prayer, you manifest. There is no God, only longing, longing for material goods. You manifest for a new car, a new house. It is longing divorced from faith and that, perhaps, is the most dangerous kind. Because it teaches that all you have to do in this world is close your eyes and plead into the void. Not supplicate yourself to the Almighty, not live in His grace, not follow His word and live a life he wants you to live—no, there's no requirement of worship at all."

I take another breath, a larger one.

"Worship is *hard.* Jesus dying on the cross for our sins is not *convenient.* Do you know who promises convenience? Who promises ease?"

"The devil," Gertrude answers quietly.

"Exactly."

I love Trinity of Pine Haven for many reasons. There are the people, of course, my Gertrudes and Big Landrys. And there is the building itself, erected in 1956, during the last nationwide enthusiasm for church construction. In 1960, church affiliation would reach nearly seventy percent, and every town was desperate for a sanctuary that recalled the past while pointing straight forward to a glorious, booming future. Easier said than done, and many ended up splitting the difference in diffuse, alienating ways, permitting the gloss of shopping-mall culture to permeate the architecture.

That same year, Americans spent over one billion dollars on church construction. Trinity came along just before that peak, when Pine Haven was at least a thousand souls larger, still swollen from Liberty Motor Truck Company, at one time the world's largest exclusive truck manufacturer in the United States. In 1973, Liberty would shutter, knocking the town back on its heels, but only for so long.

Trinity is a partial colonial revival, carrying with it the hint of midcentury nostalgia for America's founding, when all mythos had to be marshaled to combat the godless Russians. Blood-red brick, white trim, a humble steeple, the elongated glass windows stained, abstracted, lovely. I often walk through Trinity dreamily, my thoughts ethereal before they harden into a needed sermon, the egg-white and blond wood swimming at the happy edge of my vision. What possibilities, when people come together—when they forget themselves, utterly. Now, many of the congregation may not forget completely—venality, tick-like, must nibble and suck—and there's liable to be snoozers and seat fillers, those who just show up to show up, who treat church like the calcium pills their country doctor told them to take. I don't resent them. Any pastor understands this is the price of doing business and there's even a necessity to such folk. They may one day drift out of this simple existence and become something more, a worthy contributor to men's group, a quasi-regular at April Kleinschmidt's grief counseling, or merely someone shaken out of their glazed morning stupor just enough to trod up for a prayer circle.

If they're here, it's better than if they're not here: another of my philosophies I always keep close, and am glad to share if prodded.

"The devil lurks," Gertrude adds, finding my eyes. "He's waiting when you've let your guard down."

Most pastors like to leave on a note of uplift. I've debated, internally, what is more effective: a reminder of God's love or His justice. We all bask in His love, but it comes with the condition of worship. It doesn't merely present itself.

"The struggle is glorious," I say. "When you allow it to be."

I close with a prayer. We bow our heads, close our eyes, and hold hands. My right has locked with April's, my left with Gary Puffpaff's. Gary, a ten-year Trinity veteran, works with Brendan at Everest & Rulopaugh in a lower-paying role, though he's been at the company longer. As far as I can tell, this doesn't bother him at all. His hand is soft, a tad moist, and I can't imagine him commanding boardrooms or even telling his wife, Kelsie, what to do.

When we're done, I stand and smile. The sunlight is broader somehow, and I can even accept the placement of the watercolor on the wall. I can accept the haphazard brushwork, the failure of shading, the riotous colors that meld in a limp, inopportune manner. My back, which had a little crick that's thankfully vanished, feels rod-firm and straight. It's time, at last, to deliver my sermon.

Today is May 3, two days after the first of the month. For anyone in real estate, that day looms with all its hope and dreadful opportunity. The hope, if you're in my shoes, is obvious enough, and the dread comes, naturally, from not being able to collect when you should. I consider this, driving alone, farmland sprawling on each side of me. The roadway unnerves me, though I've never admitted this, even to Daniella. A two-lane east-west artery, it pits you against oncoming traffic at all hours, typically trucks and campers hungry to make good time on whatever expedition has taken them out into roaming country. One wrong twitch or wince and you're over the double yellow and into the grille of a much larger, possibly faster vehicle, your bones mashed in with the hot, twisted steel. I've played out this scene many times in my mind—the exploding glass, the bursting blood, lithe EMTs swarming my long-dead body. There's an assumption that a pastor can't fear death, and that's just not true. I'm *comfortable* with where I'm going, but I'm not, necessarily, in any hurry to get off this Earth.

It's true that in one sermon, I said just the opposite. It was six months ago, trending into Christmastime, and I wandered onto an anecdote about happy Christian funerals. My contention, which was well received by the church, was that you won't see as many tears and frowns and crinkled expressions at truly Christian funerals. There is outward joy, not sadness, because the dearly departed loved one is now going to meet Jesus. There can only be so much to lament, I said, because so much love awaits you. This was, in no way, an endorsement of death or what they might call suicide ideation—it was an observation worth making. When you believe, you secure an inner peace that can deliver you through the worst of life, a belief that slowly strips your fear away.

Fear, though, is on tap for a bit longer, until I can veer off onto East Putnam and drive the three miles to the Breckenridge homestead. Daniella has Chloe and Austin at home. Theodore Jr. is on a playdate—well, he's too old for it to be called that, but that's what I still think of it as—with Garrett Hannon, Brendan's second oldest, and they're probably knee-deep in cheese puffs and ice cream, playing lurid video games on Brendan's forty-three-inch LED, F22 Series, smacked snugly against the oaken side wall of his supremely finished basement. A house I sold to him, which was no easy feat given that Brendan's credit and cash flow were a bit more tenuous than expected, at least in those days. This was before his promotion at E&I that vaulted him gracefully two tax brackets upward. Now he entertains my oldest in style, and I drive alone to repair a leak. At least that's what Gertrude called it over the phone.

I approach East Putnam slowly, sure not to yank my Chevy too far to the right, lest I hum into a muddy ditch and start kicking up dirt on a road barely large enough for my four-door. Dust clouds dutifully swirl, hanging like dragon breath, and I click my tongue, an old habit. If you're conscientious around here, you're taking your automobile in for a weekly deep cleaning, and I'm six days out from my last trip to Chip's Wash on Huron. Time to get on with it and I wish I weren't approaching the Breckenridge homestead in such a soiled vehicle. I like coming out here with a gleam, a near sparkle, and I can only imagine what the cold-blue swabbed Chevy would look like under a heavy late afternoon sun.

It's a straight shot on East Putnam, past two glum intersections, corn flanking me on all sides. There's nothing quite like the high after a good sermon, the trace it leaves in your mouth and stomach. It must be something like the buzz of a ballplayer, a job well done, a synchronicity that nearly transcends words.

Driving through the country has reminded me I don't want to live in the country. I am glad Trinity of Pine Haven is situated on prime real estate near the college, that the founders had the wisdom to build near a secular liberal arts institution. If they resented the godlessness of Pine Haven—that's the college, neatly named for the town—they at least understood, intrinsically, it made most sense to own tax-free land two streets away from its outer border. I don't like the overt emptiness of the country and the darkness that encroaches. Lonely farmers, even those engrossed in prayer, are a particularly mournful lot to me, and I wish they could all congregate nearer the warmth of a municipality—a city in the technical bureaucratic sense, a town to anyone who is functioning there—that will remain around nine thousand until Jesus Christ's return. The country here is stripped of hills, of right angles and jagged edges on the horizon, and the flatness in twilight can bring a man real low, like he's soil-bound in the face of a starshine he'll never reach.

In town, I know where I am. I know it teleologically. I know I am closer to God there, too. It is why, as much as we may pray alone, we're ultimately bunched like bugs on Sunday, clustered under one roof. I don't want to preach to myself, but here, in the corn, that's all you can do. You collapse into your homestead. Gertrude hasn't succumbed to this, but poor Harry has. Harry, now laid up in Luce Memorial, that staph infection taking a nasty but manageable turn. He's four months younger than me, thirty-nine teetering on forty, and I know he doesn't want to start a new decade this way. I've gone three times to visit him there, where he's now sequestered in a stepdown unit with an ornery roommate, a fiery seventy-year-old Episcopalian from Mount Pleasant who's recovering from a heart attack. Harry has a television he can stare at straight above when he adjusts his bed just right and the last time I was there, he was intently watching a *Jeopardy!* rerun. He wants, more than anything else, to get back to his farm, where work can drown out all the noise that comes with merely existing.

They have one child, Aidan, who's thirteen and already liable to wander; there's a scissor-flash in his eyes and I don't trust him very much. He'll mutter about wanting to beat it from Pine Haven altogether, though there will be no better place for him, nowhere that will ever care so much for his future. Harry, at least, has chosen to recede into the life he has, while Gertrude, with limitations, ranges about. She drives into town every weekday to sit in the admissions office at Pine Haven College, answering telephones with two other ladies. And if Aidan hasn't already, he's probably planning on getting into drinking, and fornication isn't far off. When I pull into the homestead, I figure this will come up and I'll need to prepare comforting words for Gertrude.

Soon, the big red farmhouse looms. I'm close. Dust swirls again and a pheasant, a highly decorated male, skirts overhead. My automobile is making a kerplunking noise I don't especially like and I take note, to get it looked at before next week.

I inch up the rambling driveway, spotting two well-fed cows and a gelding beyond a picket fence. One of them is named Fredrick, and I forget if this gelding, the color of chocolate left in the sun, is him. Harry's truck and trailer are farther up the driveway, as well as Gertrude's Wrangler. All the vehicles are parked slightly askew, as if a microburst had tossed them around a bit, and I chalk this up to country folk ways I'll never quite understand, no matter how much I come here. I park far enough away to give the Wrangler a wide berth for escape; suddenly, I'm assuming it has a mind of its own.

There are no doorbells on the homestead and Gertrude isn't one for texts. *I'm here* won't suffice. I knock on the soaring wood door twice, hearing my own echo and enjoying the feeling of skin in hard contact with material that long predates me. The homestead was built by Harry's maternal great-grandfather in the 1910s and it'll have to be Aidan's someday. A child, always a son, has inherited it, and Aidan can only flee his birthright for so long. Kings abdicate, but not farm boys due their treasure. Land, excepting God, is the greatest lure. I listen for Aidan's potential pitter-patter, hoping he's not home, and hear nothing as I wait on the cramped porch, which was grafted onto the two-story some decades ago.

Sounds behind the door, a solitary two-step, and I know I'm fine. In my right hand, I have my leather pouched tool kit, good for fixing the kind of penny-ante kitchen sink leak Gertrude needs help with today. I dabble in minor repair work. I would never call myself *handy* or pit my limited skill set against the men with round, firm guts who tinker away weekends on their F-150s and craft their own hunting blinds, but I'd like to think, here anyway, I can hold my own. A man has to know what to do with his hands, particularly in a world like this one. Daniella likes that I can install showerheads and lay tile. None of this was taught, just as the men vanished beneath the undercarriages of their F-150s had to learn most of what they do on their own unless they were blessed with daddies who took the time to helpfully guide their grease-soaked hands.

"There you are," Gertrude says when she opens the door. I peer behind her briefly, checking to make sure that there are no sounds of a wayward son.

"On time, just through the dust clouds."

"You always hurry when you're needed. And you've got a bit of sweat on your brow already. It was supposed to hit seventy today, but never did."

"Weathermen deceive, or they talk out of ignorance. I still find comfort in them, though. I wait for the five boxes. Monday partly cloudy, Tuesday chance of rain, Wednesday clear, humidity inching up. I feel you can set your watch to it, even when it isn't right."

"You want facts for facts' sake. Even when the facts are incorrect."

"I do think we'd all be calmer if we all agreed to collectively watch the weather forecast every night."

"We'd be calmer if the television told us all what it really thinks."

I follow her inside, enjoying the lightest jousting, what's possible when two people are alone and allowed to perform. At church, a crowd (a lovely one), and at home, another, also lovely, three children, a wife who is languorous until she isn't, and a stack of bills always hitting our kitchen table. None of that here, in Gertrude and Harry's shadow-sunken foyer, smelling lightly of sandalwood. In here, the sunlight dribbles in just right through the leaded glass windows, leaving a wide, crescent-shaped pool on the grand piano. Our feet creak over the hardwood, no carpet anywhere, and I'm grateful for the sound. We make way for the kitchen.

"How is Harry?" I ask, straining to summon up worry.

"Harry is complaining about the food. He thinks Luce Memorial wants to poison him to keep him there indefinitely, to soak him dry and steal the homestead."

"That would be quite the scheme. Workable, in some sense."

"I'm going to see him before it gets dark. It's best visiting him at that time of day."

Gertrude is a crisp, trim thirty-six, her dark brown hair slashed at the shoulders, her eyes a curious milky hazel. Her name belies who she is and what she looks like: even around here, she's the only Gertrude under sixty, and neither of the surnames she's possessed in this life—Howell, the maiden, or Breckenridge, the married—lend any credence to her relative youth. She's never Gertie, either. She and Harry joined the church four years ago and have been regular attendees since, Gertrude's devotion increasing over the past year. That's when she joined Bible study.

"Let's see that leak."

Gertrude is dressed for a run. She's the only person I know of who jogs the country roads, risking her life on choking dirt and gravel, no shoulder to dip into, drivers comfortably lured into committing manslaughter. Right now she's in dark Lululemon high-rise track shorts and a sleeveless Nike top, her upper arms thin and lightly toned. I can't tell if she's about to run or has already. Exercise or not, she doesn't seem to sweat. That's its own talent.

"I don't think it'll be too much trouble."

I've never pressed Gertrude on why she and Harry only had one child. I have my theories, one of which she has alluded to: one child was enough. Neither Gertrude nor Harry, despite the pressure of their environs, longed for more. She was twenty-three when Aidan was born and could be presiding over a teeming household by now, four or five at least barreling through, a brood not far off from what the Muellers have brought forth. Three is enough for me and plenty for Daniella; we're satisfied. I'm always surprised Harry, so in need of a descendant to care for the homestead, didn't demand more. What passes between them is still unclear to me, even with the time I've spent with her, turning over her relationship. If they were a city couple, I wouldn't wonder much at all. Apartments are filled enough with childless couples, let alone three children stomping through, and no one can feasibly afford an apartment with four bedrooms unless it shows up in an area that has just suffered a dire fiscal crisis or seismic crime spike. A house like this is hungry; it aches to be filled. Right now, we'll do.

I bend down and inspect. There's hardly a leak at all. Well, of course. And how many tools are actually in my tool kit? I grin to myself, in the semi-dark around the piping, and slowly rise. I'm six-one or six-two depending on the day and who is measuring, and Gertrude comes just up to my chin. The leather pouch rests at my foot. There's an interior weight to this house I've always liked, of lives lived and fortunes sought, and I spy an oversized metallic wall clock against the kitchen's far wall, ticking away softly. It's nearly a quarter to four.

"No trouble," I say. "Water is hardly dripping at all."

Longer ago, I could savor the anticipation, the silence heavy between us before fast action. Gertrude's face is warm yet impregnable, like a poster board for a vanished icon only I can recall, and I glance downward, toward her flexing calves and shoe tops. Daniella has a white pair of Adidas she wears for walks that are not so different than these.

"Good, Teddy."

I forgo whatever ceremony is left—the lingering gaze, the breathy intake, the heartbeat at a nice hop—and kiss her on the lips, harder than I intended. I always enjoy this taste. If I haven't been chewing gum, she has, and I catch the aftertaste of something cool, Eclipse or Extra, and let it settle on my own tongue. Her eyes are closed, as usual, and I kiss her again, biting her lower lip, feeling the light, delicious click of her incisors.

"Upstairs," she says.

I watch her on the banister, careful, and we go to one of the guest bedrooms. My favorite, where we typically end up, has the best view of the verdant farmland, two lace curtains parted for miles of surging corn. The sheets are an off-white, cottony, and the mattress has a good spring to it because so few (other than us) sleep there. She hesitates slightly at the top of the stairs—a cramping in her calf? a second thought?—and veers left, thankfully, to our spot. I slide after her like a furtive child, my toes soft on the hardwood, and I'm mouse quiet behind her. There's no reason to be, really. Only Aidan is a threat to return and Aidan has better places to be on a Sunday afternoon. If he returns at all, it'll be at sunset, when Gertrude will start calling him on the cell phone Harry bought for him last year.

"I'm glad we're here," I tell her as she undresses and I'm unbuttoning my trousers.

"This house?"

"This room."

"Oh, I hate it."

"I love it. Look at the view."

"You can only look at it so many times."

"You want a view of town."

"I don't want that either."

"A straight shot to the Pine Haven College clocktower, the sprawling quad, coeds with Shakespeare tucked under their arms."

"The college is hell-bound."

"Not all of it."

"Oh, Pastor Starr has done a survey, examined every last soul."

She's drawn the curtains and soon I'm on top of her. Usually, she wants to rush under the sheets, but not today. We haven't even shut the door.

"Realistically, in a school of fourteen hundred undergraduates, there are a few who've accepted Jesus Christ as their Lord and savior."

"If they said it, they're lying."

"Don't underestimate the human heart, Gertrude."

I take my own survey of her naked body. I hope, in those distant eyes, she's doing the same of mine.

We slide under the covers after we're done. I have my hand on her breast and she's noodling with my chest hair. It was one of our best yet, and I'm trying to recall, almost desperately, how many times we have been together. Suddenly, this catalog matters. If a memory can't be summoned, did the experience ever produce it? This is why, perhaps, we need God. God is always watching and God can remember for us.

"I meant it about the college," Gertrude says.

"We can pull up stakes and move Trinity then. Maybe the Breckenridge homestead will have us."

"I'd like that. Harry would finally get that heart attack he's threatening to have."

"Pine Haven College was founded by Presbyterians. At some point, they gave up."

"I don't like Presbyterians, but I wish they stuck with it. I can't go in there every day and listen to these people."

"These people? The students? The coworkers?"

"All of the above. They're a hive. They want to rewrite history, rewrite the human body."

"It's the fad of the moment, but I think it's giving way. The social justice enthusiasms."

"They are all filled with hatred. No one hates more than a Democrat at a liberal arts college. No one burns more. No one aches for more blood."

"They believe they have clarity, even if their vision is confused. That can be a dangerous thing."

She sits up slightly, her hazel eyes flitting in my direction. Whatever I've said, it's not good enough.

"You speak about it with such detachment."

"Not at all. I'm only saying, they're confused. A liberal mind builds a church without God. A church of deconstruction, a church of, well, academia. It's a *confused* church, since it lacks a center."

"I need to get out of there. But then I'm here. I'm on this farm. Do you know something, Teddy—what I think about sometimes?"

I'm still in a state of postcoital placidity, my eyelids slightly drooped, my groin tingling faintly. I could fall out for a few hours, doze until nightfall, though curling up here is simply not an option. Daniella will set dinner by seven, Theodore will be home, Chloe will be asking for Daddy, and little Austin may want to be held. Images of the very near-future rush through me and it's hard to focus on what Gertrude is saying. I want to give over myself fully, as I might at Trinity, particularly when she raises a thorny theological matter. Gertrude is a close, close reader, and I appreciate her surgical precision in all matters of life. But here and now, I'm not sure I want her to tell me so much about herself—about the homestead, the college, Harry. I understand it well enough. It's all weight on her she'd rather shed.

"What do you think about?"

"How it would be great if it all burned down."

It's advice I should give and it's advice I don't necessarily have. Not now, anyway, not in this state. I can rack my brain for a Bible passage but I know that's not what Gertrude requires from me. She wants wisdom from a friend, a lover, even a therapist, and I can only be all three for so long. I counsel several couples at Trinity (not Harry and Gertrude) and their difficulties, which are common in long marriages, are not quite so charged, so rage-flecked. Their unions have a sort of irritable ease that is salved by more communication, empathy, and prayer. CEP (hard C), I call it privately, and I can offer a dosage a week and stroll out of there arm in arm with man and woman if I so choose.

Gertrude does not want, I assume, to communicate with Harry. She does not want to empathize with him. She will pray alone, undertaking her own winding and very private conversation with God. This is the first time she has told me she wants to burn down the homestead.

"You shouldn't burn down the homestead."

"Who said I will? I never will. It's a wish for an act. I don't want Aidan or Harry to be home."

"When does Aidan get home?"

"You'll be long gone by then, don't panic. I know that's your worry, Teddy. You didn't bargain for this. It's like when your real estate clients want to talk God. If it bothers you so much, you should get two cell phones."

"It doesn't bother me at all. I welcome such talk. You can tell me anything. I understand you and Harry are in a rough patch. It can be hard, at times, to get along. Have you told him how you feel?"

A ludicrous suggestion, and I know it the instant it leaves my mouth and hangs between us. I've been lured into an exchange I'll have to abort soon. Typically, Gertrude is not this way, her resentments toward Harry buried stomach-deep, out of view. The hospital stay, if anything, was supposed to short-circuit such chatter completely and give us more running room in our time together. He'll be at Luce Memorial at least another week, from what I understand. Beyond that, Harry is a problem I cannot solve. I won't recommend divorce. It's not as if a sizable minority of the congregation hasn't been divorced already or is living together unmarried—and I'm not such an obstinate goat that I wouldn't advise separation, under such and such circumstances—but I won't be in the business of actively encouraging disunion, even if it adds to the cleansing side of the ledger. Aidan, deluded as he might be, deserves a married father and mother. This homestead won't be haunted by Harry alone—Gertrude would have to leave, and that's clearly what Gertrude wants—and it won't be my responsibility when that balky scenario inevitably devolves, an unmoored single father barely tending to the corn as the child spins off into nefarious orbits.

"I tell him all the time. I tell him every week."

"Direct."

"He's somewhat like you. He's comfortable in abstractions. Maybe that's why I'm here. You can tell him something twelve consecutive times and he won't believe you because it hasn't yet settled into the makeup of his universe. It's neither right nor wrong—it just doesn't exist."

"At some point, it will exist. You just have to wait for it. You have to wait for it to settle. He's that species of livestock."

"I don't have that kind of time."

True enough. God can call us up whenever he decides; He is the only timekeeper of relevance here. No one has a *kind* of time. They have a ceaseless ticking forward, sometimes deadening, sometimes sprightly, and you hope to sniff out the worthwhile moments in between. Mostly, I hope, those are at Trinity. I do believe most of the congregation, even Gertrude, views it as *a* peak of the week. When I preach, I want them all to feel relevant. They are the hum, the news, what the worthy talk about. They are onstage. God is watching and they must be celebrated. True worshippers know they are being watched and they cherish this knowledge, hugging it close like they would their own children.

Gertrude has stood up and I follow the unsunned undersides of her thighs as she hunts for her discarded clothing. I should do the same. At the foot of the bed are my trousers, my leather belt still hooked in, and somewhere down below my argyles. My unbuttoned dress shirt, an understated clamshell white from Ralph Lauren, has fallen down too, and I mimic a blind man as I reach for it on the floor. There's no good way to depart, really—certainly not from here.

"Remember," I say, when I've got my shirt buttoned and my pants up, "the people of the college can't change you."

"And I can't change them."

"Their time will come."

I say this, nearly believing it, and decide now is a good enough time to get home to my wife and children.

2

The drive to Utopia Gardens takes sixteen minutes from our house. It's a perpendicular eastward shot from downtown, over the Spruce River and past the Shell station and the crepuscular Chinese buffet, where the lights are forever too low for my taste. Go any farther and you're ramming into the western edge of Madison, the hotel and motel strip, all of them surviving on the month-to-month folk, not the travelers from out of county. If you're headed to Pine Haven and you've got a savings account and an IRA, you're checking into the Drawbridge downtown, the homespun inn that is de facto property of the college. You're nowhere near Madison or the freeway. Sometimes, I wish Utopia Gardens were nudged a little farther downtown. I know that's like saying the stray mutt you rescued should now transform, through sheer will, into a goldendoodle. That longing won't take you very far.

I turn up the Christian rock station being beamed from Wayne County. It's not my first choice of music, a few at Trinity know this, or at least suspect it from my stray remarks. There's an idea that middling, guitar-heavy rock with plaintive and gravely vocals must be the music of the Lord, and that all of it somehow manifested nearly two thousand years after the birth of Jesus. What does it say in the Bible about amplifiers? I have a cultural view and I deliver it at the pulpit well enough but I don't plan to wage war against the godless Left with Switchfoot and Relient K at my side. Still, on my way to Utopia Gardens, I'm working the volume nob on a Christian band I've never heard of, their lead singer bellowing about seeing the light after a dark night.

Music offers a mood and you take it. I feel almost settled. This is not my favorite activity, driving into Utopia Gardens and knocking on a few doors. I'd rather be with my children or riding a bike down the nature trail. I'd rather be at Trinity or penetrating Gertrude. I can reel off ten to twenty activities I'd choose before this, slowing now as I reach the wide white sign hammered into the soil, the well-painted announcement that I've arrived.

UTOPIA GARDENS, WELCOME HOME. That was my own touch, to insist on a repainted eight-foot clarion, a welcoming message. Green lettering on white, small renderings of tree leaves framing the U and the S, the faintest chiaroscuro around each word. Four days ago, I saw Gertrude, and now the memory is candied and I've got a smile on my face. It was Daniella's father, Del Justice, who told me this would eventually be my fate. Big Del, a former state senator with a slew of LLCs that make him the third-largest landowner in Luce County, has more words for real estate than anyone except myself, perhaps, or one of our audacious eager-to-please junior associates down at the main office. Big Del is the sort of person to tell you, with only some jocularity, that he's forgotten more about real estate than you know. I can't say if this is true but I can appreciate his ingrown ambition, the little burning ball inside of him.

Del is in my brain now, with his little yodel. He likes to talk about how Ohio is the most godforsaken state on Earth. "I was born there, so I know. Spent nine years in the Cleveland public schools." One of his dreams, he told me, was to buy a service plaza off the Ohio Turnpike. That was where Ohio pressed whatever advantage it could over Michigan. According to Del, the Ohio service plazas are underrated marvels, their geometry flawless, the chain restaurant selection impeccable. He says the piss crackles off the urinals. Thinking about this brings me a small comfort. I'd rather have Del rumbling through me than whatever is on tap in the next twenty to thirty minutes. If I had my druthers, I'd build a small visitor lot for Utopia Gardens, something to psychologically encourage visitation or at least the idea of it. I've always wanted a mobile home park to be more of a *park*. Hope and a nickel will get you on the subway, Del likes to say, having traveled all across this country and rumbled through New York's underbelly in the carriage of a flesh-choked train. He has little regard for my flights of fancy and that's why, maybe, I respect him so much. When I was courting Daniella, he made it plain: the world could be screwy, but always have a plan.

I never needed to ask him for the money for Utopia Gardens. Knowing the man he is, he would have liked to have been asked, so that he could give. He's someone who says, in all earnestness, *that's mighty white of you* or *that's jake* at the end of sentences. He's got a combustion engine voice and a motor oil glimmer in his gray eyes. He can swear up a good storm, too. My good friend in the mortgage division says he's worth five million easy.

One piece of advice I learned long ago is to do the hard stuff first. I'm sure Big Del would've imparted that to me if he got the chance to do it first, if he didn't sense I understood it already, on the level of marrow. Run right at your troubles like a giddy rhinoceros and then keep going. Rosebush Lane is where I'll start then. If I razed twelve or so American chestnuts, I could have that lot and then meander over to Rosebush, whistling a little show tune. But I haven't done that and that means I've got to rover in more confrontationally than I'd like. The Chevy will need to purr onto the lip of the driveway and I'll have to kill my engine right there, at 43 Rosebush.

Not a tableau I'd favor. Automobiles inevitably put a tenant ill at ease. They never come with good tidings, unless they're ferrying the pizza man from Little Caesars.

I notice the divot on Rosebush that was supposed to be patched up three months ago is still plenty present, despite the contractor's insistence that the work was done. That will be a phone call before nightfall. In the yard across from 43, two boys are passing a basketball back and forth, no hoop in sight. They are thin, lunar-skinned, and ten at best, their eyes fixed on the ball. Through a partially open floral-printed living room curtain I can see a large woman in muumuu-like attire, her body in repose. This could very well be the mother of one of the boys and it looks like she's watching a television attached to the ceiling. I can't see the TV and it's possible she's asleep. Yet there's an alertness to her figure, even if she's unmoving, that leads me to believe she's watching everyone.

Catching Kelly Unger at home is never easy. He works an erratic schedule at a small wholesaler in Sebastian, hoisting boxes in a back lot. There's a chance, usually, his wife, Madison, is at home, surveilling their mud-colored pug and two boys and a girl, though the boys and girl should be at school. I kill the engine and check myself in the mirror to make sure I'm smiling and there's no food in my teeth. All clear and I'm out, a small hop in my step, my loafers soft on the dewy grass. No rain in the forecast and I'm grateful. You want to be arriving on a sunny day, whether you're showing a place or collecting. Old resentments can die speedily in sunshine.

There's a ceramic, crenulated flowerpot set out near the front door to the Unger residence—a single wide with silver and blue vinyl—and I admire the craftsmanship, assuming it's Madison's handiwork. At the minimum, it doesn't look Walmart-bought. The curtains are drawn and it's impossible to tell if anyone is home. I listen for the telltale sounds of daytime TV or a child's thumping feet. Inside, at least for now, is a few decibels below whatever I can catch.

Shave and a haircut, two bits. I do this twice and wait. Two knocks are enough to start. You never want to open with three. That was a rule Del Justice did impart to me. Three can be a hostile number. Two is an approach, a hearty hello.

The Ungers are lucky to have a handsome oak on their lot. I can't help but admire the shadows cast, fit for a Rip Van Winkle nap. I wouldn't mind sneaking twenty minutes in the grass either. Good sun will do that to you. The boys, across the street, have stopped passing the ball and are now huddling, discussing arcane sports strategy, girls, or something entirely mysterious.

"Hello?" I offer.

There's a low thud, a *tap-tap.* The Ungers have beige carpeting, I remember, which tends to swallow footsteps. Across the street, the curtain has opened more, and the muumuu-clad woman appears to be stretching, each arm splayed wide, her lips at a slight quaver.

"It's Pastor Starr. How are you?"

The thud is louder. The Ungers don't attend any church, as far as I know. I have half a mind to pull them into Trinity, figure out if they can meld there, and give them, slowly, what they need. It would take time. These usually aren't the circumstances where I make my pitch and I sometimes wish I had a dab more of the missionary zeal, the need to spy converts in every weed and bough. That's a talent as much as an urge. Maybe now is the day to start. I'm certain there are footsteps and they belong to an adult. My luck has turned enough.

The front door swings back behind the screen, which has a small zigzag gash that needs repair. It shouldn't cost very much. A member of Trinity could even come by and fix it, on my dime. I'm rotating through possibilities when a faded face dips out from the shadow and rises toward me. Brown eyes with large irises, a bony nose tugged outward, shoulder-length hair with blondish highlights—it's Madison Unger, unsmiling. Her lips are buttoned together. I really need to get her into church.

"Yes?"

"It's good to see you, Madison. I'm looking for Kelly. I've been a little worried about him."

Kelly handles all finances. Madison works too, tending to a checkout counter at the Meijer near the freeway. If I see her in the store, I tend to avoid her line or dart straight for self-checkout. Simpler that way.

"Kelly's at work."

"Ah, day shift."

"Always a day shift."

"I remember when I came by a few months back, around dinnertime, you told me he was headed to work."

This elicits no response. Madison is not quite looking at me. I imagine there's a sparrow or maybe a boa constrictor up on a tree branch that's captivating her attention. She is somewhere around thirty, on one side or the other, and her skin, in the light of day, is near translucent. A tattoo of mauve script peeks out near her collarbone, a swooping phrase I can't make out. She's biting, softly, at her lower lip, and I almost want to console her.

"So, the reason I'm here is that today's more than a week after the first. I wanted to check up and see how everything is doing."

Again, no response, and no evidence these words hold any meaning. An outside observer, from another planet perhaps, would conclude I'm speaking English and she was raised to not understand English at all. In situations like these, you have to repeat yourself, but I'm suddenly not certain that would make any difference. God could grant me a thousand years here to tell her it's more than a week after the first of the month, and she would stare up at me like I was telling her the best breakfast food is sparrow with a side of boa constrictor.

"Unfortunately, you are—Kelly is—behind on rent again. I wanted to make sure everything is all right, that it's on the way very soon."

Madison stops biting her lip. There is a faint sound of daytime TV, several women and a man gabbing. The door is still not completely open and I can't see much of what is behind her. Across the street, the boys have gone inside, the basketball left ominously behind. Sitting there, sunken in the overgrown Bermuda grass, the ball looks native to the environment, a late spring plant that needs tending. Someone will come and pluck it out. I scratch at a globule of sweat forming on my cheek.

"He's at work now."

Madison grew up here, I know that, yet she has an improbable Texan twang, or the approximation of one. Perhaps she learned it on TV. There are immigrant boys who grow up speaking like outer-borough mobsters because they learned English watching *Goodfellas* on repeat. There is a logic here, even if I do not agree with it.

"It's very important that he sends his rent check in soon."

"I'll tell him, yes."

"You wouldn't happen to—" I stop myself. Requesting this would be like opening up *The Tale of Genji* and reading it out loud to Madison in Heian-era Japanese. I was about to ask if she had the money or access to it, maybe the checkbook of their joint account, maybe the ability to *write* a check from the joint account. And they do have one—I remember the Unger family checks—but there's no doubt Kelly has ahold of it. He's doing the printing and signing in his gnomish scrawl. There's no chance, in fact, Kelly has left a checkbook out in the house. He seems like a man who would pin a checkbook inside his coat and take it everywhere. All of this is a reminder that I've been lagging on getting a vendor to set up an online payment system where my tenants can pay through credit with ease or I can automatically deduct from their accounts on the first of the month. We were supposed to be online in March and now it's spring tumbling into summer, and I'm here at the threshold of the Unger home, straining for a rightful payment that is not here and may never be.

"Mhm," she answers or exhales or expels, a noise that's anywhere from a firm agreement to the equivalent of an oral fart. She hasn't edged out any farther, the door still covering at least half her body, as if the white Trimlite is a shower curtain and she's naked behind it. I see her suddenly in her brackish mid-teens, earbuds jammed in ears, small Goth trinkets wrapped around her wrists and drilled into her lapels, a chip-toothed boy texting her a blurred picture of his swollen penis head as she tries to do algebra. Bleak, bleak. She and Kelly are both graduates of Pine Haven High School and, like most graduates, never achieved exit velocity from Luce County. Not that there's anything wrong with that—the most upstanding members of our community are PHHS graduates. Madison still has a chance to join them, along with Kelly. I've seen couples in far worse shape. But it starts here, at the baseline, making payments on time.

"I'll really need to get that payment soon."

Madison nods at half speed.

"Kelly should be home tonight."

"Tell him he can send it first thing in the morning."

"He's gonna tell me money's tight."

"I'm happy to work out a payment plan with him. He has my number, I think, but do you want me to give it to you again?" Before she answers, I'm pulling out my Starr Realty card with office and cell phone printed clearly, along with email. "Call me anytime."

I hold the card out and she regards it without moving either hand. I'm convinced, for at least a full second, she will never take the card and I'll have to tuck it into the flowerpot. Finally, she inches the door back and her right hand crawls out to take it. Her nail polish, a ruby red, is flaking away. Her fingers are almost as long as mine, only more spidery, more committed to their joints and tendons. She seems like someone who can bend her fingers backward and forward in uncomfortable directions.

"He'll be back tonight," she says again, as if I didn't hear her. I'm not coming back tonight. I'll be eating dinner with my wife and children and then sleeping.

"Is there a particular time he's usually home, if I have to come again?"

Her eye contact, again, is nowhere near mine. There could be a wind spirit traveling around my skull and she's struggling to lock eyes with it, to take whatever devilish power it's got on tap. Her boredom is enervating. I consider turning around and leaving without waiting for an answer. This would be nonsensical and confrontational, and word would get around Utopia Gardens that Pastor Starr behaved in such a queer manner. In communities like these, or in Pine Haven writ large, you never want to become the curious person. You do not want to create conditions where you are imposing, without even realizing it, distance between yourself and others. Most interaction is about predictability, of approximating automation, and the longer you seek disruption, the poorer and more alone you'll be. The Ungers should heed this lesson. Maybe I will try to get Kelly and Madison into the church.

"It depends. It's hard to say. Schedule really depends."

One of the boys has come outside for the orphaned basketball. He picks it up and glances right and left, checking for nonexistent road traffic, and heads back into the darkness of his home. It's a shame I don't know the families who pay in a timely fashion. Sometimes, real estate is all too much about squeaky wheels and grease. The Ungers squeak among the loudest. Their decision to mail in late payments is deafening.

"I can try six o'clock in a few days, maybe. But of course, it's all moot if the check is mailed in before then. If you don't mind me asking, while I have you, do you have a church you're currently worshipping with?"

A light tremor passes through Madison, a signal that she has offered a response, though I can't possibly discern what it is. If it's a *yes*, it's among the weakest I've ever seen. If it's a *no*, it's as far from commitment as possible without deploying a *maybe*. But this might be a *maybe*. I'm going to have to ask again. A migraine aims like a woodpecker at the underside of my forehead, and I feel a succession of sharp aches. This may be psychosomatic. I can't tell yet.

"Yes?" I ask.

"Over in Orchard, sometimes. Orchard Church of Christ."

"I'm gratified to know you and your family are godly."

"Yeah."

"We need that in this country."

I'm not sure why I'm still talking, considering there are still several delinquent homes to visit. The Ungers were never going to give way, not this easily. The money arrives, just never when it's supposed to, no logic or rhythm to the check reaching my office. Real estate, like religion, is something of a horizontal business, and you have to keep in mind the long stretches, the greater journey. Utopia Gardens is an investment in tomorrow and the next day. Land appreciates; it's why I never dealt in automobiles.

"I suppose I do have a question." Madison says this with her eyes dipping to her toes wriggling in Dollar Tree flipflops, plastic and ungainly. "The lot rent . . ."

"Yes?"

"It was $614 when we moved in. Now it's $702."

Her expression hasn't changed. It's too drained to be described as puzzlement or befuddlement; it's more an anti-expression, her lips flat, her eyes fastened on a point that is still not particularly close to me. There are several ways to answer her. Del Justice would either favor tact or aggression, or maybe a quick and painless lie to throw her off the scent. I try to summon his exact words and come up empty. Scripture, obviously, is no help here, and that's a shame. It's as reliable a lubricant for conversation as any. I could describe inflation-adjusted facts and figures, the ebb and flow of a market, the sewer investment I decided to undertake last year or the need to fatten a fund for future beautification projects at Utopia Gardens. Over time, costs must rise—that is an American law,

I'm told—and there is nowhere that chickens don't come home to roost. If I were deranged, I would lower her rent to zero dollars and zero cents, or consider a symbolic five-dollar charge so Kelly Unger could feel he wasn't living scot-free, which can be important for some men.

"Unfortunately, a series of vital infrastructure projects over the last quarter, combined with rising overhead—inflation has driven up the cost of fuel and other materials—made an increase necessary. I am committed to making Utopia Gardens a place anyone would be proud to live in, and part of this is investing in the infrastructure and ensuring the highest quality. The future roads are paved with the intentions of the past."

Madison begins to open her mouth and then closes it. The TV behind her purrs through a commercial break, and I can hear a man with a mid-Atlantic accent pitching a type of laundry detergent.

"Okay."

Her eyes, for the first time, rove directly into mine and I don't particularly like what I see. It's time for me to go, and that's an underrated talent wherever you are—to understand when it's time to eject and head on to more fruitful pastures. I can give a smile and a wave and be on my way. Lon Snowbin's house is next and Iggy, who lives alone, is even more recalcitrant than the Ungers. Another urge, though, rises in me, and I feel I'll need to upchuck a few more words, this time more cheerily.

"I'll be honest, Madison," and I've never trusted anyone who starts a sentence this way, "I never want to raise the rent. This isn't an easy business. But I want to build a community here, a community in Pine Haven—I believe in it fully. I believe we are blessed by God. I want to bring great changes here. A rising tide lifts all boats. Before I came to Utopia Gardens, the lot rent *was* cheaper, but the weeds were higher, the roads looked like Baghdad, and brown water oozed every which way. You might remember it, and it was probably when you moved in. . . . It was not the way a community should be. Uplift is difficult. I believe in giving back—giving back to you and everyone else here. And to do that, to make Utopia Gardens the little community it deserves to be, we need to build for the future. Does that make sense?"

Posing it as a question is a mistake. I can see that now, by the way Madison's dim face curdles. There is every virtue in escape. With some people, slipping out of a conversation presents its own riddle—there are threads to revolve, thoughts uncompleted, implicit demands made. I've reached enough of a station where few question, in Pine Haven at least, what I do within a conversation, how I maneuver, when I need to drift or even go silent. Madison is my tenant, after all. I nod and wave.

"Give Kelly my best."

I back away and spin-turn, my loafers clopping on cement until I'm safely ensconced in my Chevy. I make a silent vow not to explain lot rent to anyone else for the rest of the afternoon. Madison has slunk back inside, the door long closed, the curtains still drawn. I'll expect a check in three to four days. My engine gives a splenetic kick I don't care for, something that'll have to be addressed in the shop next week. Lon Snowbin's is a hard right on Olive Lane and another right on Robin Drive, two roadways that barely accommodate more than two cars at a time. I slow down to twenty-five and take my time. If Snowbin doesn't ask about lot rent, I will consider the day tolerable.

A realtor is a showman, a handmaiden, an advertiser for your arriving life, the one you want to live. When I show homes, I always try to dream my client into the living room, the primary suite (or master, as we used to call it), the bonus room, the basement—finished or unfinished—and the grassy tongue of backyard. Just as they are projecting themselves forward into a structure that is still heavy with the residue of a past they have no stake in and never will, I am doing my own psychic forecasting, a forward-flash of image-making to suit what might unfurl before me, if the transaction proceeds accordingly. Realtors trill at the economy's baseline, its happy underbelly, and typically sniff out expansion or contraction before the economics reporter of any reputable news organization catches wind. When I sell homes at the clip I prefer, I know the weeks ahead will have a saccharine aftertaste for all involved. The hushed intimacy of an empty home on the cusp of a sale, buyer and realtor huddled together, is one node that defines, one way or another, the quality of the country that we'll eventually inhabit.

A landlord is no less essential, only uglier. Land implies an unholy dominance of nature, of the untrammeled wild that is supposed to be shared in communistic fashion. And when you put *lord* after it, the word is just feudal malevolence with an alliterative kick baked in. A landowner is no better. And that's what I am, an owner and a lord, a single man bundled into an LLC extracting a monthly fee from people who are, in theory, operating under far more tenuous circumstances than myself.

I say in theory, of course, because I do not have access to their savings accounts and I am not, unlike others in my position, hostile to the concept of renting. I keep pamphlets in my car from the office like "Rent or Own: What's the Real Deal?" that lay out plausible arguments for each based on your income, ambition, and outlook. Really, it's up to you. And I never want my renters behind the eight ball. It's why I'm out here, checking in, checking up, ensuring we aren't two or three or four months behind and eviction, another very ugly word, is suddenly in our vocabulary. No lord of land wants to evict, including me. I'd relish it as much as an appendectomy.

Land appreciates. Recessions, depressions, and pandemics can't undo land. The business of land is the only worthwhile business, if you want to get down to brass tacks about it. You can lose with land, but you'll probably win. Gambling is sinful but it's also foolish—there is, of course, something known as speculation with land, but no one who spends long enough buying and selling property is taking much of a gamble. You hold and you win. Like any venture, you're sunk if you fall behind and panic. Really, you buy and wait, like a rattlesnake. Buy and wait.

I slow down in front of the Snowbin residence. It's Lon, alone, no wife, no family. He was here when I bought Utopia Gardens and I was warned he was fickle. In particular, the old owners, a consortium of bored energy dealers out of Maumee who wanted to dabble in Michigan real estate, had created a quasi-intuitive internal system of red and yellow cards to denote tenants who proved, over time, problematic. Snowbin flitted between red (most severe) and yellow (rather severe) with no discernible rhyme or reason. He was not seasonally late or early—winter or summer could produce similar lulls—and none of it seemed to depend on work, which he had reliably picked up at Quaker State, where he changed oil on weekends and some weekdays. This is the third time his rent has been late since I took over and this will be the second time I've visited his trailer, a gray-striped single-wide with a customized porch in faux oak. An American flag flies on a diagonal from a bracket screwed into a panel next to the framing of his front door. A second flag, that of the Michigan State Spartans, hangs in a neighboring bracket. There is no wind, so the flags are quiescent; from my vantage point behind glass, they may as well be plastic. I step out of the vehicle and head to where I need to be, ready to knock and knock.

The first time I met Lon Snowbin, I was not asking for rent. I was introducing myself at Menard's, where we were both coincidentally skittering through the lumber section, as his new landlord, though I didn't refer to myself in that fashion. I used the term *property manager* and was sure to let him know I was the pastor at Trinity of Pine Haven and he was always welcome. By then, I knew about the red and yellow cards, and considered it a stroke of luck I could strike up a conversation with him in a space shuttle–sized hardware chain. Snowbin had a shag goatee then and purpled rings beneath his eyes; he smiled up at me with ocher-tinted teeth, specks of tobacco plain enough. I shook his hand, thick and calloused, and he held mine a second too long.

"If you have any problems, feel free to come to me," I told him. "Don't hesitate to call."

Snowbin never called and I didn't expect him. As far as I could tell, he attended no church, and divided his time among Quaker State, his home, and the Log Cabin, Pine Haven's longest-tenured bar. For a time, I almost prayed for his redemption, that he would be, for me, the tenant who never earned himself a red or yellow. I ended up scrapping the system entirely for a simpler internal checklist, no colors required, and there seemed to be a number of months where Snowbin intuited a system switch and behaved accordingly. He approached the status, briefly, of a model tenant. Then slippage. I'd like to think, contrary to scripture, he wasn't born with sin.

I reach his doormat, a dark brown monogrammed forty-eight-inch, soft underfoot. If he's smart, it's one hundred percent coir. A tongue of beige paint is peeling off the door. I knock, shave and a haircut, adding two bits for good measure. There's no sound of a television playing. Snowbin's cranky maroon Camaro is parked out front. He's here. It's just a matter of waiting.

No sound, and then footsteps. There's an unseen rustle and additional movement. I half expect him, cinema-style, to press apart the blades of his dusted venetians and peek one yellowed eye through the window. But the door is shaking and opening and there he is, in an imitation mohair and denim jeans, staring. A swollen pair of black Bose headphones are wrung around his neck. He heard me, to his chagrin, because they weren't yet around his ears.

"Yeah?"

"I wanted to say hello, see how it's all going, make sure everything's all right. I haven't heard from you in a little bit." *Heard from you* is the personal check hitting my mailbox. I offer my hand for a shake. He reaches out and shakes back, his grip far looser this time.

"All good over here, Pastor," he says, his ruddiness almost welcoming. I can't place Snowbin on any internal ethnicity matrix. English? Scotch-Irish? He's shaved his goatee, leaving behind a dark starfield of stubble. I don't smell liquor.

"Well, I am glad to hear it. I really am. I was just over at the Unger residence . . ." I'm not certain why I've told him this or why it matters. "And I wanted to check in here. It seems you are a bit behind on the rent. I wanted to make sure everything was well with you and see when we could be expecting the rent."

"*We*?"

"The management company. I'm the principal, but we have employees, a board, an accountant, an attorney. I like to think of it as a team and we are one."

"A team, huh?"

"Like the Tigers, except we can't all hit quite as well." I remember the Tigers, from my cursory interest, are playing below .500 ball and are inevitably not hitting all that well. This may be why Snowbin is not smiling. "We're not fireballers either."

"What happens if it stays late?"

"The rent?"

"Yur."

"We assess a fifteen percent late fee, which would be a real shame, since you're paying a fee you really shouldn't have to pay."

"And?"

"What do you mean?"

"Are there more fees, after the fifteen percent?"

"Well, it's fifteen percent on the month, and another fifteen on the subsequent month until the duration of your lease expiration.

It'd also be within our legal rights to initiate eviction proceedings. I don't think that's going to happen. I know you to be a good, respectable—"

"Cigarette?"

Snowbin slips out a pack of American Spirits from the front pocket of his mohair. He pinches one and lights up, blowing a small cloud to the side, away from me.

"No thank you, I don't smoke."

"A pastor, right."

"And I struggle with the taste. Once in a while, a good cigar."

Snowbin continues to smoke. He leans against the siding of his trailer, taking in a scene that might be of more interest to him than to me, his eyes falling to the roadway. He is my height, give or take a quarter inch, and his hard belly gives him an extra twenty pounds. His hair, which I've seen pressed beneath ball caps in the past, is an unruly thatch of chestnut.

"A good smoke on a cold morning, you don't know how good it is."

"Listen, I really don't want to intrude. I hate doing this. It's just you're very late."

"And you need the rent."

"That's right."

Snowbin takes another drag on his cigarette. When he's done, his chest inflates slightly, as if his next point must germinate there first, among the blood vessels and tendons swirling around his breastbone.

"My daddy used to take me to church. Every Sunday. He was a church elder. Maybe you knew of him, Ray Earl Snowbin."

Snowbin must know I'm barely forty. Few ever assume I'm *older* than I am. A meticulous skin care regimen and careful sun exposure has kept wrinkles at bay, absent genetic frown lines. My hair has yet to thin. Yet Snowbin imagines I was a contemporary of his father's. I consider whether to make this point gently, that his curiosity is implausible. A light correction. Snowbin is older than *me.*

"I didn't know him, no, though it's fantastic whenever someone decides to give back to the church community like that."

"My daddy talked to God every day. Do you, Pastor Starr, talk to Him every day?"

"I do, yes."

"Talk. Do you *talk*?"

"Yes, I do."

"What is it you talk about?"

"Questions of faith and the soul."

"Questions of faith and the soul," he repeats, turning the sentence over in his teeth, infusing it with his own syrupy fury. "Those are large questions. You get your money's worth."

"I hope you're talking to Him too. He's always listening, you know. Even when you think the door is shut. He wants to hear you."

"God wants his lot rent."

"There are temporal matters we do have to tend to, from time to time."

"If I pay now, do I owe you the fifteen percent?"

"Not yet. But very soon, you will. That's why I try to stop by. I don't want anyone in Utopia Gardens paying a late fee. I know, sometimes, money can slip anyone's mind. I know I'll forget about a utility bill, the water." I've never forgotten any of these bills. "It does happen."

"Indeed, life does happen, Pastor Starr."

"I'm glad you understand."

The cigarette now dangles from Snowbin's lips, desperado-style, and his left hand is toying with the pack, bopping it against his denimed thigh. I struggle to imagine what it is, right now, he's actually thinking.

"There's a smell here, you know," Snowbin finally says. "A smell all around."

"I don't smell anything in particular. Do you mean in the whole park, or inside your home, or a gas leak?"

"All around, man. You smell it once, you smell it always. It's like the burnt ass of a thoroughbred. You ever smelled that?"

"I've never, no."

"Here's what we'll do. You want a check. You're a pastor who wants to get paid. I can respect that. The last owner, he just sent us angry letters. You come in for the personal touch."

"Listen, we're all people here, and I just want to make sure you're all right, Mr. Snowbin. I want to be of help."

"You want to be of help, Pastor Starr?"

"Yes, of course."

Snowbin stubs out his cigarette. He has me in his sights now. No glancing right or left, no surveying a mythical scene beyond my shoulders. His left hand has steadied and the pack of American Spirits is back in his front pocket. A pair of northern cardinals wheel overhead, their feathers a filmic red. The sky is still quite blue.

"Why, you can pay it for me."

Perhaps I should have prepped for this turn all along. Most tenants understand the logic undergirding real estate enough to never venture such a request, even of a pastor. They are properly accustomed. The Ungers know they've signed a binding lease. Snowbin must know too. I would ache for him if I had heard Quaker State decided, one week ago, they no longer needed men to cheerily change oil. I would ache if the job market were so loose that even handy men couldn't labor at auto shops any longer. I would ache if I were an anchorite locked away from the world, with no comprehension of temporal economics. Lon Snowbin, with his American Spirits and T.J.Maxx denim, would have my charity, and I would rush to the Chevy's glove compartment and find my checkbook.

But that is not his reality. He believes he is playing from a strength, not a weakness. He has money socked away somewhere, just not for today, just not for lot rent at Utopia Gardens. He's betting I'll fold in, that walking with God is somehow a sign that he can have what he wants and get back to his American Spirits and midday masturbation. I've met many men like him. They take the church for little more than an assemblage of rubes and suckers, worshipping the invisible, and they profess an interest in God only when it furthers whatever transitory political agenda they may pursue on the expressway to hell. They vote Republican and that, they figure, should be enough. They last opened the Bible when they were ten and they last spoke about the teachings earnestly when they were eight. Their grasp on the matters of the body politic is not any greater than their understanding of Jesus Christ. A pastor who collects rent isn't to be taken seriously as a landlord; he *preaches*, so how can he be owed anything? Pastors are too busy unraveling Exodus to understand a land contract in the state of Michigan. Pastors don't scrutinize pronouncements from the Federal Reserve or consider the ROI on a distressed property.

Pastors don't stand in your doorway, unmoving. I grin back at him. There's a band of warm sunlight hitting my neck just right. Snowbin doesn't know how eager I can be.

"That's an excellent suggestion. I'd be happy to take a peek into your accounts and tax returns sometime to see whether you qualify for rental assistance. You may be eligible, depending on your prior year returns. And if you don't want the government involved at all, I can consider a bridge loan. It would be a favor from me to you because you've been at Utopia Gardens for a few years now."

"A peek, huh?"

"I'd have our office review the paperwork and I'd personally oversee it all so we can process you in a timely manner, assuming you'd like to be processed."

The gleam has faded. He has, like a butterfly forced backward into his cocoon, assumed his natural state, a man with a circumscribed aptitude for the affairs that involve any movement of money. Bar math is easy, and so is Quaker State math. Lon Snowbin is the kind of man who thinks it's clever to ask your height and then tell you he didn't know shit could be piled so high. I could save him if he let me, but he will never let me. He will slink through the years, maybe give the wrong state trooper the side-eye, and do a jail stint he'll have to explain away when he's sixty.

"I'll have the money," he says quietly.

"I very much appreciate that. And you know what? I think I'll have a cigarette, after all. I've heard good things about American Spirit and it's been so long."

Snowbin does not want to reach back into his mohair, fondle the pack, and hand to me, the man extracting monthly lot rent from him, one of his prized cigarettes. He silently offers one, a light tremor in his fingers, and I give him the smile of a man with plenty. It's my curtain-raiser, extra wide and bright, like the one I normally tuck away for the pulpit.

"And if you could give me a light, please."

Snowbin passes his teal gas station lighter. I hadn't noticed it until now. Teal is a color that holds your gaze. "Thank you."

I hold the lighter in one hand, the cigarette in the other. I put the cigarette to my lips and slowly, slowly, raise the lighter. Snowbin is watching and I have to be sure he's watching, that he doesn't lose interest or drift behind his door, never to be seen again. But his cigarette is involved—he'll keep on me, too despairing to look elsewhere. The cigarette is soft between my lips.

"Ah, well, you know what? I think I changed my mind, Mr. Snowbin. This may be rougher on me than I thought. It's been so many years since I puffed one of these."

I pass the lighter back and keep the cigarette cool and crushed in my mouth. If Snowbin had the wherewithal, he'd be calculating precisely how much money he had wasted on me. He would torture himself for days.

After the full second passes, I pluck the cigarette out of my mouth. "My apologies."

I let Lon Snowbin's worthless cigarette drop to the dirt and walk back to the Chevy, my time with him through.

On Saturday, I take Gwennie, our lemon-and-white beagle, on a walk around the old Nyman Park. It's early, just after six, and in a few hours the whole Starr crew is headed up to Orchard for the annual Flapjack Jubilee. We're missing the race and the free eggs and flapjack breakfast, but we plan to bob and weave around the carnival, gobbling elephant ears, cotton candy, and popcorn. The kiddos will ride the rides and I'll watch them ride the rides. Most of Pine Haven converges on the grounds of Orchard High, where the Flapjack Jubilee is held every year, usually the third week of May. Orchard is half the size of Pine Haven, little more than a smattering of churches, general stores, and a public school system, no liberal arts school, no downtown for the liberal arts school to slowly consume.

Pine Haven now has a Starbucks, a used record shop, microbrewery, and a wine store. There's hardly any need to go into the city anymore.

Nyman Park, plunked southwest of downtown, was, for many years, something of an emblem of the pre-commerce Pine Haven: easy to idealize, unworkable in the context of the twenty-first century. When I started at Trinity, Nyman Park was a partially untrammeled expanse of switchgrass, some of it nipple-scraping. On the west side, the Spruce River brought the occasional fisherman, and honking wild geese mounted their attacks across the cratered walking path that took you around the perimeter. What I remember from the old park was the varieties of shit the geese inevitably deposited on the path, and the game you could play hopscotching over whorls of gray-green, hoping one piece never went kersplat on your new soles. At the center of it all was a soccer field, sometimes utilized by the local PAL league and the middle school, and I suppose there's a reason to miss that, even with superior fields across town.

As part of the land acquisition, Everest & Rulopaugh agreed to build a new walking path. Now the cement is bone-white and blemish-free, and just enough grass has been left behind if Gwennie gets an idea to give chase after whatever wildlife crawls out of the river. Theodore didn't like the loss of the field and I can still recall the talk I gave him, about the beauty of change and progress. He was younger then, just nine, and I assume my words will echo with him when he has the maturity to give shape to them in his years of near-adulthood. "Building is what we do, as people," I told him. "It's what God wants of us. To strive—to exist, as gloriously as we can, in His image."

I'm amazed at how fast Everest & Rulopaugh can work. In one year's time, practically, they made Nyman Park into their pontoon paradise. I like to think, in my small way, I played a part. That's the wonder of a town versus a city—a *real* city, not what Pine Haven remains, a census-designated city that exists, in the only way that counts, as a town. Here the interlocking and intermingling—the collaboration that gives us meaning—is possible, which allows humanity to thrive at its intended scale. Inevitably, many of us in Pine Haven wear two or three or four hats: other than Lon Snowbin, maybe, no one rubs an eyeball over a pastor-realtor. Brendan Hannon, in addition to serving in my prayer circle and running point on logistics at Everest & Rulopaugh, is the commissioner, unpaid, of the Pine Haven Soccer League. Part of the dream of Everest & Rulopaugh's expansion was Brendan's; part was mine; and part of it was Mayor Zeke Street's. Zeke has owned and operated Tried & True Hardware in downtown Pine Haven for twenty-eight years. Multiple hats, see. Anomie is only possible if you're nesting with sociopaths.

Today, I would give a different speech to Theodore because I do believe he is old enough, at thirteen, to understand the glory in mundanity, the grayscale switches and hubs—the metaphorical circuitry, unseen—that make up any grand plan. Boys will bemoan, bemoan, bemoan—they are, still so close to their births, sensitive to small losses. They don't yet understand a point in time cannot be fixed and extended outward, in perpetuity.

Theodore, who likes booting his soccer ball and tossing the frisbee with Gwenee, very much wanted Nyman Park not to change. He didn't understand the pavers and diggers and cyclone fencing, which has remained. He didn't understand the disappearance of his switchgrass. He didn't understand why supposedly open space could be, in the matter of a year, so closed, property that seemed to be his now belonging, at a rapid clip, to another, a faceless venture that had nothing to do with Gwenee, soccer, or frisbees. *Faceless* is my approximation of his thinking; he knows Brendan from church and, even then, mildly understood Brendan had a job with the pontoon factory. Brendan has been to my house many times for dinner. Still, it can be difficult for a boy to meld a conception of Brendan from church—Brendan, with three boys including one, Garrett, a grade ahead of Theodore—and a corporation building atop Nyman Park.

Theodore, today, would hear from me about shared prosperity. We have many fields of grass in town, but only one Everest & Rulopaugh, one of the most successful pontoon manufacturers in the country, right here in Pine Haven. They can go anywhere and were threatening, four years ago, to head to Georgia until Mayor Street intervened and told the city commission it was a time to grant Everest & Rulopaugh the tax abatement they deserved for their years of service to the town and greater Luce County. Losing them would have gutted us, economically and psychologically, and I don't think the latter can be discounted. This, I would have to couch to my son carefully. The psychogeography of a particular place can, over the years, shape its destiny. A man's feelings for his town can become his town, and a mass of men act accordingly, either in fits of ambition or outright desperation. Opioids have not racked Pine Haven; the usual ills of deindustrialization passed us over and we never devolved into an anecdote for a northeastern newspaper straining to explain, to its Amtrak readership, why the country has grown so alien to them. The stasis of prosperity: my goals, and those of the town, are implicitly intertwined. The tax abatement vote was unanimous. In the matter of three weeks, the business was done.

Mayor Street does not attend Trinity—he's a longtime member, out of loyalty to his mother, of West Superior Christian—and I know not to try to lure him my way. Rather, we go out together during hunting season and I make it my mission to stop into Tried & True at least once a week, whether I'm pursuing a home improvement project or not. The mayor is good to those who do business with him, and he has what I'd like to think of as a *land* perspective to most matters. He understands what it can do, when placed in the right hands. In his visionary flashes, he saw what needed to be done with Nyman Park.

Gwenee races around the polished cyclone fencing. We're at the perimeter, where we once set out blankets to watch soccer games, and now the pontoons crowd. There are, by my count, at least fifty pontoons parked there, a nifty whirl of sporting, luxury, cruising, fishing, and double-decker. I spy the Venture 88 Cruise IV, a port and starboard bow bench and extended seating without the portside gate, and the 89 Quad Lounger, a twenty-seven inch. Both are beaming white with swoosh accents, a subtle stars-and-stripe theme, and I shift closer for a better look. To the left are a pair of luxury Excalibur Quad Loungers, each equipped with Medallion touchscreens, eight-speaker audio systems, and GPS. I'm not a boater myself. What I am, however, is an appreciator of those who boat, of ideas and concepts and propositions, the promise of an organized day on the lake. Whole lives are made in these boats. From a distance, they seem almost alive, napping orca-like creatures ejected from far-flung worlds, fresh sunlight twinkling off their aluminum snouts. Gwenee barks at them.

The abatement was paired, unofficially, with the land acquisition. For $50,200, the city sold the acreage to Everest & Rulopaugh, approved a quick rezoning, and the storage capacity for hot-off-the-assembly-line pontoons ballooned just in time for next summer. As a citizen of Pine Haven, my interests are bound up in the success of the pontoon manufacturer, and I've also got my own stake, which perhaps would have softened the blow to Theodore at the time, if he understood what it would mean for the quality of his Christmas presents or the renovation of our beloved in-ground pool. Several years back, with Brendan Hannon's urging, I joined Everest & Rulopaugh's board of directors, where I had the pleasure of perusing quarterly reports and occasionally participating in strategy calls.

My sense, from joining, is that the men at the top wanted less boating expertise and more discernment of the town they had headquartered in for the last fifteen years. There was something of a siege mentality—of a company unsure of Pine Haven's intentions, of a town wary of what a pontoon manufacturer promised—that I hoped to quash, and eventually did. I proposed a local hiring program and the easing of a college degree requirement for the office side that culled, in my view, too many deserving Pine Haven applicants. I told them they needed to start sponsoring a Little League team and help fund a new grandstand at the Blossom Avenue ballfields where they play. Brendan should toss out a first pitch. At every parade—Memorial Day, the Fourth, the Halloween assemblage—Everest & Rulopaugh needed a float, a tent, free candy for children, and attractive T-shirts (also gratis) for adults. Beyond Pine Haven, they needed to be the most prominent sponsor of the Flapjack Jubilee 5K. All of these upfront costs, I explained, would repay themselves easily and lay the foundation for even greater gains. More than anything, I argued then, Everest & Rulopaugh needed to be perceived as a *family* company, and I proposed, on the north wall of the cozy office park, a mural of children laughing and playing schoolyard games, to be painted by talented students recommended by Pine Haven High art teachers. All of it was done.

Pontoons, pontoons, pontoons—as far as the eye can see. I circle once more, making sure Gwenee gets her exercise. She won't be coming to the Flapjack Jubilee. I'm near the office park when I see Adrian Mueller walking his burly schnauzer. He, like me, is an early riser, and he's looking especially fit today in his Under Armour tee and mesh shorts. It's not even sixty degrees, but he seems unbothered. Just as he sees me, I wave at him, and Gwenee rushes headlong toward his schnauzer, Achilles.

"Good morning, Pastor!"

"Adrian, always a pleasure catching you with the early birds. Are you going for a run? 5K's in another hour and a half."

"Oh, I know, Jessica wants to get a move on. Talyn and I are running it this year. One of these years, Pastor, we need you in there. You've got what it takes."

"I haven't run that far since I was eighteen, and I don't plan to again."

"We'll be seeing you, then, at the carnival. Jessica is selling her crafts. This year, she crocheted all of these cute kiddy animals—baby crocodiles, bears, and raptors. She's selling them for twenty-five dollars a pop. I told her she should list them higher, but that'll do for her. Come by our table."

"You bet I will. You know, I'd do the 5K someday to get those free flapjacks and eggs."

"That's the perk. And the T-shirt."

"Thinking about it is getting me hungry."

"Oh, I bet."

We're both betting now. "Daniella, you know, will be interested in those crafts. She started up crocheting recently. I'm out of the house a lot and when the kids are at school, she needs fun and challenging hobbies. I've seen her toy around with it. Jessica, I'm sure, is a real pro."

"Women amaze me sometimes. Such ingenuity. I didn't think we'd have eight—I prayed for five, and we were blessed with three more—and sometimes they're more than a handful. But Jessica keeps this steamship running. I try to get everybody enough attention between all the screaming. It'll be good for Talyn to get up there and run today. He's got a real shot to make varsity cross-country fwhen he gets to be a freshman. I'm sure he'll be looking forward to seeing Theodore. Those two have gotten thick as thieves."

"Theodore and Talyn are at that age. Manhood in grasp, yet they're still boys, and the future can't extend past the gym class next period. He wants to go out for the basketball and baseball teams when he gets to high school. I told him, either way, he needs to be ready for the practice, the rigor. This won't be booting balls around the grass at Nyman Park. You're closer to the big leagues."

"Oh yeah, Talyn used to like running around here too." Adrian turns his head toward the cyclone fencing and surveys a row of pontoons now resplendent in the sun. "This was a fun park while it lasted."

"It was, for a time."

Adrian continues to stare at the pontoons.

"Well, I'll be seeing you, Pastor. Say hi at the crafts table."

"Be good, Adrian."

The world needs more Adrian Muellers. Tidy players, tidy thinkers. Life, if it's to be successful, is about ironing out the knots. Adrian's on a smooth express lane to a comfortable retirement, little traffic ahead, every metaphor right in place. He ambles on at a relaxed clip, Achilles silent at his side, no leash needed. I wait for him to turn the corner out of the park and decide it's time to get home. I'll be driving everyone to Orchard. Daniella doesn't have a crafts table—I should really encourage her—but she's good for forty minutes of wandering there, picking over the handcrafted doodads like an archaeologist. I prefer the rides, the attractions, the faded splendor of any good carnival. I'll be walking Chloe and Austin around, buying over-sugared lemonade and fried Oreos, playing dad.

In the meantime, a sermon comes to me. Tomorrow's is already planned, but there's always tinkering to be done, themes to be intertwined or disregarded. Preaching is not so different than writing or politicking. Your words begin as a bridge to reality and become, with enough effort and execution, reality itself. God creates, but you are in His shadow, imbued with his universe-shaping wisdom and grace. A pastor is called. There are those who aren't called who preach anyway, grasping onto the temporal authority or the paycheck. Many take annual salaries and strain for pay bumps. When I started at Pine Haven, I told them I was going to preach on commission, with my rate increasing if we grew the church. If growth wasn't evident, they had every right to reduce my compensation. Daniella didn't like this at first—she's not one for risk—and I explained, patiently, this was how success could be achieved. You place your trust in God and *then* you place your trust in yourself. It's a bromide, but bromides are often true. You'll be successful if you decide, largely, to live by them. Folk wisdom endures for a reason.

Some of my favorites: don't bite the hand that feeds you; what goes around comes around; a penny saved is a penny earned. Can you argue with any of them? As I sit in my car and drive the five minutes to my home, this thought competes with the sermon—I want to turn over Ephesians, perhaps three. Most priests, reverends, and pastors who claim to have memorized the Bible are lying. I preach mostly from NIV these days, if I prefer King James; I have committed enough of both to memory, though I'll never lie about knowing more than I actually know. *Put on the full armor of God,* Paul commanded. *For our struggle is not against flesh and blood, but against the rulers, against the authorities, against the power of this dark world and against the spiritual forces of evil in the heavenly realms.* It's such an alluring image, marching in God's armor; Paul dreamt, in his own way, of battle. *Stand firm then, with the belt of truth buckled around your waist, with the breastplate of righteousness in place, and with your feet fitted with the readiness that comes from the gospel of peace.*

Ephesians passes from memory to my lips. I am speaking soundlessly. Nowhere in the Bible is there talk of fairness—not from God, his son, and his messengers, anyway. Fairness is a human creation. The justice of the courts is not God's justice. God created all of it: goodness, justice, fairness. God can bend an arm backward, make red turn blue, make debauchery a virtue, not a sin. He exists beyond light and darkness because he filled the void with both. Most men of faith underestimate God's power. They lack the ambition to conceive of what it might do, what it is to shine in God's universe. They've never felt the weight of His armor.

How can I get Trinity to feel that weight? That, in some respects, is my greatest task. To make them understand what it means to armor yourself against the forces that seek to unravel a community like this one. I will tell them some of this on Sunday, once I straighten it all out for presentation. I want to say something about the danger of mixing social justice with the church.

But first, I'm home.

Theodore is my only child who remembers what it was like to live anywhere other than Hearst Road. For Chloe and Austin, this is their only home, and I prefer it that way. Memory is a fickle mistress and can incite all kinds of confusions and agitations, unspool narratives that cling in unexpected ways. Theodore is old enough to have known *ascension*, to see his own financial station evolve.

Before Hearst, we lived near the river, in a two-bed, two-bath that was built in the early 1900s. It was insulated well enough to prevent frostbite and little else. By late fall, clouds of breath hung in the bathroom; when snow piled up on the roof, in January, it seemed plausible that the bulk of it would collapse straight through in a matter of days, drowning us in meltwater. Stray dogs danced far too close to our porch. Bats wheeled around the detached garage. As soon as I was able to get us out, we got out.

When I bought 48 Hearst Road, interest rates were nonexistent and the market was in a long cooling-off period. I pity my buyers today, and that's why I'm so committed to helping them land without immolating their credit. At the time, I took a fifteen-year mortgage—in today's game, you're paying double value if you go off a thirty-year interest rate, and even a decade ago, the logic of taking a thirty was equivalent to firing off all your bullets from a limp crouch—and paid it off aggressively, having already put almost forty percent down, much more than the recommended twenty. I had cash to spare and wanted a lower rate. It was rare, then, for a Pine Haven home to sell for north of $250,000, and I blew past that. My market value, if I ever bothered to sell, has likely tripled since.

Consider that real estate is location—you know this already. Hearst Road is just within the city limits, a short drive from downtown, and abutting Pine Links, the most desirable golf course in Luce County. Sometimes, when I'm out on the back patio, I can hear the little *thwick* of a well-struck golf ball through the hedges.

A few minutes ago, I was dreaming of my helix-shaped driveway, a gentle and immaculate curve to the front door, and now my automobile hums on it passing through on the way to the three-car garage in the rear. A petroleum engineer, with the help of an architect reared in the Prairie School, built the house in 1964, plumping the six-bedroom, five-bath sand-brick beauty on prime green, sweating over the hipped roof, overhanging eaves, and the horizontal band windows that drink an evening sun so well. If I weren't a pastor, a realtor, or a property manager—and if the outside didn't call to me so frequently, for the business of the town is the business, ultimately, of life—I'd be content to putter around indoors, drinking a cool Coke at the marble fireplace or entertaining Antrim and his pals at the wet bar. The butler pantry is a favorite touch. The game room, on the lower level, is built to Theodore's desire, and we've sanded away afternoons knocking around the billiards balls. When I bought the house, it came with a commercial-grade backup generator.

The gunite in-ground pool is the gem, in my view and Daniella's, though she isn't much for a swim. She prefers to sit poolside on a white fabric chaise longue and read novels, mystery or romance, titles I can't recall. When we moved in, there was no pool, and we had it built and customized, a slight undulation Daniella sketched out with a pen and pad and flashed at our contractor. The aggregate finish, more my idea, combines colored plaster mixer with shards of granite, quartz, and glass beads. At sundown, there's a Martian glow I can bask in for hours.

Around here, pool season runs from the end of May to the start of September, and you're paying to not use it for large stretches of the year. This isn't Los Angeles. Many a pool owner has gotten the blues in October or February, staring out at the snow-covered tarp, wondering why he bothered in the first place. Pools taunt and pools kill. Other than owning a gun, there's no greater predictor of untimely childhood death than a swimming pool. Children trip and children drown. I followed Theodore like a hawk in his first few years and now I trust him to keep an eye on his younger siblings if I have work to do indoors. Pool management is risk management. I do believe it's all worth it, because there's little more glory than the end of May, poolside, spring pouring into summer. I've sketched out sermons poolside and closed more than a few deals. Daniella has caught me napping too, a hint of saliva on my lips.

"Theodore, Austin, Chloe, let's go!" I call out when I trundle through the front door, Gwennie in tow. The living room is back to hardwood after we ripped out the carpeting and I'm pleased with the new finish, the light glint. In the kitchen, Chloe and Austin are bent over bowls of Kix and Frosted Mini-Wheats, each child blending the cereals with a healthy heaping of milk. I don't see Daniella, who is probably getting ready in our bedroom, and I fear Theodore, given his age, is probably sleeping. The youngest boys and oldest men have little trouble waking at dawn and embarking on whatever business they might have, whether it's cartoon consumption or a gentle walk to the post office. Come ten or eleven, these powers recede, and budding adolescence demands heaps of sleep and ornery wakeups. Theodore is there, though I'd prefer he'd forestall this phase a little longer. This is obviously my first brush with adolescence as a parent, but I've gabbed enough with the other fathers at the church to know a bit of what's in store. Marijuana, for one, is now legal in the state, and it's not hard for a freshman in high school to talk a senior with a fake ID into procuring beers from one of the lax rural gas stations up M-70. I'm a wilier adversary than Theodore thinks; a thirteen-year-old may believe forty is *old*, but youth is still not difficult to conceive at this age. The generational wall isn't made of iron. I can punch through when need be.

"Where's Theodore?" I ask. My children, still hunched over cereal, shrug. "And Mama?"

"Bedroom," Chloe murmurs.

"Theodore is in his bedroom?"

"Mama is. He said he wanted to walk and Mama let him."

"Mama just let Theodore go for a walk?"

"Mama was tired and said it was okay. She told us to eat breakfast. I poured cereal for Austin."

"You did great."

I'm no longer feeling leisurely. Letting Theodore strut out of the house, unattended, was not part of the plan. We're all due for the Flapjack Jubilee well before noon because finding parking, for the only time all year, is a challenge. The high school lot fills fast for the 5K and temporary town ordinances forbid all manner of street parking. Homeowners blot out available spaces by pulling their automobiles out of their driveways and preemptively leaving them out front. Others post passive-aggressive handwritten notes on traffic cones. Three years ago, my fate was to inch at ten to fifteen miles per hour on local Orchard streets, craning my neck in vain for anywhere at all to stop driving and walk the three to five blocks to the carnival. One reason to not live in a city is to avoid wrenching experiences like these.

"I'm going to say hi to Mama."

The master bedroom down the hallway off the living room, with windows facing out toward the backyard, where we have three quarters of an acre of greenery. The door is closed which means Daniella is inside. Daniella prefers a courtesy knock and I give one before edging in, quickly smiling to show I mean no harm. I'm here for inquiry and clarification, and little else.

"How goes it?"

The skin of Daniella's bare back peeks out of her walk-in closet. She's rifling for clothing, trying to make the right pick for a day on the town. I can empathize. If you aren't what you wear, you're an approximation, a strong echo of whatever churns inside. Her back disappears fully into the closet and I'm left to stand, arms akimbo, in our sprawling oblong master, earnest morning light forcing its way through the blinds. Our bed is still unmade and I wish Daniella would tidy it already.

"Any idea where Theodore's off to?" I try again.

"He wanted air," a voice that belongs to my wife replies, from deep inside her closet.

"He wanted—not *needed*. We're on a tight, tight schedule today, dear. The jubilee is rocking and rolling already. And here we are."

"We'll have plenty of time to be there, to roam," the voice answers.

"That's all relative. You know today is the one day of the year the rural reaches of the Wolverine State become Times Square."

This reference probably irks her; we took a family trip to New York two years ago and Daniella found herself turning and turning in the widening gyre, unable to hear the falconer, mere anarchy loosed, the blood-dimmed tide washing over her shoes. I enjoyed it, personally, and I think Chloe and Austin got a kick out of the ferry ride we took around Manhattan Island. It was a city of godless liberals, though the sheer abundance of churches, Christian and Catholic alike, could almost dispel that notion. Daniella seemed to resent, in particular, my insistence that we travel to an Orthodox Jewish or *frum* enclave, Borough Park, to see how another Abrahamic people went about their days. There are as many Venusians as Jews in Pine Haven and I thought it would be ameliorative to go there, like taking a trip to Paris or Japan, to see black-coated, black-hatted, black-bearded, white-skinned Jews hurrying about their crammed chockablock quarters. And hurry they did. There was an industry to their gait you don't see much around here, a craving to erase the distance between Point A and Point B. Daniella did not like the Hebrew scrawls, the kosher butchers, the yellow cheese buses—crammed with yarmulke-clad boys—groaning around double and triple-parked automobiles. Daniella didn't like the pigeons either.

I tempted fate by being there. But that was how comfortable I felt.

"Teddy, I . . ." and the voice trails off.

"Where exactly did Theodore go?"

"He'll be back soon. He has his phone. He wanted to walk to the trail and back."

"It's almost as if you think he has all day and night."

"As I said, he'll be back soon."

She is out of the closet now, in one of her frilly black bras, and she's yet to apply any of her signature makeup. There's a lovely ghostliness to her face now, thinned out in a half shadow, and I notice, as she turns toward me, the imprint of her rib flashing through taut, creamy skin. Daniella, five-two in her stocking feet, has dark brown eyes and lighter brown hair that tapers at the breastbone; when she's like this, I'm reminded why I wanted her in the first place and why, at times, I need to drift off and recalibrate at the Breckenridge homestead.

"You should have told me you were letting him take a walk, dear."

"I was not going to call you to tell you this."

"It would have taken a simple second. We have cellular devices for a reason."

"Perhaps your son feels the need, in this particular instance, to not be called—to walk, to enjoy. We will get to the jubilee and we will have the most precious parking space you can imagine."

"You're being chippy."

"*You're* chippy. You just consider anything you can't immediately agree with or even contextualize as chippy. I'm here getting my clothes on. Chloe and Austin are eating breakfast. Theodore is walking. Quite frankly, at this age, we should be thankful he wants to take a walk early in the morning—that if he's going to have a vice, it's *this*, not calling you on the phone."

"Theodore likes to disengage. It's hard to tell, sometimes, what he's thinking."

"And it's harder to tell, at times, what you're thinking. He inherited the floating sensibility from you. The feeling that other people may or may not be there, even when they are, even when there isn't a debate. You could talk a tangible object into being intangible. Now I'm going to the bathroom."

Daniella walks past me into the master bath and I suddenly feel a longing for the Jacuzzi, a bubbly spray at my chest. This isn't how I wanted the morning to continue. When I left, Theodore was still sleeping, and I assumed he's still be sleeping when I returned. I don't know anything about this walking habit. Daniella is an *in medias res* kind of person—she supposes it's fine enough to not know the backstory if the present itself, to her at least, makes enough sense—and I doubt she knew anything more than I did about Theodore's sudden love of unannounced strolls. But she can pretend to, and that irks and irritates. If I tell her this, we could break into open warfare, and I've made a vow never to fight in front of the children, always keeping my voice at a steady octave, a smile never far away. Daniella's rage is hushed anyway; it travels at an undercurrent, surfacing with long-forgotten grievances when you least expect it. Two weeks from now, we'll be discussing this.

Either way, where is Theodore? I'm his father and I *can* call him. I never entered into a covenant to let him simply bandy about. I was ambivalent, at first, about Theodore even getting a cell phone, and it was ironically Daniella who was more in favor of the idea, believing we were setting him up for social failure if we didn't at least provide him with a means to communicate with his friends outside of school. Internet access is severely limited (something Daniella and I agree upon, at least) and I chose for him a Samsung over an iPhone, in part because I didn't want him to make a false idol out of a brand. Apple shouldn't have any apostles. I don't know of Samsung, a fine Korean corporation, having any. He'll have one of the Galaxies until he moves out of my house.

I press Theodore's name on my phone and wait. One ring, two ring, three. If he doesn't pick up by three, this usually means he won't pick up at all. The voicemail, which he set up at my insistence, clicks on, Theodore uttering *Hi this is Theodore, leave a message thanks* in an oddly throaty monotone, like a bit of mucus was lodged deep in him that day. I don't leave a message because even

I know this is foolish. I pound out a text, *We're leaving soon, time to come home*, and wait for a response. If he doesn't answer in ten minutes, I'll call again.

Austin and Chloe are too young for cell phones. They're at ages where personality is still not a fixed construct. They can be, on any given day, different people, though I sense where their temperaments are headed. Chloe has a wit. Austin speaks softly. I think they're going to be children who answer their phones, once they have them. I hope they are children that do not take sides; I hope, in particular, that they are not against me.

Is Theodore against me? I know his phone is on and I know he would see that I'm calling. He keeps a loud ringer. Perhaps, last night, I could have communicated to him better how important it was for all of us to get an early start. Daniella knew. She just didn't care.

"We have to get going soon, dear, the kids are still around the breakfast table," I call out to the bedroom, where the door is half open. I wait one beat and then two, hearing nothing. "Can you get the kids ready?"

Austin has started in with his tablet, playing a racing game with cartoon characters I barely recognize, and Chloe is still fiddling with the cards. It's as if time were the most irrelevant construct, a mere suggestion or something that could be manufactured at will, like cotton candy. They take after Daniella, in that regard. Sometimes, I wonder what it would be like to be so breezily indifferent. Wondrous, childlike—fine for Chloe and Austin, who are literally children, and maybe Theodore, who is verging closer to adulthood than he thinks, but not for Daniella. No, not for a woman of thirty-seven, a mother of three, the wife of a pastor. When you lead a church, you gain a greater understanding of the movement of time. There is no such thing as lateness when it comes to delivering a sermon or counseling a couple in distress. Adrian and Gregg and Brendan and Big Landry would not follow me if I regarded time the way Daniella does, if I merely drifted and hoped for events to coalescence in an agreeable way. She has still not come out of the bedroom. A spout of metaphorical bile is surging somewhere up my innards and I stifle my language, sanding it down to, "Daniella, *please*."

Nothing. I call Theodore a second time. Ring, ring, ring, ring. *Hi, this is Theodore.* I miss the sensation of hanging up on a landline. We still have one but never use it. Before I angrily click, I leave a voicemail. He won't check it. "Theodore, this is your father, it's almost nine o'clock. Please come home. We're getting ready to drive up to Orchard." It's actually six minutes past nine. I'm not sure why I lied. The children are still puttering, tablet and cards, and Chloe seems to have invented her own game. Cold bowls of milk begin to warm. Boxes of cereal are still out and I decide, at least, to put them away.

"Chloe, Austin, go to your mother."

I send them toward her bedroom where she'll have to handle their needs, dressing and toothbrushing and hair-combing. I've eaten, I've brushed, I've dressed. All that's left is the family and, crucially, Theodore. Daniella can process the children quickly, get them up and ready and fired out of the chute when she commits to it. It's Theodore, who was permitted to gallivant, to gather air on the one day he could do so on our schedule, get his calves flexed and breathe lusciously through his nostrils at the Flapjack Jubilee, where we're supposed to be. Half of Pine Haven will be transported there and it's all but guaranteed there will be no parking near the high school at the rate we are progressing.

"I'm going outside to see if Theodore is coming," I say in Daniella's direction, imagining her nodding in agreement. Our front lawn, on a second inspection, is not as immaculate as it should be, and I'm going to have to call in the landscaper sooner rather than later. Quadrants of our Kentucky bluegrass and perennial ryegrass have been lightly trampled, Chloe and Austin clearly not heeding my call to avoid the front for play—they have the whole sprawl of the backyard for their games, day and night—and Daniella not admonishing them like she should. She is here far more than I am. This will be discussed.

Theodore is not coming from either direction on Hearst Road. To my right, past another row of homes on each side, is the elementary school and then the biking trail, where Theodore might be. I debate whether to, against my better instincts, head into the Chevy and cruise up and down Hearst until Theodore emerges. If he's on the biking trail, I can't reach him—and if he's not, he should be emerging soon. There's still some time, a diminishing amount, when we can arrive in Orchard and hope to nab a spot in the high school parking lot. Each minute that slips by, though, will make it less likely.

Theodore is nowhere. I lean against my Chevy, arms crossed. There's nothing else to do. My phone has no missed calls, no texts. Thoughts of Gertrude drift back, whether she'll head up to the jubilee without Harry—it's always been the three of them there, and Harry's still laid up at Luce Memorial—and when I can make it out again to the homestead. Perhaps in three or four days. Will Gertrude be there with Aidan, aping single motherhood? Harry isn't the most attentive father anyway. It might be good for Aidan to have time at the fair. Gertrude and I could watch him on the Tilt-A-Whirl as Daniella takes Austin for a pony ride.

"Where are you?" I hear a tinny voice from inside the house. I turn and see I've left the door ajar, allowing the voice to travel to me. It's Daniella's. "Where did you go?"

"I'm outside."

"Why?"

She's moved through the threshold and is staring at me. "I'm waiting for our son," I say.

"He's on his way."

“He hasn’t told me this.”

“He told me he’ll be back in ten minutes.”

“Ten minutes. I didn’t hear this.”

“He texted me. You weren’t here when he left so, in this particular interaction, I’m his point of contact.”

“Are Chloe and Austin ready?”

“They’re ready.”

“Very good. We need to get going very, very soon.”

Daniella turns back into the house without saying anything. Again, I’m alone here, still perched on the Chevy. My son is nowhere. I glance at my watch, a silver steel forty-three-millimeter TAG Heuer, and I decide to count down seconds and minutes. Beyond my backyard shrubbery, I hear the soft click of a golf ball and know we’re in it now. The old boys are golfing and we’re not early for anything anymore. There will be no parking space at Orchard High School.

Does a pastor think about God all day? Many years ago, when I was just starting out, the small child of a parishioner who has since moved to Indiana, Buster Van der Platts, asked me if I was *always* thinking about God. It was not accusatory; the boy was genuinely curious. He was pudgy, coal-eyed, a bit of drool peeking out from his corner lip. At the time, he might have been seven. And I answered, in full view of Buster and his wife, *yes.* God and his son are always, indeed, on my mind. We are formed in God’s image, I said, and I am tasked at this church with communicating the word of God to you and your parents so I must be thinking of Him—His glory and His message. Had his parents not been there—had the question not been posed in our fellowship room, in view of five or six parishioners—I might have sprinkled my answer with addendums. God is everywhere, and inside me and you, and since He has created all of us, even the movement of our thoughts are, naturally, a product of His work. But mankind, being born into sin and an unshakable wickedness that is noted rather plainly by God in Genesis, will drift from Him in his daily ruminations.

I was thinking of my children, Orchard High School parking spaces, Daniella, Gertrude. Where was God? Where was his son? In there, sure, churning about, but not supreme, in those moments, in my consciousness. But God blesses all of it—that I know from prayer. For my work, this bounty. His wisdom is unquestioned. His wisdom has brought me here.

To my right, at Hearst Road's horizon line, a small figure emerges on the roadway's shoulder. He has black mesh shorts, weathered white sneakers, and a navy-blue T-shirt falling down to his thighs, the logo still unintelligible from this distance. It's my son.

He is coming lightly, slowly, no hurry at all in his gait, his eyes drifting to a treetop or a flock of birds. I stand ready at the hood of my Chevy. The T-shirt is an oversized number we bought for him at a Tigers game last year; I can now see the stylized Old English "D" in white at his left breast. He sees me now and this has not increased his speed at all. I decide, at first, to pretend I don't see him. I glance at my watch and hold the glancing, counting down seconds. At fifteen, I look up again, and Theodore is slightly closer, bent down toward the phone he's holding in his right hand. His thumb is twitching over the screen. By now, he's seen my text. Perhaps he's deigned to respond.

If I am guilty of not thinking about God as much as I told Buster Van der Platts's son, I know I have to do much more work to ensure Theodore is even thinking about God at all. I watch him in the pews. He sits on one side of Daniella, Chloe and Austin on the other, and he battles back sleep. I've watched his eyelids grow heavy, his forehead dip forward. When he was younger, he had a growing, preternatural understanding of scripture; I remember, at nine, he was posing questions about Colossians, Paul's labor for the church, his mind happily darting toward obscurities. Over the past year, I've seen his interest in the Bible diminish, his church attendance and general participation more rote; the Mueller children, for example, seem to care much more. Why has he grown so slack?

I've asked Daniella versions of these questions. And she sees fit, almost every time, to disagree. "Theodore loves the church," she says. "All boys get a little sleepy on Sunday mornings."

He's spry now, checking his phone, ambling closer. He has the energy to come to me as quickly as he chooses. Now that he's seen me and I've seen him, it's up to me to break the standoff. I'm his father. There's lately a new geometry to my interactions with my oldest son, circumstances requiring fresh angles and gradations, the plane or slope of Y equaling whatever X Theodore is bothering, in this particular instance, to report to me. His eyes are still downcast into his phone. He's managed to walk many meters without looking up.

"Oh hi, Dad," he says, as if I've just landed in front of him with a magic flying umbrella.

"Where were you?"

"I walked over to the trail. I told Mom to tell you. Didn't she tell you?"

"She told me you took a walk."

"Then you knew, yeah. I wanted to walk before Flapjack Jubilee. I like going out to the trail."

"You know we are on a schedule, Theodore, and you didn't tell me beforehand. I was worried."

"You were gone when I left."

"That doesn't matter, Theodore."

"You were gone walking, right? So, I wanted to walk too. I would've walked Gwennie. What route did you take?"

"I want to know why you texted your mother and not me."

"She was home."

"You can text me as well. I'm your father. I have a say in this household."

"I'll walk Gwennie next time, if you want."

"I never said I needed you to take Gwennie for a walk. I need you to follow a schedule and listen. I need you to understand you've caused me a great deal of consternation. You've caused this family a great deal of consternation, heading off without telling me."

"But I told Mom. And I don't think Chloe and Austin care if I take a walk."

"You tell your mother and me. Do you understand this? This is protocol. You tell us both."

"If you're home and Mom is not, I should tell her too, tell her something? If Mom is at Walmart and you're home, I should text or call her at Walmart?"

"You should always tell me. You can't just do whatever it is you want, on any timeline. That's not how this functions. You aren't a free agent."

"Dad, I should get inside, right? We've got to get to going. I want to put on a different shirt; this one is sweaty."

"I don't know if there's time for that anymore."

"It won't take a long. Ten seconds."

"Wear your Detroit Tigers shirt. Have regional pride."

"It's *sweaty.*"

"You walked; you didn't run. You shouldn't have perspired that much anyway. It's barely sixty degrees."

"I walked in the sun."

"You're lying to me."

"I'm *not* lying."

"You couldn't have walked only in sun if you took the bike trail. There's too much tree cover, too much shadow. You're passing in and out of shade for miles, particularly in the morning."

"I feel sweaty."

"Feeling sweaty is not the same as *being* sweaty."

"Why does it matter?"

"It matters because you aren't telling the truth."

I want to torpedo this deep into my son and keep it lodged there: you do not lie to your father. Not large lies, not white lies, not the passing misdirection, the withholding of the every day, those little bits of dross. *Nothing.* If he can't tell me the truth about the sweat, he can't tell me the truth about whatever else he may do in the subsequent years, whether it's drugs, alcohol, or even greater blasphemies. Slopes don't have to be slippery; gravity handles the rest. And I hate the undignified *whine* creeping into my son's voice, that adolescent crackle, and I want to stamp it out fast. I know, for whatever youthful reasons that is not worth discerning, Theodore doesn't want to wear his oversized novelty baseball shirt to the jubilee. He wants, perhaps, apparel more stylish, and he has plenty of it. The path of least resistance would be to nod happily, like a sitcom father, and send him on his way, where he can hunt out whatever he believes conforms to his expectations for a day rambling about. I don't know and I don't care. What I do care about is that he has wandered off without telling me—defiance, rather unvarnished, though he believes otherwise—and that he thinks I'm a fool who believes it's possible to sweat buckets on a shaded morning walk. I almost want to seize him by his collar. *Just tell me you don't want to wear the shirt anymore.*

"I'm telling you the truth. The shirt is sticking to my back."

I see the front door has opened and Daniella is again craning her head outward, this time fully made up for the day. Behind her, I hear the soft squeal of children.

"Theodore, let's get inside now. Your father wants you to get ready. We're leaving in fifteen minutes."

Like that, my son is summoned inward, and goes to where he is told. He doesn't say anything more. Daniella follows him and I'm left here, still at my Chevy, blinking dumbly in the sun.

My father was a failed man with pharaonic ambitions. He returns to me at uncertain, craggy moments, when my mood is misaligned or my family is proving rebarbative. He's with me as I'm driving north, fifteen minutes to Orchard, now in the passing lane so I can take us past eighty and ensure we aren't parked in cornfield ten miles away. Daniella is not speaking and Theodore is not speaking. Austin is bopping away at his tablet. Chloe is slashing at a coloring book. After a brief conversation starter—ready for the fair?—I've given up, and decide it's best to let them brood. Daniella has turned the brood into an art form, elevating it beyond the sulk, and she knows exactly how to marinate in a silence, let it become her own. The air has certainly thickened. Theodore's nose is pressed to the window and he's wearing another navy-blue T-shirt, this one fitted slightly better on his slender torso. A slogan, LET'S GET READY, apparently advertises a sneaker brand on his chest.

I stomach far more than my father did. I do not beat and I do not bellow. He had the patience of a flitting little insect, or a finch, if I want to be polite. He had the fists of an orangutan. He only hit stationary objects like walls and tables, and others he would make, through force, nonstationary. When I explain to those who ask that my father was an actor, very active in local theater, they naturally imagine such traits couldn't be imbued in such a homespun little artist. What is more benign than volunteer theater, the director the cozy matron, the leading man and lady both members of good standing in the Kiwanis Club? The Mackinaw City Players would put on as many as seven shows a year, a bulk of them musicals, and it was my father singing lead as much as he could. *Guys and Dolls*, *Camelot*, *The Miracle Worker*, *The Odd Couple*, *Man of La Mancha*. There are more I'm forgetting. My mother did not act or sing, but she made sure to attend as many of my father's performances as she possibly could, bringing me from early childhood. It was important, she said, we be there for him, as if we were all that stood in the way between my father and chaos.

I sensed, as soon as I reached my teenage years, my father very much wanted out of Mackinaw City—and always did. I don't hunger to leave Pine Haven; everything I want and need is here. My father, born in the UP, believed the journey south to Mackinaw City would be one step in a multipart and multimodal journey that would land him on Broadway or in Hollywood or at least in Detroit. He was never supposed to stall out on the cusp of Lake Huron, overfed tourists clogging the streets each summer on the way to their appointed ferries, hoping to scoop up fudge and take a bike ride around Mackinac Island proper. He was never supposed to have to earn extra money as a reenactor of nineteenth century pioneer scenes on the island. He was never supposed to have to rely on my mother, a gentle ex-Quaker who ran a moderately successful souvenir, doodad, and trinket shop two stone's throws away from the Maritime Museum. He was supposed to be, somehow, a man apart, and he never was.

God rest his soul—and hers. I've spent twenty years now without either of them, missing my mother's dotage and my father's barbed love, his calloused ape hands running through my boy hair, telling me I could be an astronaut if I wanted. Why did he tell me this when I hardly spoke of space at all? One memory surfaces: my father gripping a vintage alarm clock and hurling it against the kitchen wall. My mother was ten feet away, making a stew, and my father did not want to scare her. The aggression was saved for himself, for some picayune failure, and my mother turned to him, an obsidian black stare on her face as she finished surveying the wreckage.

"Nothing will ever be how you want it," she said quietly.

"Nothing is as anyone wants it."

The winters were an assault, of the like my children won't ever fathom, forever free of sparsely heated cottages. They'll never know the blade of a lake wind or the heat of a father's wrath. They are blessed to live in the house of someone who is glad to be exactly where he is—who would change nothing.

We make it to Orchard and I'm grateful traffic is light, the main drag of Poplar bearing us at a reasonable velocity toward Blue Jay Lane, where I'll hang a right for the parking lot. We pass the ragged open field where novelty helicopter rides will begin in an hour, the H130 silent and waiting for now, a smattering of children ogling its potential. At the four-way I pause, catching Ricky's, the burger-and-fries stand, and their giddy lamb logo, its painted fleece winking in sunlight. At the next corner, one before we turn, is the pony ride and petting zoo, replete with goats. Daniella will take Chloe and Austin there before they enjoy the town proper.

Orchard is about half the size of Pine Haven and flanked entirely by farmland. There is no liberal arts college to anchor it and, therefore, fewer of the distortions that might come with such a collision of populations—the sons and daughters of Grosse Point bankers having to brush up against tow truck drivers getting their lunch jerky at the 7-Eleven, these same drivers growing perplexed at the opening of a Starbucks across the street from campus. In Orchard, each resident is equally poor, basically. Anyone with means prefers to live near Pine Haven College or CMU, another ten minutes or so north on 127. There aren't any golf courses in Orchard. No equivalent of Hearst Road.

The jubilee is their Super Bowl, if resented more for the commotion it brings for locals unaccustomed to a weekend crush. Most who partake are from other towns in Luce County, those who wonder why they haven't been blessed with their own three-day festivals. I'm a bit hazy on the history myself. Still, it feels, at the very minimum, egalitarian enough. What else, exactly, would Orchard have?

"Do you want to ride the ponies?" I ask Chloe and Austin, the Chevy finally inched onto Blue Jay Lane.

"No," Theodore replies, his eyes now on his phone.

"I'm speaking to Austin and Chloe."

"Okay."

I await my younger children to respond to my cue. Chloe is gripping the coloring book tightly, as if foraging through it for biblical cues. Austin has not broken from his tablet. Their nonresponses irk me more than I care to readily admit.

"Chloe? Austin?"

"Yes, Dad?" Chloe answers first. She still hasn't looked up from her coloring book.

"The pony ride. Do you want to ride the pony? And pet the goats?"

"I'll pet the goats."

"And ride the pony?"

"I don't think so."

"Why not?"

"Where's the pony?" Austin asks.

"We just passed it. I'll take you there once we park."

"Is it a horse?"

"A pony, as you know, is a baby horse."

"I want to ride a horse." Austin has set his tablet down.

"You aren't old enough to ride a horse."

Daniella has not said a word. If she didn't continually blink, I wouldn't know if she had been swapped for a waxen lookalike. I'm tempted to wave my hand directly in her face.

"Isn't that right, Mom?" She hates when I call her Mom. "He's not old enough?"

Daniella's blinking has increased and she takes a lacquered fingernail to her chin. "Horseback riding can be mastered at any age. The issue is training. Austin would have to take lessons. Austin, honey, do you want to take lessons?"

"Yeah!"

"There's a riding school out on Eagleton, past the furniture barn. We'll sign you up there," she adds, "if you stay this excited."

"I will, Mom. I want to ride horses."

"This is the first I'm hearing of that," I say.

"Austin loves horses," Chloe replies without looking up.

"So do you still want to do the pony ride?" I try again.

"I don't know. Maybe."

"Honey, you probably have to ride ponies before you ride horses. So this could be good experience," Daniella says.

"I want good experience. Okay."

A crossing guard points me into the Orchard High lot, which is accessed through a congealed road that takes us past the gymnasium, temporary home to the crafts. On any ordinary Saturday, let alone a weekday, this lot would be far too vast, paved optimistically for a school-age population boom that never arrived. For the Flapjack Jubilee, the lot is pressed into service, like a state hospital that finally scrapes its capacity during a deadly epidemic. After the breeze of earlier traffic, I'm now in line, trailing a white Ram ProMaster. Another crossing guard has materialized, redundantly pointing us in the only direction we can go. Soon, we'll be in competition for what of the fair remains.

And what is left, so far, is what I predicted and what I feared: phalanxes of automobiles wedged together, two by two per row. Spaces are filled obviously or filled deceptively, a brief gap that sends a tickle through my heart amounting to little more than a size differential between vehicles, the vacant parallelogram of cement a mirage. Daniella doesn't care, the children don't care. They aren't driving and the time ticking down is meaningless.

"Hey, do you think I can get out here? Before we park?" Theodore asks.

The request temporarily stuns me into a sort of half-silence, a babble coming from my lips that will, in one beat, have to be a response.

"What?"

"Garrett's here. He texted me. He wants to meet over at the rocket launcher, you know, that fair ride."

"This is a moving vehicle."

"Right. But can you stop? We're near the fairground anyway."

"Theodore, I'm looking for parking."

"I really just want to get out of the car."

"You can as soon as I stop. I need to find a space."

"Stop over there, Dad. Up by the fairground."

Garrett Hannon, Brendan's fourteen-year-old son, is a pallid, thinly muscled junior varsity basketball player, the sort of person I am happy to have Theodore around. Next year, they'll be in high school together, and under almost any circumstance, I'd be elated to deposit Theodore with someone who isn't another sleepy-eyed, bat-eared teen addicted to fast-twitch memes and pornography. They play video games together in Brendan's basement, no doubt shoot-'em-ups and fighters, but I'm willing to tolerate it for now as a bulwark against far greater depravities. I trust Garrett, as Brendan's son, to be of a certain pedigree and ambition that will keep Theodore from swerving off any dubious exits on life's turnpike.

Given that, it would be easy to, on Theodore's command, release him to Garrett. All logic points there. But fatherhood isn't governed by mere A and B logic, one point transiting to another, requests made and answered. A father isn't a vending machine, with buttons to be mashed, bags of Funyuns to be dispensed. A father can't only assent. Push and pull, push and push. This is how Theodore will learn.

"We'll stop when we park, son."

"I just want to get out right there. We're pulling right by the entrance, look—"

"First, we park."

My gambit is that I can placate a fuming Theodore in the next ten minutes. The lot is likely at capacity, but there are small gaps to be hunted out, quasi-feasible places, where I can leave the vehicle. All of this, of course, *is* Theodore's fault, and that's one lesson I'll have to teach here. Had he not taken his walk and disappeared unaccounted for—unaccounted to me, at least, and I do head this household—we would have arrived here in a timely manner, with ample parking. This scenario would not and could not exist. He deserves this mild, low-hum suffering of his fresh-born adolescence. It has been earned, and he'll sit here, buckled with his siblings and his mother and me, until we are properly parked.

Will we be properly parked? My confidence decreases with the minute, as the gambit becomes more of an optimist's lark than I would have liked. Here we go, in chiseled rectangles, bumpers glittering in the sun, bulky vans and mud-slung trucks and even a Mini Cooper occupying precious asphalt, fairgoers puttering about in my periphery. Austin, still tablet-bound, is blissfully unaware, and Chloe has started in with a second coloring book I didn't know she even had. Daniella is on a scroll through Instagram, checking up on the rival mommies, no doubt contemplating her place in this precarious digital universe.

Theodore's raw anxiety is palpable, unnerving even to me, and he's taken up a habit I despise, nail biting, which he inherited from Daniella's side of the family since I've seen old Del Justice nearly gnaw a thumb off his hammer teeth, taking skin and blood with him. Theodore has one eye out the window.

"Lot looks full," Daniella says without looking up.

"I am not surprised. Not surprised at all." And I'm not. We're crawling back through town, against traffic, passing a succession of lemonade stands with variable pricing. One stand, held down by a trio of knobby boys in crewcuts, charges one dollar for a half cup and two dollars for a full, which is somewhat obscene to me, given all cups should be properly filled. The next stand, two houses over, is overseen by a single girl with long blond hair, her arms crossed over the table. Several adults, some of whom must be her parents, sprawl in camper chairs in the shade, massaging their phone screens. We're running behind, but I slow the Chevy anyway.

"Anyone thirsty?" I ask. "I'm going to hop out and get some lemonade. Who wants some?"

"Me!" Austin cries, still downcast into the tablet.

"Lemonade," Chloe says.

"Two cups then. Daniella? Theodore?"

"I'm fine," Daniella answers. Theodore, of course, says nothing.

I slow the Chevy in front of a hydrant and cut the engine.

"Three cups of lemonade," I say. "We've got a thirsty bunch in the car."

A handmade sign dangles off the table, the blue marker scrawl indicating the price of the cups and offering a short message below, in the unsteady handwriting of a grade-schooler: *saving up to buy a bike*. There's an attempt at cursive before a default to print and I admire the effort. The girl can't be older than ten.

"Trying to buy a bike, huh? That's exciting, I bet you want one right in time for summer."

"Yes. I want to ride around the lake."

I don't inquire about which lake. Behind her, strangely, are at least five bicycles, one of them electric. Several are leaned against the porch, while one is tilted over into the overgrown grass. I suppose the girl wants a *new* bike, since, evidently, the household is in possession of many of the used type. Her sign could be more specific.

"Are you close to hitting your goal?"

"Not really, no. Though it's getting hot out now. I hope we'll get it. My mom said when it's high noon, whatever that is, we'll start to get a lot more money.

She pours gingerly. Once, a few years ago, I tried to entice Theodore to do this: to start a lemonade stand on Hearst Road. I wanted to instill in him a sense of industry, of what the market brings to bear on all of this; I wanted to give him the experience of *waiting* in the sun for business, the ache of time's passage that is essential knowledge for any adulthood. This girl will march well-armed into the world. In addition to the necessary quarters, I deposit a dollar.

"That's for you. For all your hard work. Keep it."

"Well, thank you."

"Walmart has some quality bicycles and the shortages are over now. I remember, a few summers back, one couldn't be had."

"A few summers back, my bike was invisible."

Why can't Theodore be this way? Many parents, I suspect, privately agonize over why their child hasn't become the child elsewhere, someone else evolving closer to the ideal. Theodore never took the lemonade stand initiative and actively repelled my hints that he should start one. One retrospective stumble of mine was buying too much of what Theodore requested, whether it be a video game console or a basketball, and not forcing him to aggressively save on his own, like this girl. Americans, particularly children, need goals. Selling lemonade, in its own way, is a Christian instinct, it is the industriousness native to those who believe.

"And now you will ride free and clear."

"The bike's the thing."

The Chevy is hushed when I enter with my three cups of lemonade, two in my right, one in my left. There's the sugary ping of Austin's tablet and little else. Daniella's phone usage has, unsurprisingly, continued, and Theodore is gazing longingly and silently like an impressed soldier at sea. Chloe has stopped coloring and appears to be dozing. "Chloe, Austin," I say, and pass over the lemonade. Austin grabs his first, then Chloe. Theodore regards us at a great distance, like a Roman god in terminal decline, his slouch suddenly pronounced. He cannot imagine why we are drinking lemonade. I swallow mine in two gargantuan gulps, feeling the sugar water course down my throat, and let out a subtle exhalation.

"Chloe, Austin, you're enjoying your lemonade?"

"Mine tastes funny," Austin says.

"Mine is good. I think I would make it less sweet if I make my own lemonade," Chloe says.

"Less sweet? Would you like a lemonade stand of your own?"

"Only if I didn't have to make the lemonade or sell it."

"You want to oversee a lemonade stand, to be a boss of a lemonade stand, then."

"I want it to say my name. *Chloe's Lemonade*. After that, it's up to the people who make and sell the lemonade."

"So you want to be a boss, not a worker."

"I want to boss, boss, boss."

"God is the ultimate boss."

"Yes, Dada."

The town is full. Every available curbside has a vehicle and threatening signs are posted everywhere near driveways, warning of towaways and law enforcement action, all genial Midwest pretense melted away. Garage sales spill into view, each house awash in lawn shlock, Wayfair and Walmart folding tables holding aloft generations of accumulated windchimes, hunting magazines, baby clothing, and rustic pottery.

At Northrop Avenue, we weave rightward to a series of streets—Opal, Dennison, Richards, Nettles—that are all beyond Orchard's middle rim, shack houses with crumbly front yards that run you $60,000, even in this inflationary mood. I see a mother and son on the front steps of one, each sipping pop, their eyes dazed in the sun. Another lawn sign asks us to KEEP AMERICA GREAT I nod along, sympathetically. Two streets ahead is the pickle lot, a roped off dirt patch thick with farm machinery and automobiles, most arrived for the jubilee.

Nothing is promising. Nothing at all. Luckily, no one, excepting Theodore, seems to care all that much, the passage of time occurring differently to most of them. Daniella rightly figures the crafts are not hurrying off in the next three hours, that a morning's perusal can easily transmogrify into an afternoon jaunt, a late lunch followed by more haggling over the handmade charm bracelets and cinnamon-scented soap. The children will eat when they will eat and ride when they will ride. I plan to be on fairgrounds duty with them while Daniella has time for herself and her girlfriends at the crafts.

Theodore is anxious. And Theodore will have to wait.

"Here we go," I declare, "a space that's just for us."

"We made it, didn't we," Daniella says.

"I want to ride the snake ride," Austin says.

"I want elephant ears. Elephant ears," Chloe says.

"When we get there," I offer, "all of it will be done. Snake rides and elephant ears."

Three minutes into our walk, past the $60,000 shacks and a blue-and-black tinted American flag to celebrate our law enforcement, I hear Theodore's voice. The syllables are garbled, suppressed in a mouth that has quickly closed shut, and he may hope none of us have heard. I've barely heard. Daniella is holding hands with Chloe and Austin, not paying much attention.

"What was that?" I've dropped pace to come side by side with my son. "I heard you say something."

"I didn't say anything. I was just clearing my throat."

"You have allergies?"

"Maybe."

"Would you like a Claritin?"

"I don't need a Claritin."

"I think you were doing more than clearing your throat."

"Think what you're going to think."

"If you want to speak to your family, you should speak clearly."

We approach a large intersection and a stand of slanting trees. There's no traffic light. We'll have to brave it against vehicles in both directions, moving ad hoc through an ill-defined crosswalk. I still want to know what my son said.

"What did you say, exactly?" I try again.

"That this is stupid," Theodore says at last.

"Theodore," Daniella offers, a small buttress for my coming inquiry. I am glad she has decided to engage.

"Tell me what *this* is? What is stupid? It's all relative. We're moving here, as a family, together. Is that stupid?"

"We were right there at the fairground and you could have dropped me off."

"Ah, so you didn't want to walk with your family. Your family that loves you."

"I was right there—I just wanted to see a friend."

"Had we been earlier, perhaps, a space would have been available in that lot and the walk would be shorter. Actions have consequences, son. That's been the case for as long as we've been the Lord's creatures. Had you taken a different action, you would have had a different consequence."

"It just doesn't make any sense."

"What doesn't make sense is going off on your own, on a very crucial day, right before we were about to leave as a family. To make the selfish decision to wander about without telling me. Your mother and I want to be told together."

"On a *group* text?"

"The medium is up to you. Just know there's a reason you're making this journey with us."

"The reason is not a reason."

"Listen to your father," Daniella says.

Theodore doesn't reply. He's not listening but he's exhausted his rebuttals, for now. I have to weigh how much I want to dig at him. Combat with your own children must be delicate, even when you occupy higher ground, facts and reason firmly on your side.

Victory is inevitably pyrrhic because you must parent afterward. The wreckage belongs to you. For that, I'm thankful for Theodore's new silence as we make our way across Reading and toward Blue Jay Lane, skipping past as many garage sales as we can. Daniella, thankfully, has not asked to stop, and she is walking beside me with centurion eyes. I say a silent prayer of thanks.

Orchard, alive! A safari of activity, lawns spilling over with early barbeque and banter. I smell burnt potato and the trace of a cigar. I can finally regard vehicular traffic as the mildly interested observer, my fate no longer bound up with the crawl. Savor this moment of liberation, I want to tell Theodore. We're walking at a healthy jaunt, the smaller two children keeping pace, only Austin moaning about sunscreen stinging his eye. Daniella can address that later. In the distance, I hear the helicopter, and wonder who exactly is strapped into the chassis. Perhaps Theodore wants a ride later. That will crack some of this ice.

"I'm going to run the rest of the way," Theodore says.

"Run?" I stumble over the word, and it dissolves at the bottom row of my teeth.

"We're close enough, Garrett wants to meet, so if you don't mind, I want to run there."

"You want to run. You want to leave this family and run there."

"It's not that far now, we're almost to the fairground."

"If you wanted to run, why not have signed up for the 5K?"

"I don't want to run five miles."

"Five kilometers, Theodore, is not five miles. It's less than four."

"Either way, I'm not going that far, the fairground isn't that far."

I hold back the roil. Rage can be frothy, and I don't enjoy displaying it, particularly with children. If I'm upset, I'm clipped. I come with facts, chockablock, and I'm sure to sharpen the edges. I want them to learn. We are arriving as a unit, the Starr family, and Theodore will be taught what it means to be a Starr. He is not going to tumble out, alone, into the jubilee, and ricochet about until he finds Garrett Hannon. He's not an urchin. I was never a pastor's son, and I imagine that comes with its own singular pressure that Theodore feels; he has more sympathy from me than he thinks exists. This sympathy, though, cannot extend to indulgence.

I think of my own father, and how little he indulged. Parents today lack flint. Too much, of course, can alienate, but little bits here and there delivered properly can achieve a great deal. If Theodore wants to ride in a helicopter later, he better stay put.

"You're walking here, with us. You aren't running anywhere."

"I just want to get there; I don't see the point . . ."

He knows he's erred.

"You don't see the point of family? That's not of interest to you?"

"Of course, I didn't mean that. I mean, we are still a family, even if I just want to run ahead to the fairground."

"Thank you for your dispensation. I am glad we are still a family."

"Ostriches have families, right?" Austin asks us.

"All animals in God's kingdom do."

"Even snakes," Chloe says. "Even when God told the snake to crawl and eat dust. He was cursed to eat dust and have no legs. But even he gets a family."

"Snakes have moms and dads, that's funny," Austin says.

"We're almost there," Daniella says to Theodore, attempting a lighter tone I don't particularly care for, not in this context. "I think I smell the flapjacks."

"I don't smell them quite yet," I say. "It may be the gasoline from the helicopter."

An orange-hued man in coveralls drives a tractor in the middle of the street, just beyond us. Trailing him is a vintage 1935 three-window Deluxe Coupe. They seem, for some reason, to be traveling together. Several onlookers have torn themselves away from garage sale tables to snap pictures on their phones.

"The snakes have daddies," Chloe says. "And their jaws can swallow whole deer whole. They don't even have jaws at all."

"Can they swallow cars?" Austin asks.

"If they try hard enough."

We pass a white clapboard Methodist church (too liberal) and a jabbering family locked in a long-range game of cornhole, red and blue beanbags bulleting each way. A few summers ago, I put out a cornhole game and Theodore had little interest. It may be time to revive it, with Chloe and Austin old enough to play. Let them enjoy it. Theodore can look on and ponder what he passed up.

But he won't. He's not yet at a ruminative age. He is rangy and loping, frenetic too, and he is going to spit at what he doesn't comprehend or what he won't comprehend at a speed that feels proper to him. I will bear it when I can. What I won't do is let him run off, alone, until we've entered the fairground together. That decision has been made. Two more blocks, three, another lemonade stand and garage sale summited, and we'll be there.

"What is Starr anyway?" Theodore asks. His question comes with no obvious connective tissue and I consider how or if I should respond. Sometimes, I've found, I can clod onward acting as if I hadn't heard anything at all.

"We're Starrs," Chloe answers.

"What do you mean?" I manage.

"Our last name, Starr. It doesn't even sound real."

"It's English. The English are very real. Do Hammersmith or Savage sound any more real to you? Both are surnames circulating throughout the world. And if you need to know a Starr, there was the Packers quarterback. He died a few years ago."

Theodore takes a long breath.

"We should have one 'r' then."

"Should, would, could. Take it up with the ancestors. I was told they were fine Englishmen. A few may have been Scots. If you're in this part of the country, you're bound to have the Scottish in you, and I'm certain we do."

"My mother is Scots-Irish," Daniella says.

"Starr sounds like it isn't from anywhere, like it just appeared," Theodore says.

"Theodore can sound the same way. Or Teddy. Ted. Theo. Why not Dore?" I'm feeling jaunty. "Why not Theod? There are many combinations out there, many realities to be written."

"We all get to write our own sometimes," Theodore replies, more quietly this time.

"We aren't writers of reality. We aren't the authors. You'll learn that. The book was written long ago, we're all in it, and God has made His determination."

"You said there were many realities to be written."

"By God."

"You didn't say that the first time."

"Mankind can strain to invent to, to write—but the realities aren't realities, only pale imitations. Again, something you will learn in time."

Finally, Blue Jay Lane, and our original parking lot, which will take us to the fairgrounds. Inside the high school is the craft hall, where Daniella will go with one or two children, depending on their mood. Or she'll go alone, and I'll take the two children to the amusements. Theodore can spin out of our orbit and find Garrett. They'll rendezvous with friends from school, friends from church, and when I call to see where they are—to see where Theodore is—he better pick up.

Next week, I remember, Big Landry wants me at his fund-raiser. I was trying to put it out of mind but obligations have a way of always intruding, making themselves known at odd moments. It's not that I'm against Big Landry's fundraiser for Buck Shasta, our indefatigable congressional representative. Buck is God-fearing, as politicians should be, and makes for a stirring tableau at our Pine Haven Memorial Day and July Fourth parades, which he dutifully attends, his figurine wave and ex-Marine muscle showing up strongly in the *Pine Register's* newsprint. I've met Buck several times since his first election, and he's never stumbled over my name. If he ever moves, I'll be sure to represent him or at least take the initiative to find him a suitable home, if he's already working with a different realtor. I've already written the $2,500 check to Buck's reelection fund; his finance professional merely needs to receive it and cash it. When the FEC publishes his ledger, I'll be proud, again, to appear among his donors. Daniella appears too, since she writes a separate check from our joint fund in her name. Del Justice likes it, anyway, that his son-in-law mingles with muckety-mucks and such. It makes him feel her selection was especially true. The fundraiser location is amenable, the Elysian, a country club and golf course a twenty-minute drive northwest from Pine Haven. I'll arrive early for an agreeable mingle.

Why think on it? Because I'd rather be here, at the jubilee, and my mind-realm too often is tugged between present and future. The present is managing Theo, managing the children, getting Daniella to her craft hall. I will, undoubtedly, see many parishioners here, much of Trinity gloriously loosed on the carnival and crafts. This demands my attention and I'll give it. Buck Shasta, for all I know, will find his way here, perhaps, and I'll have yet another encounter, a chance to search his memory, to see if he can recall what he discussed last, in passing. Let's see if he knows I am the pastor of Trinity of Pine Haven. Let's be sure he doesn't mistake me for a Methodist. (Certainly not a Catholic.) Let's see what Washington, DC, that marbled bowl of iniquity, has taught him.

"Can you take Austin and Chloe?" Daniella asks me. "They'll enjoy the rides and games more than the crafts hall anyway."

"Happy to. My thoughts exactly."

"Good. I know some fathers who would insist I have one of them."

"Name names."

"Theoretical fathers."

I want to kiss her on the cheek, and do. Let the children witness spontaneous tenderness. It will do them good in the coming years.

We've made it to the parking lot. It's vaster, of course, when you're taking it on foot, the asphalt an uneasy moonscape under our feet. It's far too late for my liking, trending closer to high noon, but I am glad this all can be completed. Everyone will be where they need to be. First, we approach the high school, reconstructed fifteen years ago as a two-story late modernist hulk in light beige, an orange and blue Orchard Comet pennant draped over one facing. In and out the swinging front doors come the crafters, Daniella's brethren, plastics and totes teeming with their homey bounty. This time, I give her a kiss on the cheek, and she knows what to do. "Come get you in an hour?" I ask. "Two," she winks, and that's that, lovely and off, and I'm guiding three children to the fairground.

Theodore is hunting with his eyes. When that proves unsatisfactory, he sends off a series of blistering texts I can't see, likely to Garrett Hannon. I imagine they're of the pleading variety—Where are you man??—and I'm immediately thankful most of my childhood and adolescence came before the popularization of cell phones. Boys and girls were unattached atoms then, careening blindly around their microverses, and all of it had the feel of a trippy, disorganized play, lines shouted into the void. Meet up later, maybe. Maybe not. Come at six or I'll be gone. Catch me at Burger King, window seat. If you missed, well, there was always tomorrow. But now there's an uncertainty, a fear built into the invisible 5G world that binds us—will he respond? Is my text seen and ignored? Seen and read and ignored? Time's passage freighted with darker meanings, life's value shrunken to time of response. Poor Theodore.

And then he has it. I see he's texting again. "Garrett's by the haunted house," he says out loud, not necessarily to me.

"Be sure to answer your phone when I call. You'll have a couple of hours before then."

"Right."

There he goes, on a light jog now, into the fairground. "Bye, Theodore," Chloe says, and we know he won't answer. He's into it, onto the next, as most children are. And I, as an understanding parent, accept it fully. My children are not merely domesticated beasts with more sentience, to be fed and leashed, watched with a rolling anxiety. Other parents embrace the surveillance mentality more. I don't want to be left ignorant and I don't want defiance—particularly when it may scuttle well-laid plans, as Theodore nearly did this morning—but I am not implanting chips into them. When they have automobiles, they can drive them knowing old Dad won't have a blinking blip on his phone tracking their trips to Dairy Queen. I'll have better things to do anyway.

Chloe and Austin are fine companions. Young children are underrated; the popular culture portrays them as self-interested mongers for affection, but that's not always the case—the tykes can stand alone, and prefer to, as inventive as they are when you let them. And they love Daddy. I take each of their hands and we amble, an attractive trinity, through the open gates. The crowd has built to the many hundreds, maybe a thousand, a healthy blend of downwardly mobile town folk and the upper income strata imported from elsewhere. They've come with their broods, larger than mine, and some hip pockets bulge with firearms. They talk God but don't know God.

First, the food booths. Clyde's BBQ Pit, Verna's Crushed Lemonade, Rainbow Ice Cream and Caramel Apples, Pizza & Ice Cold Pop, Mexican Fiesta (Tacos and Taco Salad), Elephant Ear Express, Fried Oreos and Donuts, Cornutopia, Fudge and Friends. Chloe points to the elephant ears and I tell her she can split one with Austin, which pleases Austin and seems to irk Chloe, who doesn't fathom how large the elephant ear—crisp, cinnamon sugar fried bread, stretched to elephantine proportions—will be when it arrives. We're in a two-sided line, one streaming to each window of the booth, that is at least ten bodies deep, and movement is light at best. Boys as young as thirteen appear to be tending the cash register and card machines. Somewhere, in the confectionary shadow, is a marginally older supervisor, pimpled with age.

"I think I want my own elephant ear," Chloe declares.

"Honey, they're quite large. You'll want to share with your brother. You'll have to trust me on this one."

"I'm hungry now for a whole one, and I can see what they look like. I want my own."

Here, an opportunity for an on-the-fly lesson: "It will upset your stomach. Think of the future version of yourself. Think of how you may feel, groaning, the ache, even an unfortunate trip to the potty. Would you want that?"

"No, I don't think so."

"Half an elephant ear will do."

Inflation has ravaged this market too as I note the price: nine dollars, or what a full meal in a passable restaurant, in the long-ago last decade, used to cost me. Memories of one- or two-dollar ears flood back, a time when the children beside me were unborn. At the cashier, a boy who appears eleven offers me a bucktoothed grin. I ask for one elephant ear and decide, at the last minute, on two small lemonades. Chloe and Austin can enjoy those while splitting their confection. There's a rabble inside the booth, other boys of indeterminate adolescence, and I notice two are wearing red ball caps for a credit union I don't recognize.

"Dada, do they chop off the ear of the elephant?" Austin asks.

"No, they're not real ears at all. They just look like them."

"I want a rhino ear, though. A real one."

"Maybe when you're older. We'll get you rhino for your eighteenth birthday."

"Rhino and giraffe ears. I want a giraffe ear."

At last, one of the boys produces the elephant ear on a paper plate, sugar and cinnamon crumbling to the ground. I make a gentle tear, trying to separate the pieces as equally as I can, and find one is slightly larger. Chloe is older so it will be hers. Austin doesn't seem to notice either way. There's no napkin dispenser anywhere.

"Excuse me, we need a few napkins over here."

None of the boys in the booth hear me. They're all engaged in the making of confections, or the illusion of their manufacture. Lines are thick on each side, glabrous parents and their more demanding offspring—more demanding than mine—pining for their cinnamon, pop, and candy crunch. "Napkins," I say again, and it feels as if my words have been siphoned into an alternate dimension with no light or sound. The boys bustle onward. I rap my knuckles for message delivery and affect. The boys are unmoved.

Finally, two are pushed across from a hand out of view, somewhere in the netherworld of the booth. I take them and pass one to each child, knowing they won't be nearly enough. They never are.

Next, I supervise. Chloe demands the Ferris wheel, Austin longs for a shoddy serpentine dragon ride, twelve interconnected cars clanging around an oval with several mild swerves and dips, and I opt for that because the line is shorter. "But Dada," Chloe says now, perhaps mimicking Austin, "I want to go up on the Ferris wheel and see the whole state." The whole state. It's a compelling pitch.

"One at a time," I offer. "We can't split up. You can ride the dragon with your brother. And then the Ferris wheel."

"But I don't want to."

"Chloe, we don't whine here."

"You say we don't whine in the house. You never said we can't whine at the Flapjack Jubilee."

"You can't whine anywhere, honey."

"Why not?"

"It's unbecoming."

"I don't know what that means."

"It means bad. Bad, bad, bad," and I take her hand, leading them both to the shorter line. Another gambit: the Ferris wheel line will somehow thin in the next twenty minutes. The fairgrounds are as dense as any Times Square revelry, salt and sugar-flecked limbs at a discomforting whirl, yowls and yippees and groans all about, the soundscape hemming me in. It would be good, for a moment, to be in the shade, and it's all a reminder that the theory of the jubilee does not always match the practice. The crowd's ambitions here are greater than I imagined. Here we are, this rabid demand for action—the last decade, in so many ways, seemed quainter. No plagues, no price increases.

We make it to the dragon. There are seven ahead of us, and four are scooped up for the next ride. The carney is a muscled Mexican somewhere in his twenties, with the gaze of a lounge singer. He has intentions, I imagine, for a different life, or at least one not here, yanking a lever to send a dragon train up and around. An easy way to quench longing is through real estate; God is harder, and this is why so few men do both. Buy or sell, and you feel the honeyed pang, of an earthward recognition never greater than yourself, but enough. And you can honor God this way, buying and selling—you simply remember your success is God's success. No one is honored with a bear market, put it that way.

Austin is strapped in his dragon. He frowns from the fifth car, gives a quick wave, and the dragon grinds on its rust-covered, concentric track. Every car is shaped like a subsection of the mythical beast, faux scales painted on the hull, and the very first car is attached to an imitation snout. The dragon jolts up his track, like he's having a little mechanical fit, and the boys and girls treat it as magic, grinning from their compartments. Chloe gives a yawn.

"I don't want to watch the dragon, Dada."

"We need to supervise your brother."

"The dragon protects him. I want to ride the Ferris wheel. Then you'll have to watch me, because the Ferris wheel isn't an animal."

"So it can't protect you?"

"It doesn't have life."

The dragon makes two loops, then three. I don't know how many are guaranteed. Austin has yet to smile; riding the dragon is a grim responsibility to him, like ferrying precious herbs and spices across the sea. He has a workingman's furrow, his cherubic hands clenched around the bar. Chloe is tugging at my sleeve, asking when the ride ends. Her perception of time varies by how much she's anticipating its passage. If she longs for it, it will never come fast enough. I suppose that's how we all can be, but it seems particularly acute at this stage.

The dragon grinds to a halt and the boy and girls are deposited back out to the fair. "How was it?" I ask Austin. He shakes his head. "It could have been faster."

"Ferris wheel!" Chloe cries out.

The Ferris wheel is of the diminished, traveling fairground variety, a creaky purple spiral with caged carriages for its jittery riders. I cajole Austin into going and tell him he doesn't have to share a carriage with his sister. It's important they both do this together, that there isn't one of them on the ground, gazing upward. That's my job. Theirs is to participate, to make the jubilee their own. In the future, they'll have plenty of time to be where I am.

The line is longer than it needs to be. Had we arrived earlier, we wouldn't have had to dawdle so long, and their electronic devices are in the Chevy. They'll have to make do with the enormity of the present. "How do woodchucks chuck wood?" I ask them. They tell me they've heard that one before. "Then say it three times fast."

The tongue twister is more of a marvel for Austin. Chloe's eyes cut away, to the rest of the fair. I'm trying to discern where she'd like to go next. As demanding as they might be, I'd rather be here than in the maw of the crafts fair, idling as Daniella parses the handmade handbags and dream catchers. In the next hour, I will make my way there, and see if they want to grab a flapjack lunch from the cafeteria. I already have the coupons in my wallet.

"All right, there you are," I tell the kids as the line eases, the agglomeration of confused bodies pouring toward the Ferris wheel, "you're up."

"I don't know if I want to go," Austin says.

"It might be better than the dragon," I say.

"How much better?"

"You'll have a panorama of the town."

"I don't know what that means."

"I've built dioramas for school," Chloe says.

"It means a great view," I say.

"A great view," he considers this, his lower lip tensing.

"Like an eagle," Chloe says. "An eagle so high, it can eat any prey it wants."

"An eagle so high, it isn't afraid of anything," Austin says.

"You'll be just like that, when you're up there," I say.

"But I want to be afraid."

Fair enough, I want to spit back, but you have to know when to let children be children, to allow them to be alone with what they've said and pick through meaning at a later date. The Ferris wheel carriages allow two riders and, to my delight, brother and sister pair up. I had worried Chloe would spite Austin and race elsewhere, leaving him to wail and scene-make. I, the beleaguered father, would have to hurry over and assure the wheel operator, a high school junior or senior with deadened, crustacean eyes, all was well, that these children could ride sans disruption, that they were the good kind. But luckily, none of that came to pass, and I can be a proud father beaming up at them, watching the wheel spin.

I feel a tap on my shoulder and turn.

"Hello," she says.

It's Gertrude, alone, her thin face lightly dimpled with the threadbare smile she's offering me. She's in a sunflower-patterned dress I've been before, probably from church, and she's tied her dark hair behind her head in an efficient ponytail. I wait for someone to emerge, her son or her husband, and breathe out when it's clear there's no familial accompaniment, just Gertrude Breckenridge in the brittle shadow of the wheel.

"Fancy seeing you here."

"I saw you usher the kids to their doom."

"Doom?"

"These Ferris wheels always get stuck."

"Then they'll have the best views in town."

"If they're stuck where they need to be."

"How's Harry?"

"He's recovering. Two more days, they say, and there will be a discharge. His vitals are good. He's healthy enough now to fight his way out, if he chooses, one nurse at a time. He can headlock them now."

"Aidan is here?"

"He didn't want to go. He said the jubilee was stupid and that he had better things to do. I don't know, sometimes, what to do with him. Do I force him? Is that important? If Harry were out of the hospital, he'd be here—that's inarguable. And he would have forced Aidan. Harry would have been a juggernaut about that, getting us all to the fair. And that may have been the right thing, even if Aidan was miserable the whole time."

"I ensured Chloe, Austin, and Theodore would be here. They all wanted to be here, though."

"Wanted, yes. And Daniella, too. She's at crafts?"

"Crafts."

"That's good. It's peaceful there. I'll probably head there soon. I don't even know why I'm out here. I think, for a moment, I wanted a corn dog. The moment passed, and I don't anymore."

"The corn dog, you know, is underrated. It has an interesting origin."

"Pastor Starr, what are you actually thinking?"

"As a lewd book once said, I'm dreaming of aurochs and angels. I'm thinking of whatever's next. These coupons for a flapjack lunch are burning in my pocket, and they need to be used. There are five of them."

"You'll be crestfallen if they all aren't used."

"It's important Theodore eats with us."

"You think it's important. He may think something else. I think I spotted him, not long ago. He was with Hannon's kid. They looked close."

"I'm glad for Theodore that he's friends with Garrett Hannon. Garrett is something of a boy on the make. A basketball player, a scholar. Parents can only model so much; there will need to be people his own age he can follow, who influence him properly."

"You'd snuff out poor influences."

"You would too. Or already do, I bet."

"If I had such a power . . ." Gertrude's eyes swing away from mine, to a flock of distant redbirds. "If you or I could really arrange their lives in such a way, what we would do. But we can't. Aidan won't listen any more than Theodore will. If you believe he's listening, you're deceiving yourself."

"Theodore listens when it counts."

"You weren't here earlier. I came here early enough to have a parking space in the lot."

"And?"

"Teddy, were it up to you, you'd be parked up against the fairground. You'd be here for hours and now be spending your time winding down, finished with the Ferris wheel. You'd be, I don't know, maybe done with the flapjacks. What kept you from that? The way you wanted it today? Your wife? Ephesians would have something to say about that, I think.

"There's a certain clarity to Ephesians."

"You're here because you can't control your son. And you never will. The sooner you accept it, the happier fatherhood will be."

We're watching the Wheel achingly rotate, the cage with my children rocking on the left-hand side, halfway to the summit. I try to make out their expressions and if either of them are smiling.

"I'm not here to let him run wild, either. If I accept, I can still impose. There's soft power and hard, no?"

"A pastor should know about both."

"Soft is always more effective. I'm sure you've found this with Harry and Aidan. Do you like it here, alone?"

"I feel I've made something of a mistake because I'm bound to run into someone from the college. It feels inevitable, like a sunset. Perhaps it's what I really want. Perhaps I want what I'm most repulsed by. That's pop psychology, from the college. Nothing in the Bible about that, as far as I've ever read or heard from you. Maybe I'm asking to have them suffocate me."

"I'm glad, either way, you're here."

"Teddy, how many other women have you slept with?"

The curve of the Wheel, a faded indigo, is lucent now in the harshening daylight; the clouds have fled, the imposition of near-summer upon us. The buttery scent of the fairground has intensified, mingled with caramel left to drip in the sun. Little drop-toothed boys shove for position at a water gun display, their tongues rose-red and waiting, like eager cocker spaniels. Somewhere, foot-long nachos are being sold and carried about like briefcases, the viscous cheese alien-bright. My children are at the very top, and they're either drinking in the vista or arguing with each other.

"How many?"

"I'm not passing judgment. It's a factual inquiry, minus the controlled fury of HR. You're free to do whatever it is and preach on Sunday. The men of God are still men. I'm only going to expect so much from a pastor."

She shouldn't be getting this way, sounding like me, almost, in the manner she's trying to pry. I don't like the line of inquiry at all. It's a tally I'll keep close to my heart. Whether she means it or not, she will judge—she's a woman, after all—and she might not be prepared for how I answer. After a relatively fallow youth, I hastened to make up for lost time, and the making up—in all its delectable degrees and permutations—would not exactly please her. And I wouldn't want to diminish the meaning of our own congress, to have her, very suddenly, weighing her hours with me against the many, many hours I've spent breaststroking through other pools.

It's time to orient elsewhere.

"Gertrude, have you seen those nachos? I've never seen nachos that enormous."

"I would hazard you have three or four others, at least. Three right now. That would seem like enough. There's only so much of a balancing act I can tolerate."

"Toleration is what separates us from the animals."

"I'm going to settle on three, yes. I see myself and Daniella vying with three others. I don't think all of them have equal time. Some are more tangential than others. Some are more relevant to the equation. Some may require longer drives into the deep country."

"Deep country. That's a lovely phrase. Let me watch you as you say it again."

"When Harry is home, we'll have to cool it. He's dumber than he looks, but his ignorance has its limits. Discernment will fight its way through. He can start to figure it out."

"Discernment is a slugger."

"I'm not a woman who likes to hear people talking."

"I haven't heard any voices."

"You don't know where to listen."

But don't I? I've done my share of ferreting and sleuthing. I've mongered gossip, or what might pass for it in Pine Haven. Gertrude is clean and I'm clean. I understand potentiality is her concern. You scrutinize a bell long enough and you come to expect its plangent ring, even if it sits there, silent and waiting, no human hand nearby. A bell, you start to believe, can ring itself. Or God will decide, on His own, it's worthy of a ring. That sort of longing, though, is never biblical; it's paganistic, as all superstition is, the devil's handiwork never far.

Gertrude's eyes hunt mine.

"I'll find a new time to slip into the homestead."

"There won't be any new times. That's what you'll have to understand. The memories will have to satiate you."

"And you as well."

"I'll watch you preach, always. I enjoy that. You have less certainty than you believe yourself to have. You speak with the slightest tremor. It's hardly perceptible."

"You're never dull, Gertrude. Never dull."

The Ferris wheel has several revolutions left, at the minimum, and it only seems to be slowing down. Once the children are done, I decide I'll check on Theodore. Better, anyway, to be in motion, to let my blood slosh around in my lower veins. I can feel one foot steadily falling asleep. Next year, we'll go up north for a different festival, to a grander and far-flung location, somewhere tucked close to a lake. Perhaps Otsego County, not far from where we keep a lakefront cabin. I haven't scouted their festival circuit nearly enough. There are advantages to clearing the exit velocity of Pine Haven and Luce County.

Gertrude and Harry, as far as I understand, don't own a second property at all. That seems, in the long term, like a financial error, given how land up north will likely appreciate in the next five to ten years. If Gertrude might believe the liberal media has manufactured the so-called climate crisis—what with every stray sunbeam or melted snowflake equating to civilizational collapse—she should be able to recognize, as I have, that, in this fallen world, it matters far less what the substance of your belief is when pitted against the outcomes those beliefs themselves creates. This is not the godly, but the material. It matters that the upper Midwest, to the moneyed liberal certain that warmer climes will destroy us, still manages a frosty winter and a delicious summer. Nattering coastal elites are eyeing their own immediate fortunes with sudden trepidation now cast their gaze out to the country they once dismissed as the flyover, landlocked now a mere synonym for storm surge–free, the wildfire blaze only irking us if Canada fails to get its act together. This is what I want to impart to her, as she prattles on and on about the memories that satiate and her desire, so abrupt, to never have me at the homestead again: buy Gertrude, buy. Get in on the ground floor elsewhere. Plant your stakes in tomorrow.

Or else, it will be you, Harry, and Aidan leaving this Earth with no more value than you put in. God will love you, regardless, yes, but He looks well on those who attempt to prosper.

"I'm going to look at the crafts, after all. Enjoy yourself, Teddy. I'll see you in church."

"Trinity is blessed to have you."

I do mean it. I want Gertrude to keep coming back, regardless of what we do. For others, her presence would be a complication, but I find Sundays would lack a necessary tension, if she suddenly vanished. Today, at the fairground, I'm happy to see her go, however; I won't lie to you there. What was a welcome intrusion became, in time, something else, that sticky human variable. Live wires will do that. I have half a mind to call it a day and take the whole brood out to Crystal Lake. Lake water, come summer, is at thick broil, and the mosquitos become engorged little hellions, nibbling at every exposed crevice. I shudder at the thought of heading there—in summer. But now, in late spring, it may just be a delight. And the jubilee is no longer stirring warmth in me, as I hoped it would.

When Chloe and Austin are off the Ferris wheel, they race toward the row of claw games. There are three, all arranged thematically: one for Marvel heroes, another for DC, and a third for glittering, multicolored octopi. It's one dollar to play and I dispense crinkled bills to my children. I want to tell them, gently, these games are a D-league hustle, and you're guaranteed to watch the dollars vanish for nothing—better I tear them up in front of them to teach a lesson. But I won't do that, they're giggling too much, and Chloe is up first, chasing her octopi. The claw clinks right and left, then wobbles and descends, floating over the mountain of stuffed and grinning creatures. Austin, at the Marvel machine, has already tried and failed with his Hulk, the fluffed green gentleman plopping like a parachuter shot dead midair, his bulk left to loll among his identical friends.

Chloe, though, has struck pay dirt. "Dada, Dada," she says, and here comes one octopus, teal and white, a grimace frozen on his face. I'm slightly appalled that such a comfort object would be marketed to children. "He doesn't look happy," I tell her. "No he is, he is," and she tugs at this underside—I don't know where she learned this—and pulls forward a second octopus head, this one graced with a horseshoe smile, and the other head disappears within the body. A reversible octopus.

"Can I have one more dollar?"

"Does he need a friend?"

"Yes, Dada."

Austin and I both watch the claw take a second crack at the kingdom of octopi. Chloe is studious at the joystick, nudging it with surgical interest, one eye squinted shut. The claw hits upon an octopus of blue-and-gold, this one smiling at the outset. The claw has him dead in the cranium. "Here we go," my daughter says, and her friend is borne skyward, halfway up the glass and to the octagonal chute. One, two, three—and it drops. I watch it limply go, and Chloe turns to me, her brown eyes hunting out mine. "I want another. I want to try again."

"One was hard enough, Chloe. I don't know. Maybe let's get some cotton candy."

"Cotton candy is yucky. It's cotton, not candy. I want another dollar."

I accede, because it will be one of those days.

Austin and I watch a second time. She is a like a bear cub after her milk, or anything with the sub rosa ferocity of the very young. Remarkably, she's targeting the blue-and-gold octopus again. The claw trembles as its drops—imbued, perhaps, with belief. God in the claw. I don't turn away and there it is, the octopus struck, the octopus clamped, and a slow rise up and out of his octopi panopticon, his pinprick black eyes surveying us all. Austin cheers. Chloe says nothing, her tongue peeking out from the corner of her mouth, a bulb of bright pink.

"I got him," she says. "I told you, Dada, I told you. And I still don't want cotton candy."

Her triumph colors our walk away, through the fairgrounds. Austin is content to bask in his older sister's success. I hold both their hands, wending nowhere in particular, passing an Old

West–themed funhouse and a line, seventeen-deep, that induces relief when Chloe and Austin show no interest. She holds one octopus and deigns to permit Austin to have the second. This is more a loan than a gift—they belong to her—but he has the blue-and-gold in his starfish grip, turning it over as we rove on.

It's Chloe who notices first because she is, ultimately, the noticer—young enough to comprehend the phenomena before her, old enough to shuck the adulthood allergy to wonder that encroaches, usually, in late adolescence and never leaves. "There's Theodore!" she cries out, jabbing the air with her octopus.

One hundred and fifty feet away, halfway obscured by a slapdash bumper car ring, is, indeed, Theodore. There too is Garrett. And there, when I squint to ensure I see exactly what I need to see, is Theodore's hand—in Garrett's. The two are near the line for the bumper cars but not waiting to board them. They are in languorous conversation, their words lost to me, their shoulders slack and their limbs rubbery, two bodies gradually melting into one. It's apparent neither has heard Chloe, whose fluty voice doesn't carry much over the fairground din.

Garrett sees me first. He's a year older, the budding basketball star, three and half inches above Theodore, his hair burnt the vapor-blond of his mother's Norwegian lineage. He looks nothing like his father, yak-like Brendan with his hair the color of an outfield warning track, much of it hurrying away from his skull altogether.

Apollonian Garrett, with his hand entwined with Theodore's.

Theodore finally sees me.

"What is this?" is all I manage at first, delivered with enough force for their fingers to unlock.

Before Theodore can reply, Chloe has broken free from me and is dashing up to her brother. "I won this octopus from the claw game. And that one too, that Austin has. Dada didn't think I could but I did. I always believed."

"That's great," Theodore answers, bending down to her. I don't like Chloe's indictment of my belief—I certainly partook in her excitement and hoped she could succeed—and I consider whether it's worth a gentle riposte. But I hold back. Theodore is my concern. Theodore and Garrett. "You're a big-time winner."

"Those claw games are hard. I can never get one of the animals," Garrett say. "I assumed they were rigged. But she proved me wrong."

"Boys," I interrupt. "How's everything? Are you enjoying the jubilee?"

"We were just walking around. There's an outdoor court and Garrett was talking about shooting around in a bit."

"Yeah, Theo is developing a great jumper."

Theo. A pet name we've never employed. It's the first I've heard of it, courtesy of Garrett Hannon.

"I didn't know Orchard High School had an outdoor court," I say.

"It's nice, actually. They remodeled it a few years ago. Repainted and everything."

"Repainted and everything. That's splendid. And how are our hands? Garrett, were you helping Theo with the feel on his jumper? Or was Theo offering assistance? A particular rough callous?"

"Mr. Starr, no, it's a game, actually." To my surprise, Garrett has a sprightly smile, the sort that can never know shame. "You know TikTok, right?"

"Yes, I know TikTok, Garrett."

"Well, it's a challenge. A TikTok challenge."

"Yeah, it's a little—you know, you see who can let go first. You have to massage with the thumb," Theodore says. "And there's this ASMR part, but it's loud here, you know, so we can't do that. It's hard to explain."

"It's dumb, I promise," Garrett says. "I think TikTok is dying anyway."

"Traffic is down, supposedly," Theodore says.

"Social in general. We're all just tired. I'm going to deactivate my Instagram unless I get some big NIL deals in college, and I don't know if that's going to happen."

"It's tough to get those deals. You have to be the best player in college football or a very hot gymnast."

"And I'm not going to be either of those things."

"Unless you really start stretching," Theodore says.

And they laugh. The two of them there, in front of me, and I am rummaging through sentences to disgorge in their direction. I can say, simply, that I don't believe them. I know enough about the internet. I was born late enough to be a child doused in its infinite glories. As the pastor of a flourishing church, it's my duty to understand the social currents rippling through my congregation, to engage as much in worldly matters as I can to best apprehend, ultimately, the enemy—Sun Tzu, heathen as he was, understood a few uncomfortable and immutable qualities of the human condition. I know TikTok. I don't know all the trends—who can, it's like knowing the names of asteroids—but I know what a trend might be on such a platform, and what they were doing would not be it. No.

Yet they are sure they have one on me. There is no fear in Garrett Hannon's eyes. There could be a hint buried in Theodore's, but he has his schoolboy mien back, a little gleam that won't be wiped away. He's learned well, perhaps from his mother. I want to bore through him, to attack at the truth, to procure honesty from them both.

Instead, banter.

"What do you think comes after TikTok?" Garrett asks.

"TrikTok. Only deception. Nothing else."

"Only what things don't seem like."

"BlipTok. If a video is over two seconds, it automatically deletes. You have to hit two seconds. If you don't you try again."

"We could do a BlipTok challenge."

"Once two-second videos are big, you'll have to come in at one or under. Under one will be the mark of a true legend."

"The video that can't be seen will go the most viral."

They both turn to regard me, surprised that I'm still here.

"You have another hour, if you want to shoot baskets, Theodore. Then meet your mother and I at the crafts hall."

"Okay."

"And a word for both of you—don't let anyone get the wrong idea."

I turn, Chloe and Austin in hand, leaving them both alone. Let them think over what they've done.

That night, I have a dream the devil comes to Earth.

He is, as to be anticipated, in human form. He wears penny loafers, a navy necktie, and a Loro Piana cashmere blend overcoat, with suede-trimmed pockets and a herringbone motif. His handsomeness is prewar, his chin dimpled, his brown hair lightly Brylcreemed. When he speaks, people listen.

He is the devil, after all.

Since he is the devil himself, and not a metaphor or an allusion, he has a simple message for mankind: he will make them all immortal.

When the devil delivers this message, fancying himself another Moses at Mount Sinai, several wise men step forward. They ask the natural question. What's the catch?

No catch at all, the devil says. Once I wave my hand, you will all be immortal. All of mankind will never die.

The men and women murmur among themselves. They know this nice-looking man is onto something.

All you have to do is say *yes*. Say, *make me immortal.*

Make me immortal, they cry out in unison.

There is a small ripple of light, and it is done. At first, the men and women feel nothing and assume it is yet another hoax. What else has there been but light? They see light enough, anyway. The ripple may have been a distant comet, and nothing more.

Time slogs on. What the billions of people all across the world find, to their delight, is that their psychic image of who they are reflects their physical being; decline had ceased. The devil has done his work. When the realization is planetwide, uproarious and oceanic parades swallow the city streets. Ten years, twenty, thirty, fifty—time has left them, but they are unchanged. All of them.

Aging is done. Dying is done. Fear itself becomes fable, like Demeter swallowed as a newborn or Icarus plummeting into the sea. There is merriment of the likes never known; of alcohol imbibed, drugs snorted, banquets arrayed and consumed, one after the other after the other.

No consequence, no death. The generations holding firm. The leaders of yesterday are the leaders of tomorrow. The men and women are grateful to still be here, gloriously persisting. They remember, now a century ago, the man who is really the devil coming to Earth.

The gift he has given.

Would immortality breed boredom? Would the so-called meaning of life be reduced? No, the horror is much more prosaic than that. The devil has made no one infertile. That is not part of his plan—he enjoys fornication, and wants more of it for his amusement. Babies are born and permitted to trundle into adulthood, where they will age into their very peak and remain: lush scalps, shining skin, buttocks tight and firm. They beam and beam, and kept beaming. They have all they could ever need.

The devil, from a remove, stifles his laughter. Look at the people, multiplying into the sun. Look at them, beginning to see what is happening to their civilizations, their bursting and bloating civilizations.

Too many people.

The newer-born are the most restless, and then the most rabid—they have the most to lose in the new order. The devil, after all, had offered no infinite boundaries. Humans may never die, but they aren't gaining new farmland, new forests, and new cities. Real estate men like myself, for the time being, could bathe in the filthy lucre of scarcity. The first families of immortality would not vacate their Tudors and craftsmans and mid-century moderns. And if they did, bidding frenzies ensued, prices quintupling hourly.

And they all still had to eat. The devil had not robbed them of hunger or thirst.

And they still could be poor.

The rich could live and live and accumulate. They could compound their fortunes or make them gloriously static, reap bounty in the new scarcity. They had first-mover advantage, and retained it. The poor, the devil saw, could only swell.

So much immortal poverty. Behold!

The people understand now. They have lived long enough; they are now shivering in mud homes and reedy huts, as beautiful as they would ever be, still scurrying for their daily breadcrumbs. The cities crumble under their weight. They feel like overfed rats stuffed through drainage piping. What have the people done? There is talk, among them, of the devil—mythos that, in this new suffocating world, feels as real as the thick sweat stinging their eyes. They begin, soon enough, to beg for death. To beseech the heavens for deliverance. Death is release. It is like the coolest water on a boiling day. It is like a dripping, seasoned steak fed to a starving man.

Hucksters emerge. They sell death in a bottle. They promise, with *this* potion, you can die. Billions consume the liquids and wait. Sickness comes, and they are hopeful; they are rheumy and hacking, blood vessels bursting in their eyes. They stagger like bullets have already been blasted through their toes. At any time, ten thousand bodies can collapse en masse, blackened drool sluicing their garments of tomorrow. Fevered, strangled, weeping, the taste of sawdust and intestinal fluid on their tongues, their teeth tumbling out, hard little kernels at their feet. They cry blood, and there is joy—they are, at last, *dying*. It is unmistakable.

Even the hucksters, in that moment, believe.

But the devil knows. He watching and he knows. The men and women will blink dumbly into the sun-scorched sky and think they have arrived. *Are we dead, are we dead, are we dead . . .* They wait. They tell their hearts to stop. They listen and hope, desperately, to hear nothing at all. *Let us go.*

The devil laughs. Now they understand. They can hear him laugh.

At this point, I'm awake.

3

I've been trying to shake the sensation that someone, somewhere, is following me. It started at least a few weeks ago—that's when I noted it, I should say, like a nit in the corner of my eye—and until now, I never had an overriding desire to remark upon the development. Most individuals of prominence feel this sensation eventually, since it's inevitable there will be a pursuer, a person far more devoted to them than they are to the stranger. And now, I suppose, it's my time, but I don't like it very much. I don't like referencing it, even. It may sound more than a tad woo-woo, but to speak of something enough *is* to give it life, and now that I've rambled on about this notion, it may have added strength.

Or maybe not. What am I even referencing? At the jubilee, I thought I saw a man watching Gertrude and I. And again, two days later, when I was leaving Meijer, that same sensation.

Finally, on the road there was a vehicle trailing too suspiciously close, like we were joined by an invisible thread. No good, I thought then. In a secret agent flick, I could run him into a ditch, giggle as the carriage crunches through manure and eventually catches fire, a flame bouquet in my rearview mirror. More prosaically, I could have slowed, waited for him to pull over, and dug out the Glock in my trunk. That would have sent him skittering.

A gun is not a man's best friend, nor a very good one, but it can be, like a dog, a necessary companion. Around here, experience teaches you that. You don't want to be caught empty-handed.

At least, since that road sighting, I haven't noticed anyone one else after me.

It's time, finally, to focus on something else.

Buck Shasta's fundraiser falls on a Tuesday. I have to cancel a counseling session and considered rescheduling a showing for a Victorian in Isabella County that I wanted moved quickly to a particularly flush buyer, plausibly all cash. It had been a genial week since the jubilee and Theodore's incident, since my dream of the devil. School, for the young ones, was nearly through, and Theodore wasn't far behind. The four-four beat of late spring was giving way to early summer languor, maybe a waltz, and I was already plotting our trip up north. Last year, I bought a new cabin for us, a twenty-five-minute sprint southward from Mackinaw City. Three-bed, two-bath, immediate lakefront access, and a private pier, for whenever I deigned to purchase a boat. Perhaps a pontoon, courtesy of Everest & Rulopaugh.

Daniella and I took the Chevy to the fundraiser alone. Theodore remained home to play video games and theoretically babysit Chloe and Austin. I told him, definitively, no guests, and he knew he couldn't buck me. This wasn't the 1990s. I had cameras enabled at the doorbell, in the living room, facing our backyard, and over the kitchen. A smartphone app allowed me to access all of them at any moment. I wasn't one for checking, but tonight I might be; it pained me to admit this, but children, my child included, weren't entirely trustworthy. I saw what I saw.

Daniella, of course, doesn't know anything, and I don't intend to raise the matter with her. Once I'm driving, I let her tune the radio to Top 40, a straightforward concession because there is little on the radio I'd like to listen to right now. Swift, Doja Cat, Bieber, the trap kings and queens, the drill rappers—all of it may course through our automobile, if she happens upon any of it. My thoughts are elsewhere.

"What do you make of Buck?" I ask Daniella, genuinely curious of what she makes of Shasta these days.

"The congressman?"

"The only Buck we know."

"He's like all politicians, where there's the dual plane of reality. You know this already."

"The public face and the private face."

"I grew up around them, with my father. I don't think Buck's any different. I think he's perfectly fit for this district at this time. I think he's a forward-trudging machine. I think, if you don't mind, I won't talk to him at all, even when you introduce us."

"You only want to smile and nod."

"A plasticine face. Something like that."

"Daniella, you have so many ideas."

"Not as many as you, dear. You whir even when you sleep."

I decide to take a local road, an M over a US, and we bisect a cornfield, lush walls of green on each side of us. The sun, though we're near the evening, hangs high and bright, thanks to the Michigan advantage of the Eastern Time Zone hugging the Central's light. The East is, figuratively and literally, too dark, and there's little more dismal than a quarter to five on a December afternoon in Manhattan, the oil-slicked sleet sloshing around your discount boots. Here, daylight is assumed, and evenings are a gradual decline into the briefest nightfall. The stars are shyer, and won't make their way out until midnight—and then, unlike New York, they will glimmer and pulse from the universal eye, no man-made machine light to obscure their bounty. All of this is obvious, but it's the obvious that draws us forward and settles us; it's the obvious we choose, what it is that calls to us first.

The obvious is not always good. But it can be.

"Shasta, I saw, was with Trump at the White House. He and the whole Michigan delegation," I say, suddenly waylaying myself in a patently political space. The thought had come and I spoke it out.

"For which bill signing?"

"I forget. The defunding of some liberal nonsense, probably, that needed defunding a long time ago."

"Shasta seems afraid of Trump. He's not the type who likes to be pulled to the mat. He's not one for a tussle."

"Well, Daniella, tussling isn't always comfortable. And if you're preaching, you're naturally tussling. Faith is not an endless fondue foundation. God did not ask Abraham to kiss Isaac gently on the cheek."

"I hate these things. Really. I'm telling you that now, Teddy. My hatred can't be repressed like I hoped it would. I may have to go to the bathroom when Buck Shasta speaks. That's what they all do, right? One hour in, when we're picking over congealing lasagna, the politician gives his speech. I hear it already. I hear the anecdote, the chuckle, the rising action—I will be in the bathroom. You can watch over the lasagna."

"There's no guarantee, truly, there will be lasagna," I begin, then swerve into meatier fare. "Shasta knows at least the war must be against the godless left. It's God against no-God, the terrain of Satan, the cultural Marxists, the literal Marxists, the people who want to kill the past dead and replace it, wholesale, with nullity. Family, culture, work, the nation—what does it mean to them? If Shasta is a dolt, he gets enough where we are and where we must go. That's why we vote."

"I don't know if I agree with you. I don't know what Buck Shasta gets and doesn't get. I think that's one of your problems, Teddy. You project onto others what you'd like them to be, or slowly disgorge parts of your personality in a bid to hand them off elsewhere, so you can see yourself reflected back."

"I detect hostility."

"I told you, I don't want to go."

"You could've told me this before."

"You are a very hard person to tell a feeling to. If you don't like it, you strain to will it away, and you usually do. That's your talent. At one time, it's what drew me in."

"At one time, she says."

"It's not meant to be offensive."

"Meaning and intent, against action. If I *feel* it, that is the reality you've created."

"The arc of the universe bends toward Teddy Starr. We know it to be true."

We pull up into the rambling lot of the Elysian. Most of the quality spots are occupied, Suburbans and Mercedes and the stray F-150s phalanxed at the clubhouse entrance. They jut out like android teeth, glimmering in orange sunlight, and I settle for the outer way, off a corner I'd rather not be. Members have reserved spots and I make a mental note to buy a membership, the peace of mind alone will be worth it, even if I won't be golfing here. Daniella and I are silent out of the car, two agents passing in the gloaming, her runner's calves firm below the hem of her summer dress. An Ichabod Crane–like presence stoops to us at the double doors, mouthing greetings, his tendril fingers ushering us inside and into a rash of air-conditioning.

Buck Shasta has booked us in the Elysian's Great Lakes ballroom, the octagonal crown jewel. When we enter, I see we have assigned seats, the tablecloths dotted with numbered cards. The ballroom is alive already, clusters and clods of conversation everywhere. Most folks are standing near tables or bar side, and I recognize several stalwart citizens of Luce County, including Big Landry and Deke Rademacher, the vice chair of the county party and the owner of a Mazda dealership off 46. I'm not yet in the mood for full-blast reverie, yarns of anecdote flung across me, hellos and hail hails and gab, invariably, of God's providence. We'll get there soon enough.

The room is America-themed tonight, red-white-and-blue bunting, a swirl of glittery and crenelated paper from the rafters. The pasta and scampi will be served from golden troughs, choose-your-own-adventure-style, bound to produce the uncomfortable ooze of cheese extract. Unguent broccoli heads and opposable thumb potatoes round out the mix. All of it may end up more appetizing than it looks and I don't want to judge too harshly—hundreds, including myself, must be fed, and this is for the cause of giving Shasta two more glorious years in Washington. He must vote no, no, no, unless when we need him to vote yes. It all starts here.

Everyone in this room, a max donor.

"Pastor Starr, Pastor Starr!"

Deke has found me, his planetary stomach threatening to blow through his sour cream–white T.J.Maxx button-down, warty fingers beckoning me forward. I give a smile to Daniella who knows to follow me, that it's logical here, even if she has little interest, to interact as a unit of two, two-on-one, Deke's wife nowhere to be found. Deke has worked a hard comb-over, his brown-black hair slick, and he reminds me of an auto salesman out of the 1970s, a decade I'll only know through popular culture. He reminds me of a *projection* of the 1970s, and all he's missing is reception room plaid and an oily moustache tacked on for the hardest sales. I'm told Deke is a powerful man.

"Deke, a pleasure, what a night it is. What a setup."

"Let me tell you, what a hassle this all can be. But we plow through. We make it great. Prices are a killer, though!"

He's bit down on his lower lip to hold back a well-placed f-bomb. Were it just the boys, it would be *fucking* hassle, and you'd be surprised how often they'll swear in front of a pastor.

"Inflation is deflation," I offer.

"That's *right*. And that old slack-jawed drooler, before we got Trump back, was actually corrupt. If he could *remember anything*—when he remembered, he stole. If he wasn't stealing or drooling all over the White House floor, he was in cahoots with Hunter, getting rich off that Ukrainian oil. The damage he did . . . what's become of this country, Pastor, I don't know. You're a little younger than me, but you know. It ain't like used to be. We got so much to fix."

"Not at all. It never is."

"Pastor, when you're on God's side, you're on the right side. Ain't that right? If we got with Him, there'd be nothing else to fear. We'd fix this country right and quick."

"I do believe that, Deke-o."

"Have you ever given the thought, Pastor, while I have you, to *running?*"

"Not since high school cross-country. I came in fifth and couldn't handle it. It's lonely, out there on the pine, if you're not tasting sweet victory every week or so."

Deke leans in, and I huff, unwittingly, his Tabasco breath. For a big leathery guy, he's too gimlet-eyed, and this upsets me. I already know what's coming next.

"You're a very funny guy. I like it. We need that. You know, Trump *is* funny. That's what the liberals always miss. The guy is like a crazy Jeff Foxworthy up there. But listen. You're young, you've got a great church, you should start thinking about it. We need God to get *into* politics, in a real way, men of God, not the frauds and pretenders. And your church, I hear, is really booming."

"You preach from the heart, they come, Deke. You know it."

"And I hear business has been good too."

"Business is business, you know."

"Listen, no need to be coy here. We're in a bit of a *business* place." He says this with a curious ferocity and a sniff the Tabasco again. "You'd be very well-positioned. Lootnaar is termed out next year. He wants his son to run for the seat but his son is drunk half the day. And if he's not, it's the whole day. The state senate is a nice place to start, if that's what you're thinking, and you can raise quickly. I know that. A man like you, there'd be donors tripping over themselves to max out."

"I'm comfortable in the church, Deke, but I do appreciate it."

"Think on it a bit. We've got some time. You're cut from the cloth to do it. And when the time comes, you can even be the top dog to replace Shasta. He hates DC, between us, hates all of it, can't wait to retire. If we lose the majority, he's definitely gone."

"I'm going to pray on it real hard, I promise. It's a lot to consider, and I do appreciate you thinking of me."

Daniella has said nothing and I realize she has peeled off to banter with one of the wives, a bleached blonde of fifty clenching a vodka and soda. The glittering troughs of steamed appetizers are drawing spectators and consumers alike, some weighing whether to scoop pasta or potatoes first. I'm not yet hungry and wary, too, of who might try to speak with me next. This is the networking hour before the speechifying begins and I can pleasantly let my mind wander elsewhere. But until then, I am here, liminal, not preaching, one more donor in a sea of the eager-to-be-seen. I should seek out Shasta, perhaps, as so many others will do—and then say what? We've only spoken a handful of times. The truth be told, a congressman does not come into contact much with any of my enterprises. I don't need Washington to preach and I don't need Washington to collect rent. If there were some thorny regulation I could protest, I would, but my concerns, at best, are with the state and the state has been kind of enough. There are times to rebel and times to be pliant and here, I feel, I have chosen the appropriate posture.

Deke, meanwhile, can only be half-serious. I've heard him engineer that pitch for others before. I admit it matters; to be asked, even as theater, to consider such a temporal elevation. The assumption always amuses me: you're a man of God, but it's *not enough*. Don't you want to grasp at something more? Or, if you're wealthy, it's presumed this wealth must be aimed at some higher purpose, some power, that is not *the* higher purpose. I almost wanted to laugh in Deke's face, to tell it to him straight. Do you know, Deke, how much power *I'd* have to give up to be a state senator? A congressman? I know what they do and what they do not do. I understand Buck Shasta, drowning in prestige, neutered in confetti, forced to fundraise for his life until his life extinguishes itself.

How much easier it is to be myself right now than what Deke wants from me. Politicians believe they have flocks, but voters are a fickle lot. They don't, collectively, have the rigor of belief. Each cycle, they seek a new god. Even lifelong Republicans float among idols, worshipping and discarding, worshipping and discarding.

I think this, as pasta piles high on my plate. I'll take much more than I can eat. It's the opposite of what women do, always demurring with their food. Here, you're a little bull, and you assert your appetite. A grand dame is to my right, picking through a custard plate; she resembles a distant Windsor relative. To my left, two men gab about oil futures, their jowls quaking. Not far off is the man himself, Rep. Shasta, in a comfortable weave of three other suited men, one of them draped in an unsightly plaid. They are laughing at whatever Shasta is telling them. It's joke season and I might have to join in. At the very minimum, I can see if Shasta recalls me.

There's an old canard about politicians and memory, that to ascend so far, you must internalize and file away faces and names, plausibly making every constituent feel special. The Clinton school, he shakes your hand, warm as an Easy-Bake oven, and *knows* you. Drink in his baby blues. There are, I'm sure, politicians like that, but none of the tin-pot variety I've encountered. Rather than knowingness, there is hurried blankness, an approximation of value and values. Sometimes, I merely sense fear, *I have to know you now.* Fear that they'll be forgotten soon or won't properly connect to win your vote and the vote of your family and the vote of your county, because each individual must be a stand-in for something.

I scour the room. Shasta is bearded and laughing, like a Jack Links commercial. I've heard he likes to hunt, that he hates Washington for its lack of hunting—that he was unfamiliar enough with Washington to believe there must have been arable land somewhere to take out a bolt-action or a semiautomatic and blow open the skulls of a few deer in the shadows of the Capitol. I know DC enough. It's a city you can approximate on one or two visits, ascertain and discard; less impressive with each visit, and a pale imitation of the Roman splendor the Founders were straining to re-create in their most frenzied daydreams.

It amuses me to imagine Shasta among them. Does Shasta read the bills? Does Shasta spend late nights with his briefings and books? His job is to be here and laugh. I'm happy, all things being equal, to be counted among his donors. I know he is someone who will appreciate a contribution. The easily impressed appreciate money. They know, to a comfortable degree, what can and cannot be done.

All fundraisers, I believe, have a plot, a conceit. Even the off-year joints. This year, it's the specter of *next year*—a presidential year, red against blue, flakes of the apocalypse. I have Shasta's stump speech scripted in my head. And I'll nod along, because there's truth in all dribble. We've *got* to beat the Democrats. If not, what? Socialism? Godlessness? The nation operates at an equilibrium that a blue rout—or even marginal victory—cannot upset too much. The substrata of this plot tonight, then, will be to *not* upset the equilibrium. We must maintain. We must have controlled chaos.

I take my seat at a large round table with gilded fringes, imitation empire stuff. Half the inhabitants are here, half are off chattering or scooping from the pasta trough, including Danielle. Several I know, though none attend my church. They are proud civic cogs, either unpaid members of a town commission or aspiring unpaid members, one rather comely, the wife of a flooring executive. I count two beats and wait for them to slowly turn toward me. In the distant background, I can hear Shasta's joyous growl, the congressman in the storm's eye. This is the simulation of celebrity he needs.

To be known. To believe, yes, they all love you—that from this wanting is love, to sublimate the transaction.

"Where do I know you from?" I ask the wife of the flooring executive, trying out ignorance. "Were you a Ms. Flapjack Jubilee?"

She wasn't, not that I know of, but there's a small whirring behind her eyes. It's a fantasy she's enjoying.

"No, not at all! I was never one of those girls. You're the pastor, aren't you? My husband and I attended the faith retreat outside Toledo last year and heard you give an address. We were impressed. If we lived in Pine Haven, we would be there every Sunday."

"Oh, I appreciate that. Thank you. Really, it's the Lord that speaks to you, and you're the interpreter. All you can really do is listen. Where do you and your husband worship?"

"Ithaca Baptist. It's very close to our house. We walk there every week, rain or shine. Danny enjoys the exercise."

Danny Blanchard, yes. A&R roofing, which pays for the small seasonal billboard off 127. I spoke with him once before, a fundraiser for the Luce County organization last year. Shasta, of course, headlined. He wanted to talk about God and then the Tigers, and I indulged on both ends. It was another rough year, no pitching, limited offense, a confused manager, and prospects mostly stillborn.

"I always say walking to church is a way to get the spirits up. You get your blood flowing, really get in the mood. Ithaca Baptist completed a renovation last year, right? I haven't been down to the new building yet."

"The architect did a glorious job. He actually came from New York City. He was the brother-in-law of a congregant and gave us a deal. The glass windows look like they're weeping light."

"Well, I hope our windows look like they're sobbing light someday. We're due for new work. I should take a tour sometime and see Ithaca Baptist, if you'll show me around." It occurs to me I've either forgotten her name or never learned it in the first place. Danny Blanchard wasn't one to blab about his wife.

"That'd be lovely. Danny can schedule it with you. He's so proud of it. He thought it would be too *showy*, but I reminded him it wasn't a sin if it was done for the glory of God. My grandfather was a preacher, actually. I know a little bit of what it takes to put together a sermon."

"It's not hard work because it's *good* work. It can only be so much of a struggle if you're called. I've been bringing our flock through Ephesians of late."

"Oh yes, Ephesians," and I'm watching the movement of her lips, plump and ruby, the lipstick with a light shine in the overhead beams. Danny will be back soon, as will Daniella, and I am momentarily amused that their names are so aligned. Danny is the kind of man Daniella would tolerate for no longer than five minutes, his breath reeking of tobacco and Frosted Flakes, and sometimes I think it's unfair the men in this county don't offer her more. It *is* a challenge, if you find yourself as a woman in the position of wanting to roam—where can they roam, exactly? Most men here are defiantly unfit. They maraud through Arby's and Friendly's and the Walmart confections cases, or test their luck with the gas station jerkies. They are immovable in fall and winter, the weeks orbiting around football Sundays and Mondays and Thursdays and Saturdays.

I've sought my advantages—I won't lie about that. Danny's wife might sense it too.

"I sometimes hope they'll say something different," she adds. "I've been to several of these. I hope to be surprised and never am."

"The point isn't to surprise. It's to, in theory, inspire, but inspiration has a flavor of surprise. Not all of it can be expected. I think the politician types forget that. They're very insistent on playing their notes. And I understand that. You can't be completely unexpected. The issues are the issues, and they're going to stay the issues. A baby's life is sacred. We've got to get God back in the schools. But you want that bit of flair, don't you?"

"I don't know. I suppose, maybe, though I wouldn't want to hear Marxism or something like that."

"You just want a fresh turn of phrase. You want a well-written speech. Genuinely well-written. Words that pop and sing. You want to *remember* Shasta, don't you?"

"I want one night to not bleed into the next."

"Ah, definition. What we all aim for, when it comes down to it."

"A memory. Something hard, something firm."

"Something, too, to sink your teeth into."

"*Give me liberty or give me death.* There's a reason we still talk about it."

"It's the movement deathward. The raising of the stakes. You want Shasta to drive further."

"And I want this pasta in front of me to not taste so bland."

We eat. What have I even retrieved? The memory itself, of the buffet trough, is fogged, and it must have been because my mind was hurrying elsewhere. Daniella is back and I smile at her and hope she'll introduce herself to Danny Blanchard's wife so I'll have a name. Daniella is always good for this sort of thing. But she's stony, casually distracted or fronting it, and I realize I'll have to struggle onward, alone in this regard.

Is Danny's wife forty? She's engineered for thirty-five, but I see the rosy incursion of age, my age, and it doesn't bother me at all. It's insidious how older men always prey on the young, as if they can only prove themselves with those who've accrued so little hard data in their lives.

Champions want a good match. I almost tell this to Daniella.

"Danny over there is so funny," she says to me, breaking a momentary silence. I watch Blanchard, now embroiled with two men I don't recognize, his face subtly amphibian; his mouth strained open like a guppy's, gobbling for sweet salt water. I decide I'll like him. Nothing is his fault, really. He is here on accord of Shasta and the party, like me, and if he wants to charm my wife, all the best. Men deserve to be commended for their efforts. I suppose I'll need to ferret out what form this charm has taken, if Danny Blanchard has managed any witticisms or amusing bromides.

"Anything in particular?" I ask her quietly, since his wife isn't far away.

"He's a man at such ease."

"Ease is funny?"

"Ease foregrounds humor."

"He used to read those little joke books," his wife says, overhearing us. "I hope he didn't try one on you."

"No, nothing so practiced." *I'm Daniella, by the way.* So easy to introduce yourself. But she's refusing. "Teddy here and I met him a little while back."

"Yes, I heard. We're all excited for tonight. We've got to make sure Buck gets back to Congress."

"Buck is on the right track," I say. "He's a fighter. He's a brawler. You need that now. God needs warriors in Washington. He's not afraid of mucking it up, right? Some people, they don't like the smell of blood. They want to theorize. Buck never lives in theories. Buck is action, action, action—I'm not saying there isn't a place for theory, for dissecting the weight of temporal things. But we need it. We need veins pumping with blood."

"He was a football player in high school, right?" Danny's wife asks. "All-State? I never paid attention. He went to a high school in a different district from me."

Daniella has turned away, toward the rapidly filling front of the room. She senses what I sense. A show is about to begin.

There are speeches and then there are speeches, and this was definitively the former. Rep. Shasta, at least, did not stare down at notes or peer, as some do, ludicrously into his phone. He was introduced by Rademacher, who had the shallow glint of a man who wished he had won a higher station in life. Rademacher gave it his all. He gave us the stakes, good and evil, the fast creep of the illiberal and godless left, the ravages of inflation, the Democrats embodied by that maladroit and ultimately brain-blasted Geppetto president. Shasta arrived to applause that was something approaching rapacious, and we all naturally joined in, Danny Blanchard clapping harder than even me.

And Shasta? I saw, somewhere inside him, the football-playing youth. But it wasn't what he wanted to display—it was the second-string tackle, the third-string defensive end, what they might have called a *pusher*, a ball of blubber in a cloud of dust. I almost felt sorry for him. He was straining with whatever cable television had fed him, his diction wobbly, all of it froth. The words, what words? Rademacher had them already.

Shasta fit well in his suit at least. It was plainly tailored, tapered at his wide shoulders, tugged tightly where it needed to be. A shade of dark blue that was almost mauve and a fire-red tie, electrically patriotic. He had shed five or ten pounds since I last saw him. He's been trying to become a Fox News regular, though a backbencher will only get so far, even from a swing state. The trouble, I'm realizing, is that he can't meet the moment. There are people like this and sometimes it gets tragic. There is a searing mismatch between ambition and native talent, the gap Huron-sized, and within that expanse is the chance to get lost and never return. Shasta at least reached *the* Congress. He was a state senator for six minutes too. Had he not achieved either—never been vaulted into elected office at all—it's conceivable he wouldn't have found a compelling reason to live.

He attempted anaphora for his finale. *This country, this country, this country* . . . He got louder each time, as he believed he should, and you could almost believe he was going to hit a stride of some sort, do what Danny Blanchard's wife hoped he would—make a memory. But then, like a wheezing plastic plaything, one of those that are squeezed at the tummy to eke out a noise, he could not sustain himself. He was waiting for another squeeze but there was no giant from above to get it out of him. He was delivering, and then he was done.

We sat, all of us, at the large table, and applauded. Our food had gone cold.

I'm standing now, minutes gone, and we're heading to the exits. Daniella is weary. Theodore, Chloe, and Austin will need supervision. Without checking, I know it's near ten o'clock. Rather than trust a babysitter, we've tasked Theodore with ensuring his siblings are in bed, even sleeping. Was this wise? It was Daniella's idea, her concept, a belief in early empowerment and responsibility, a boy rises to meet a task, et cetera, then you give him more. I'm dubious, but I let her lead here, and I'm willing to endorse if the outcome is what we prefer.

"Good night, I hope we can see you soon," Daniella says, pleasantly enough, to Danny Blanchard and his wife.

"Yes, it was a pleasure. Anytime you're in Ithaca, let us know," Danny's wife replies. A phrase comes to mind, a shopworn expression—*give us a shout*. But no one says that here.

"We'll have to see the renovated church," I say.

"Absolutely. Anytime, anytime," Danny Blanchard himself chimes in, and we're off, the four in a pocket of more, the gilded doors of the Great Lakes ballroom shoved open. Beyond the atrium, we meet the cold. Danny and his wife are in the valet line and I'm thankful we were early enough to avoid this luxury. We're about to bound down the steps when there's a tap on my shoulder and a laugh, and I know who it is.

Big Landry wants a last snatch of chitchat. I'll oblige.

"Well Pastor, how about it? Didn't Buck bring the thunder?"

"Thunder brought all right."

"Boy oh boy, can we get him a promotion? Senate, White House, or at least a talk show too, you know? Like Limbaugh used to have. Get him out there, booming and booming, spreading the good word, like you do."

I note Daniella's discomfort and pass her along the car keys. I'll be a few more minutes and she can wait, running the heat.

"Listen, anytime we can support a man like that, someone on God's side, we're in business, aren't we, Landry?"

"That's what we need, an army, Pastor. An army for the Lord. We're getting afraid of a fight. Well, *I'm* not afraid. I know you're not. That's why I'm in your church, Pastor, if I'm being honest. You know I've been around the block. You know I've circulated, tried on different pastors, different pulpits—I've seen it. And I know you're rising up, you're not afraid. That's why I'm sticking around."

"I very much appreciate that, Landry. A pastor is only as worthwhile as his congregation. And your energy is what's going to get us through . . ."

I'm ready, now, to head back to the car where Daniella is waiting. I appreciate Landry, but only in doses, and once a day is fast-acting and all you should really ask for. I smile warmly and widely—I want him to know he *does* matter—and place my hand on his right shoulder, like a coach would for his star tailback. No matter how old men get, they want gestures like these, to know that their place in the world is assured. Landry will always be *big*—Big Landry, our dynamo, our hard-charging vassal.

"I'll see you on Sunday, Landry. You drive home safe."

"You too, I'll be there bright and early."

I turn and take four, perhaps five, steps in the direction of my car when there's another tap, this time on my back, too light for Landry. I decide, in the lurch of the first second, it's an accident and take another step. Who taps?

Except it happens again. In the distance, I can see Daniella through my windshield, her jawline camphor-white in the glow of her smartphone.

"Yes?" I ask, expecting another congregant I didn't see inside or, more hopefully, Danny Blanchard's wife, here to share her name.

"Reuvain? Reuvain?"

The man is asking this, asserting this, through a heavy black beard and bitty kernel teeth, his breath wafting toward me. What is it, bratwurst? He is my height, stooped, and he paws at the air, hands lagging behind speech. I decide to wait, to let another second settle between us.

"Excuse me?"

"Reuvain—Reuvain, it's *you*."

"I'm sorry, I don't understand."

"Yes, you shaved, I see, but it is you, Reuvain. . . . I found you. I found you. I thought you might be—but why here?"

I begin to back away, slowly enough to not startle him. "I think you may be confused. I don't know who Reuvain is, and I really need to get back to my wife. You have a good night, sir, and I hope you find who you are looking for."

"But it *is* you. Please, just listen to me, I am not here to make trouble. I come just to say hello, to talk. I miss you. Your brother misses you, don't you understand? Your only brother."

"I don't have a brother." I am half-turned toward the Chevy and Daniella's glow, and all I need to do is complete my pivot and be gone. It'll be simple. No one expects me to be this accommodating, not to someone who looks like this. I have every right to say nothing else.

"It's *me*. It's Yaacov. I promise I won't make trouble. I've come what, almost a thousand miles to see you. I've been driving, driving, driving through this country, and my information, after being bad so long, was good. I know it's late. Can we talk tomorrow? Where are you living now?"

"I said, I don't know who you are!"

The sound of my own voice surprises me. It's balky, shrill, almost teenage—a sonic retreat, *weakness*. What broke from me? If I spoke like that in front of my congregation, they'd all desert. I watch his hunting and wanting eyes. As I move back, he moves forward. He won't quit. There are people around us, the hastening tide of Shasta devotees and donors, and I hope one of them will catch me in conversation and bear me away. That will be easiest, to lock eyes with someone I recognize and fall in with them until I can make it to the Chevy. It shouldn't be very hard. In another beat or two, I'll be free.

"It's okay, Reuvain—really. You must believe me. I will not make trouble. You are safe. I am happy to see you. It's been so long, so long. If now is not good, I understand, maybe tomorrow? We can go to a restaurant, your choice, and we can—"

"Paul! Lila!" I call out to a diffident couple passing into the gutter, their hands interlocked. Paul is a developer who has been trying to build a hideous tract housing on the site of the old Pine Haven High, and Lila is his wife. They are mid-forties, play in

Republican politics, and will happily speak with me, as a man of God and a man of land.

"Teddy, there you are, I thought I saw you across the room!"

And I'm off, into the parking lot, leaving the sputtering, bearded man and his bratwurst breath behind. Paul fortuitously parked his satin steel metallic Tahoe three spaces from me, and I can tie up our thread—Shasta, the outrageous interest rates, a promise for lunch by the end of the month—while easing myself into the Chevy. I bid them a lusty farewell, tell Lila I love her necklace, and we're off.

Daniella has looked up from her phone.

"Who were you talking to?"

"Oh, you know Paul Goffnet and Lila, his wife. Paul's been trying to redevelop the old high school property for the last decade, getting nowhere. The environment has gotten real rotten of late, with the spiking rates and cost of materials, and labor, wow, you don't want to know what it costs just to set up—"

"*Not* them. I know them. That man with the beard. He seemed to know you."

"I didn't recognize him at all. He must have been mistaken thinking I was someone else."

"I wonder who he was looking for."

"I don't know, I didn't understand him. He must have crawled out from somewhere, or been drunk. I hope he gets the help he needs."

"I doubt he was drunk, Teddy. He drunk drove here? Wandered off the two-lane country road with no sidewalks? We're five miles from any house, any bar . . ."

"Your point?" I've started up the Chevy and we're crawling out of the lot, behind a row of sickly brake lights.

"He looked plenty sober, and intentional. It bothered me."

"He was confused. You can be intentional and confused."

"Did he say his name?"

"He was mumbling. I don't know. I've told you that already."

"He didn't seem like he was mumbling. He seemed, I don't know, *animated*."

"Dear, you were far away, in the car. He was a deranged man and we'll never see him again."

When we're free of the Elysian, the Chevy hitting seventy-five, then eighty, then eighty-five, I promise myself I'll never set foot inside of there again.

4

Danny Blanchard's wife is named Genevieve. I find her the next night, in a quick property records search. Danny and Genevieve paid $349,500 for a three-bed, three-bath colonial two years ago, just as the market was heating up. She is a loan processing officer at GrahamCo, one of the local credit unions, and she has worked there for seven years. Her birthdate is March 28. She roots, naturally, for the Spartans, Lions, Tigers, Pistons, Red Wings. She graduated from Pine Haven College but posts about Spartans basketball on her Facebook page.

I consider how I'll see her again, absent Danny. There are conceivable scenarios. I might have business at GrahamCo or find my way to Ithaca, where I've been rehabbing a property, a two-bed, one and a half bath, to flip in the next two to three months. Gertrude Breckinridge's alleged departure—I don't truly believe she's finished—might make this all a bit more necessary. And if I'm being honest, after the night at Elysian, Genevieve could be agreeable fodder, a way to roll a few days into a few weeks and put some distance between myself and what happened out there.

Last year, I decided to rent an office downtown, paying an irksome premium for a storefront that was supposed to offer, at the minimum, a modest advertising boost for my firm and has, in fact, offered none—business is good, but not because of this space or whatever stray eyes have been attracted to my bespoke, red-accented sign. It can be a good place to be when I have no sermon to work on, no property to visit, no tenants to cajole, and no particular childcare duties to take on. That's why I'm driving there now. I need to find some sort of work there, plow myself into it, and consider the benign riddle of Genevieve, and how I might get closer to her.

It's a sunroof day, and I drop it down, rays of light baking my crown. Traffic is light, as it always is, and I pass the community theater, the first of two hardware stores, the Liberty Café, Ace Antiques, and the Pine Haven Brewery. Downtown is on a casual upswing, the college beginning to realize its possibilities and slowly colonize, everything student-inflected. The locals might resent it—the liberalism of the college is troublesome in too many ways to count—but it's a boon for anyone in the land profession. Rent is up, value is up, and builders hover.

I know what I've got to do.

In the front of my office sits Sue Piffle, sunny as always.

"Hello, Pastor," she says to me as I enter, the little bell jingling above.

"How are you, Sue?"

"It's been a quiet morning for the most part, you know how it goes. You've got a call about the Douglass property. There's a real fixing to sell, I think."

"Seen any good animal documentaries?"

Sue loves these, especially when they're about the endangered.

"Herb found one on the Greenland shark and we've been devouring it right up. Do you know they can live to be four hundred?"

"What a blessed species."

"I'd love to know what's in their heads, with all that living, all that swimming." Sue has a half-consumed California Cobb salad at her desk, and there's dressing splattered disconcertingly on her keyboard. "What do you think? What does God think?"

"God doesn't make mistakes, so whatever He thinks, it's for this Greenland shark to persist here. Perhaps He wants us to learn from the shark. That's a mystery to unravel."

"Herb hopes they bring one to the Potter Park Zoo. Do you think they'll bring one out? I imagine it'd be very expensive."

I have a private office in the back and I very much want to get there, now. Sue Piffle means well; she's forty-five, married twenty-five years, a semi-regular at Trinity. She has a gourd-like physique and talks often, too often, of how she'll have to start using the Pine Haven College rec center but a membership, *can you believe it, is three hundred dang dollars a year.* I debate whether I want her at my church more or less. Churches are built by Sue Piffles and occasionally destroyed by them. Her faith is slack, but she works well here, and I've never found her to be unreliable as an answerer of phones, a sender and forwarder of emails. She is a chipper face for whoever wanders in, and there isn't much more you can ask for.

"Oh, I don't know, Sue. It's possible. They're doing amazing things these days. You can bet on Potter Park. I'll be in my office for a bit to work, if anyone calls for me, tell them I'm in a meeting."

"Will you be in a meeting?"

"No, I won't. I'll be in my office."

"Okay then. I'll make a note of that. You just let me know if you need anything."

"I sure will, Sue. . ."

Out the window, across the street, I see something I absolutely do not like. I squint, remembering I need to start wearing eyeglasses more often, that there is nothing attractive about nearsightedness. The details, swimming, come into focus, squiggly lines making a man, *that* man, passing between Pizza Sty's and Weller & Weller. He is hunched, in a slight scuttle, wrapped in a dark blue blazer, his eyes hunting. He does not see me; that I am sure. But he is hoping. That awful beard again, and if I wore my eyeglasses, I could see his corroded teeth too.

"If anyone comes in here, tell them I'm not here."

"You're in a meeting, got it. Not here. Not at all?"

"I'm visiting a property. I'm gone."

"What if they see your car?"

"Excuse me?"

"Well, Pastor, a guest might come and see your Chevy parked out there and if they know you, they could say, 'You know, he might be fibbing.' I know you wouldn't do a thing like that but that's just the risk I thought about, if I say you're out of the office."

"You can tell them I'm in an associate's automobile. Tell them I'm with Finny, visiting properties."

"Finny, got it."

Before he can see me, I've dashed into my office and quietly, through broken breaths, locked the door. A back window looks out to a parking lot, mostly unoccupied, and I close the blinds. My wall is comforting: the Degas reproduction, my pastoral care and counseling certificate, portraits of my three children, and a silver cross that once belonged to a Lansing congregation in the mid-1870s. Sound penetrates, but just barely, and all the world is nothing more than Charlie Brown cartoon voices.

Now I can think. Genevieve, unfortunately, will be the easier riddle to solve.

The goatish man with the beard might come here. He might walk into this office. He didn't just leave after the night at the Elysian. That stubbornness isn't new—no, it's reared up before, and if I'm not careful, it'll come again.

There's a hot, crablike clenching in my chest. If I had the right watch, it would tell me my heart rate is alarmingly elevated. Sweat beads crawl out of my eyelids. It's still morning, what should be a bubble of quiet, and here I am. I don't like it at all. My desktop computer is like a black mouth. I snap at the keys and bring the login screen to life.

What would Gertrude Breckinridge make of all this? I have an asinine hunch to call her at her office at the college and ask. She would give me time on the phone, we can run through scenarios, try to reach an accord—a solution. *A man thinks I'm someone else. He's not to be trusted.* Gertrude has a knifeblade logic to her. She does not easily cow. It's what I've always liked about her; in that sense, she's much like Daniella, but I've never found that quality in Daniella especially alluring. If anything, it frustrates. She wouldn't indulge any of this. I'm not going to tell her I saw the man today.

I pick up my telephone and strongly consider it—calling Gertrude. If reasoning is an apartment house, it's basement-level logic to make this call, basement mania. A penthouse brain hangs up now. I know what I'm supposed to do. Wait, wait, wait . . . it's what, after all, I've been good at, and it's patience that has brought me here. Patience has granted me a congregation, a company, 48 Hearst, three children. What I'm doing now, *calling* Gertrude Breckinridge, violates the spirit of all of this.

At least I settle for her cell phone. She might be taking an early lunch break. On the fourth ring, I hear a muffling, the start of a syllable, and then a voice.

"Teddy."

"I'm glad you've got my work number in your phone."

"I don't. I just remember it."

"Is now a good time?"

"Good and bad don't have much to do with it. I'm walking between buildings on the quad. The next building has lousier service than the one I've departed from."

"If you're busy, we can talk later."

"It depends what this is all about. If it's on certain matters we've closed off, then I'm busy. Harry is home. If it's something else, if you want to discuss scripture or why it's still a good time to sell, given the punishing rates, I'd be open to hearing about it until my service gets scrambled."

"It's on neither of those topics. I'm being followed."

"Well *of course* you are, Pastor. We all follow you."

"You should try out for the Groundlings."

"I almost know who they are."

"A man has been stalking me. First at a fundraiser. Now outside my office."

"Has he spoken to you?"

"Yes, he has."

"What has he said to you?"

"He's accusing me of being someone else. He's very confused, mentally ill, likely dangerous."

"Perhaps you should contact the police."

"The Pine Haven PD is useless. Five cops who couldn't hack it in Wayne County and came here, plus a few locals who barely made it out of Pine Haven High. They do underage drinking arrests, barely. For this, they can't deliver."

"Then what do you plan to do?"

The question is the most obvious one, yet it gouges me. I don't know how to answer. I'm here, sputtering stupidly on an office telephone, hoping for wisdom from Gertrude, as if she has experienced this all already and can walk me through, step by step, what to expect in the future—as if she could tutor me, like I'm a small child taking tennis lessons.

"I haven't figured it out yet."

"The man may wander off. He could go up north. It's getting lovely now. Maybe he scoops ice cream at Traverse City for the summer."

"I don't like that I've seen him twice. I think he's going to come into my office."

"You'll have to stay there until he leaves, I suppose. But did he threaten you? Pull out a gun? A knife? Does he know your dirty secrets?"

"He didn't make any threats. And my secrets aren't *dirty*. No more than yours."

"I didn't vouch for mine."

"Gertrude, this is all more serious than you seem to think it is."

"Then why are you talking to me? Do you want me to ask Harry? He's got a nice new shotgun. When he's feeling up to it, he'd probably love a good vigilante mission. When he's bored, he gets ambitious. The hospital was good for him."

"I want—" And then there's the muffled voice of Sue Piffle, out there by the door. I hear her and know what it is. "Gertrude, can I call you back?"

"I'm going to be occupied through the early afternoon, at least. You can try after four."

"After four, fine. I'll speak to you later."

"Goodbye."

"I do appreciate you."

She hangs up after that. Sue is on her third or fourth sentence, rapping lightly. I'm not one of these moguls with a buzzer. We're a small office and if she wants me, she can come fetch me or send a text.

"What is it, Sue?"

"A man is here."

"Tell him I'm out, like we discussed."

"He insists you're not."

My ear is pressed up against the door. "What does he look like?"

"Look, well, he's a gentleman a little chunkier than you. He has lonesome eyes, I'd say."

"Does he have a *beard*, Sue?"

"A beard? Oh yes, he certainly does. A thick one, very dark. Almost like one of the Amish."

I battle back a tidal urge to take the Lord's name in vain. I once did, I used to, there was a time when it was easy to spit it all out, from Father to Son, to curse their names casually. I was different then. Now, I'm pressed against my own office door, plying Sue Piffle for physical descriptors, weighing how possible it might be to slide out the back window. It *is* possible, if I press out the glass and shamble out, slowly, slowly, and no one sees me. It might hurt, but it also might be worth it.

"Tell him to leave, Sue." My voice does not crack. "He should not . . . he should not be here."

"Is he an associate of anyone's? Is he a buyer? Should I note his appearance in the log?"

"Just tell him to leave. He's no one."

"No one, okee, got it. No one. I'll tell him you're out and about."

None of this should be hard. I remember an old banality, breathing and counting to ten, and decide I can do this. I can go one, I can go two, I can go three. . . . There is God, too, but He strikes me as unnecessary here. I can command His strength but I shouldn't have to pray for direction. The direction is obvious. The man needs to leave. And he will.

Sue is talking. I can't make out what Sue is saying. I abandon the door and land back behind my desk, as if I have something to do. I wave my mouse and the grandiosity of Paris appears, an automatically generated desktop background, Montmartre at night. Desktop icons dully beckon me. There are leasing documents to distract me, old profit-loss sheets, blueprints to a scuttled mixed-use development in Orchard. I've even, somehow, crammed a photo folder from a family trip, two years ago, to Great Wolf Lodge. Chlorinated memories, for the crackling seconds, almost lull me.

Then nothing. No Sue, no man. I'm in a void. For all I know, the front of my office has broken off into a new dimension, and I'm still on terra firma, mulling my escape. The sunlight glinting off the parking lot asphalt is sickly sweet. It is almost summer. The end of Gertrude and me is for the best, I figure now, because she never wanted to get the air-conditioning unit in her bedroom repaired. The homestead was too ancient for central air.

Sue? Sue? I should peek out. I should have a camera installed in here so I can see the front of my office. Why haven't I? What's stopped me? I have no personal qualms against surveillance. *God* surveils. That is, even for the heathen, the worthy takeaway from the Old Testament. I need Ring cameras, Nest cameras, a sturdy panopticon that keeps me informed of all that slithers in and out. What a failure, then, to not prepare—to not be ready for a day like this.

I'm relying on sound. No Sue Piffle. So why hasn't she knocked? She could tell me the coast is clear. Threat level averted. But she also doesn't comprehend the threat, the invasion. Sue is ebullient. Sue charges into the big bright future. Her world is secure; therefore, all worlds are.

"Hello, Sue?" I manage, hating the tremolo of my voice.

A beat passes, then another. "Yes, Pastor?"

"Is the man gone?"

"Oh yes, he walked out a minute or two ago. No problem. I said you were busy and out on an inspection."

"Did he say anything?"

"Oh no, he didn't say much at all."

"*Anything?*"

"Let me think." I shove the door open and meet Sue's sprightly gaze. "He said he was looking for you and hoped to discuss business but didn't say anything more. I told him you'd be back later."

"Later? Why?"

"Well, it's true, you can't be on property inspections forever and ever."

"Sue . . ." I resist the urge to dramatically pinch the bridge of my nose. "This man, he's dangerous. We need security. Can you put in an order for Ring cameras, Nest cameras, any cameras, charge them to the account. I want cameras on the front of the office so I can see everything going on from the back."

"You got it. I'll get on it right now! Come to think of it, I didn't like him much either. Before we married, Rodney had a beard and it made him look like, one of those, I don't know, communists. It wasn't a good beard. I like a big, hearty, hunting beard. Not an untrustworthy beard."

"Agreed."

I can't stay here any longer. I tell Sue I'm going out for the day and not coming back. *I am going to drive by a few properties after all, har har. I might end up with Finny! You never know!* Sue's smile is large as I leave, fastened on neatly, and I bound into the Chevy and speed out of town.

The Starbucks is on my right, as well as the China King takeout, still celebrating its "grand opening" nine months later. I rocket straight for the country, notching sixty-five and then eighty-five. The sky is nearly cloudless, astounding blue cornstalks soaring on both sides of me. I swerve from pavement to dirt, and I know I'm about a half mile from the Breckenridge homestead. This time, Gertrude is not home—no one probably is—and there is nowhere to retreat. At least the bearded man can't follow me out here.

Out here, he's useless. Useless against the cornfields, the haystacks, the sky drained of cloud cover. This is why they call this freedom. This is why I need to become a country man—move out here, acquire a farm, live off land and within myself, the hushed voice of God in my ear. Let me dig in here. Daniella and the children would learn to love it; for Theodore, it might even be necessary, a way to free him from deviancy. I can do this. Rates are high, but so what? Date the rate, marry the house. I can refinance later. This is the American dream.

I spin the Chevy left at the fork and head onto West Putnam, then off, another road calloused with mud. Did it rain recently? I can't recall the weather. The Breckenridge homestead looms, gently, on the horizon line. Without intending to, I'm driving past it, and stolen scenes fill me: Gertrude's bare breasts, her behind pointing skyward, a low moan as we finish. I can turn them around, polish them, refine them. She'll be back. And if not, Genevieve may offer promise. My hunches usually aren't wrong.

A lone figure stands in Gertrude's long, dusty driveway, clenching a clay-colored basketball. His eyes are like gun slits. I slow the Chevy, just enough that I know he can see me, though he seems to be lost elsewhere, an indeterminate hoop out of the reach of my vision. Aidan, Gertrude's son, is home on a weekday. It's almost summer, but there's still school. He might be sick but he doesn't look sick. Then he is faking—or he's here with his mother's permission. None of Harry's vehicles are in the driveway. There is Aidan, the lank sphinx, his fingers clenched, ready.

I almost call to him.

When I'm accelerating, there's an alien thud against the trunk. Brakes pounded, I spin and see nothing. Whatever has hit has gone but it was loud, boulder-like, and I pounce out of the Chevy about a hundred and fifty yards from the Breckenridge homestead.

There's Aidan, in the middle of the road.

"You're Mom's friend."

I don't like children beyond my own. They are, on the whole, untrustworthy, and there's a danger in the growing years, when mind and body are absorbing the nascent violence of adulthood but haven't learned any limiting principles. Preteens are goblins, and teens themselves are hothouses of sin. Aidan—I don't know him at all. He has the slope of his mother's forehead and her milky skin. His hair, a muddy blond, hangs nearly over his eyes. When I walk toward him, I see he is my height already, either completing a growth spurt or preparing to surge right past me, though neither of his parents break six feet. Harry is a stub, with an armadillo posture. I wave my right hand and smile brightly.

"Hi, yes, you're Aidan, aren't you? It's Pastor Starr, just driving through."

"She's at work."

"Yes, of course, it's a Wednesday."

The basketball has come to a stop at the outer edge of the roadway. Aidan makes no move for it.

"She's busy and Dad's busy."

"You threw this basketball, didn't you?"

"Lucky toss."

"More than lucky."

It's an old Wilson NCAA model, an outdoor ball that can be had at Walmart for fifteen dollars or so. I nudge it with my toe and then pick it up; it bounces, but air has been leaking out, and I can tell he hasn't been very careful about keeping it pumped up. I haven't played a pickup game in ten years, maybe more, and it's good to feel the ball on a light roll off my fingertips. Aidan doesn't expect the pastor to be dribbling toward him.

"Funny how my Chevy is the hoop now. I can appreciate the skill it takes to strike a moving automobile, though."

"I told you, it was a lucky toss."

Children unnerve because you can forget how they think. Their thoughts are like peculiar amoebas, ill-formed, reaching in all directions. What capacity for disorder a child on the cusp of adulthood truly has. Aidan, as far as I know, has never been home when I'm with Gertrude and his mother wouldn't be foolish enough to intimate anything. But does he know? Can he? Is this loyalty for his father? Is Harry Breckenridge's honor seizing him up? I smile at him, carefully at first, and we're soon within five feet of each other. He's in denim and a striped, blue-and-white T-shirt, likely polyester. His lips are thin and closed, betraying nothing.

"Let's just keep this between us, then. It might not have been a lucky toss if it caused any damage. Come to think of it, I haven't been around back to inspect. I stopped the car and came out here. It was a strange thing, given your basketball hoop is probably that way," and I point toward the homestead, "and that's how you're going to get better at this game."

"Who says I have a hoop?"

"Who says, indeed. I was making an inference. I'm a bit older than you—when I was young, they played basketball with basketball hoops. New wonders might have come to this decade I don't even know about. AI hoops? The ball tossed into VR protoplasm? Anything is possible, right?"

"I suppose."

"Do you have anything else to say, Aidan?"

He has made eye contact with me, which is a surprise; most boys, particularly when they sense trouble, gaze sideways or to the ground. Theodore certainly does. Aidan might not sense trouble at all. Maybe he's an innocent. Maybe he's deranged.

The longer I'm out here, the less beneficial it is.

"Say?"

"You struck my car."

"Lucky."

"You could have done damage. You could have hurt someone."

"You."

"Yes, me. You might have shattered my back windshield."

"I never would have tried to. That's messy."

"Is that all you're concerned with? Making a mess?"

And here he gives me his little goblin grin, and I see that I am the fool here, marooned temporarily outside the homestead. He wanted me to stop. He knows exactly who I am and what I've done. He knows, somehow, about his mother. And no, Harry's honor has nothing to do with this; his goblin grin doesn't say that either. It's a cocktail of subtle rage and evident glee. It is how, I imagine, the suicide bombers smile. The look of a job well done.

"If you apologize, I promise to keep this between us."

"My mom can know, it doesn't matter."

"That wouldn't be good for you. I know she wouldn't appreciate it."

"It depends."

"Depends on what?"

"Well," and I can see his goblin grin start to break, for something else to take its place—insolence, the snarl of a boy who hasn't quite grown up. "It depends on what I want to say."

"What you want to say. You think you know something important."

"I *know* I know something important."

"Importance is all relative. What you might think is most pressing, most vital—what seems like leverage, to you, in fact might not be. And you might be confused. Do you know what a trump card is, Aidan?"

"Yeah, I do."

"You think, right now, you have one. You're clenching it. You're excited. You're trembling, practically, with excitement. You hurled this basketball across space and struck my vehicle—have you considered trying out for the baseball team? What an arm. I know Coach Tiptree, he occasionally worships at my church; I could, if need be, put in a good word. But I don't know if you're interested. Are you interested?"

"Not really."

"Not really. You're more interested in *this*. Your information. Your secret. You're ready for the damage it might cause. Or you're *not* ready. That's my truer sense. You have no idea what you're about to do. Are you going to talk to your father?"

"I—yeah, I could."

And then I see: goblinism as a farce. He is more predictable than he seemed at first. He is more boy than man, bluster masking confusion, one lucky hurl of a discount basketball, one petulant cry of rage. This boy is going to tell his *father* about what his mother has done with me? He's going to march upstairs, to the master suite, and tell dear Dad what's been happening for the last nine months, what he has apparently borne witness to or apprehended through some mutant adolescent intuition? Here is where age has its advantages. He is still staggering through the dark, imagining courage he doesn't yet possess and might never.

Tell him, Aidan, I very much want to say. *Tell your daddy*. Scale those steps and make yourself heard.

"You could. You could give it your all."

"I saw you, I saw Mom, I saw . . ."

"Do you think your father will believe you? You don't know what you saw and you don't know what you know. Assumptions can be combustible. You might be on the verge of something great and terrible."

"I could tell him."

"Maybe *I* should tell him. What do you think, Aidan?"

"You can do what you want, sure."

"Sure?"

"Listen," and now he's looking away from me, up into a patch of sky, "I'm going inside. You didn't have to stop."

"But you wanted me to, Aidan. Give my regards to your mother and father. They're lovely people. And I look forward to seeing you more at Trinity. We need young people like yourself worshipping the Lord."

I turn and walk back to the Chevy. I'm done here and Aidan is done, in the sense that he's out of moves. He's learning. It's proof, perhaps, he'll be a man someday because a man knows when he's beaten. He's considered what it would mean, for his mother, to confront his father with the reality of her time spent with me. In seconds, the family dynamic would be immolated, and his homestead would lose its comforting somnolence, what he has known all of these years. He's likely thinking about whether his father would *leave* his mother. Harry is a man who thinks in absolutes; if he feels wronged, he's gone, and he'll happily evict his erstwhile wife. It's the *Breckenridge* homestead, he's third generation, and Gertrude would be turned out by nightfall. Men like Harry only need women for so long. Once they procreate, they move on, and

Harry isn't hungry for an available sexual partner, anyway. That's why Gertrude found me. Aidan, in his own manner, understands this too. His father doesn't *need* anyone. It's his checkbook, his savings account, his land. He can subsist on memories and hand jobs and nights downtown, drinking a solitary beer. Or he can hunt his troubles away, felling bucks if he can ever shoot straight.

This was good. Providence, even. After the events at my office, this ended up, strangely enough, being welcome. And now I can drive and think and maybe go home. Genevieve is still out there, and so are others. Soon, it will be time to prepare my sermon for this Sunday. We have plunged into Leviticus, Moses consecrating Aaron and his sons as the first priests, the dawn of the Aaronite privilege.

I'm going to be fine.

5

The first thirds of films are my favorite. Establishing shots, exposition, world-building, character development—I revel, to a degree, in all of it, and I have this longing to know how something happens before it happens. I want to know about the wave before it breaks. I want to see its shadow cast. To know what we were like before we get on with it, before the narrative carried us away.

Genevieve sits up in bed, glancing my way, almost sparrow-like. She is a twitterer, a flincher, nervy, and it was exciting to see her writhe, when she finally let go. Gertrude was more assured. But we can't all be that way and Gertrude is occupied.

It's sunny, another Monday, and I'm glad I found my way to Ithaca.

"What's new?" I finally ask her.

"Danny has a habit of looking through the camera footage. He likes to watch them while playing music. When he's bored."

"He takes footage of the bedroom?"

"There's a camera and I told him, a while ago, I wanted it off. He agreed. But there could be others. Danny is like that. I'm going to have to get creative later. In two or three weeks from now, he might know you came here."

"I came to give my greetings."

"Pastor, this is a mess."

Even in bed, *Pastor.* Not like Gertrude. It is our first time. We are naked, sitting several inches apart, murkily reflected in the

Insignia forty-three-inch flatscreen. I smile at her, my erection still in bloom.

"It's not a mess if we've just had a great afternoon."

"I don't want Danny finding out."

"Danny is not going to find out."

"He does. He finds things out."

"I can tell you're experienced."

"As are you! And you should know, these things can unravel."

"They haven't yet."

"For you."

"Are you on thin ice with old Dan?"

"Oh, the reason I'm even here is because he's had his fun. I've had mine. Naturally, he feels we've sort of evened out, and he'll leave if he knows about this."

"Yet you're here."

"I am."

She doesn't say this with as much satisfaction as I'd like. I touch her bare thigh and leave my hand there; she regards it like a trout dropped from the sky, perhaps from the beak of a large bird. I know she enjoyed all of this and we're now on to the *second thoughts* phase of the interaction. Gertrude was like this too, in the beginning. It takes time, dear, I told her. It takes time.

"I never quite understood the camera obsession even if I have them," I say. "It feels like a grasp toward an unearned status; security was for a certain class of wealth, of fame. We run cameras at Trinity but I've never watched them. I know that."

"Danny thinks we have to be ready."

"Does Ithaca have a home invasion problem? Pine Haven certainly doesn't. The crime statistics aren't as extensive as they can be—a lot of lax reporting at the PD—but anecdotal evidence is an acceptable harbinger, here. No complaints."

"He talks about the end times."

I turn to her, my hand finding the lovely dip of her shoulder, and begin a slow massage. Genevieve, who keeps fit, has a small knot.

"Cameras will not keep Satan out. I can promise you that."

"Danny worries. He makes me nervous. Which is why, I've decided, we shouldn't do this again."

"We enjoyed ourselves."

"Now we're done." She surprises me by sliding out of bed and reaching for a towel. Before I can catch her in the nude again, she's wrapped up and headed for the bathroom. "I'm taking a shower," she adds behind a door, her voice now muffled. The water hisses out.

What to do, what to do—I don't believe her, but it's important to afford a new relationship space. If I do want to return, I can't press. Women like Genevieve will begin to miss the lick of adrenaline and want another afternoon like this one. I knew, once I saw her open the door, I'd be successful. I understood her longing. But longing competes with fear, and fear can triumph, at least temporarily. Genevieve is going to want to wipe or doctor, at least, those cameras. Danny Blanchard won't appreciate what we've done in his marital bed.

But there will be explanations, if need be. I don't fear Danny. There's no need to. He is, in his own way, like Aidan. Surety will give way, soon enough, to trepidation—to the realization of what he ultimately lacks.

"When you're out of there," I call to the shower, "I'm heading to lunch. You can come with me if you'd like. I want to go to the Mennonite café." It's called Harvest Oven, but in Pine Haven we all call it that. "I may have the famous pecan roll or the famous raspberry cream cheese roll."

When she doesn't answer, I dip my head in the bathroom and repeat myself.

"I'm not going out with you," she says through the spray.

"Oh, but it'd be nice. You have the day off anyway."

"I can't be seen with you."

"It's more suspicious if you're *only* seen with me here."

"I can't, I can't."

"One famous raspberry cream cheese roll, on me. You're saying no to that?"

"I'm saying, I'm saying . . ." and her voice goes tinny in the hot spray and I decide it's best now to retreat. Even lunch is more than she's ready for and that, for now, I'll have to accept. But I'll get lunch. I've got my next appointment, a meeting with a flock of antsy realtors at four, and then a couples counseling session with Big Landry and his wife, of all people, at five thirty.

Nearly a whole half day, a nice little undulation, stretches before me. If Genevieve doesn't want to partake, it's her loss.

I dress at shutter speed, my signature classic tan iron-free Dockers slipped on first, argyle socks second, and wrinkle-free Ralph Lauren, sky blue, third. It'll be a minor scorcher outside, so I roll up my sleeves. "All right Genevieve, I'm getting around and going out for that cream cheese roll. You take care," I tell her, louder this time, and she chirps back in the affirmative, some mix of "got it" or "bye." I find my Beckett Simonon tasseled loafers and glide out into the open-concept kitchen, which Danny had remodeled last year. The tiling isn't to my taste and my sense is Danny's contractor overcharged him, as they know how to prowl for that unfortunate blend of eagerness and ignorance. The living room smells like feline and that's the price, sadly, you pay for carpeting.

Outside, summer is plotting its assault. The sky is cloudless, and the sun a fist of pulsing heat. I drop the Chevy's temperature to sixty-six degrees once I'm seated. It's a mile and a half to downtown; Genevieve is nestled on Oriole Way, part of a bird-themed section of the town's back nine, all within walking distance of the high school. It wouldn't be my choice of locale, not with the pots-banging, jailbreak energy that comes with school dismissal times. When clients ask me *where* they should live, all else equal, I almost always suggest as close to a golf course as possible. One, golf courses preserve property values because the buy-in to play is high enough and, let's be frank, a certain element will not be playing golf—not now, not ever. Two, it's a hushed sport—polite clapping, nothing else—and there's an abundance of order. Children don't go to golf courses. It is the spiritual antonym of a public school.

Had I stayed longer with Genevieve, I could have educated her on this, but Harvest Oven calls. I would prefer to share a cream cheese roll with her but I try to understand her burbling paranoia. What if she's *seen* with me? Never mind that I'm a pastor, a realtor, a property manager; I am seen with people all throughout the day. My life is people. Gertrude understood this. In time, Genevieve will too. She's a smart woman.

I park in the back lot, wedging the Chevy next to a Ford Explorer caked with dried mud. Harvest Oven is dainty, red-bricked, and hexagonal, swallowing up the corner of St. John and Northern. A candy-striped awning offers precious shade for the outdoor diners clustered on their moss-green patio furniture. Were I with Genevieve, I'd request a booth, but here I'll have to settle for counter service. I sit and wait for a plump waitress not long out of high school to ask me what I'd like.

"A cool glass of water and one of your famous raspberry cream cheese rolls," I tell her.

The Mennonites are misguided. I've long wondered if their operation of a scrumptious eatery is more than an employment scheme for those in the community who need to earn cash, in the way the diamond business always underwrote the Jews—or, more perniciously, if it's a recruitment tool. Is the Mennonite population growing? It's something I should know more about. The Anabaptists are a curious number, and their interpretation of the Bible rests on several delusions. I've been tempted here several times, while nibbling my cream cheese roll, to tell them this.

Eschew infant baptism and grease the gears of hell. Their pacifism curdles, too, under closer inspection; must you lay down your arms against the demonic forces of this Earth? Must you putter around a horse farm while baby-murdering atheists seize all the pivotal elected perches? Where is the virtue in *that?* Mewling, flaccid Christianity isn't Christianity at all and is doomed, in the long run, to failure, even if it props up a well-appointed eatery in the meantime.

The waitress, who is not a Mennonite, returns with my glass of water with ice.

"Do they pay well here?" I ask her.

She regards me like a puffer fish at an aquarium glass wall, gazing up at the aerated Great Beyond. Her elongated eyelashes fall up and down. An uncomfortable spittle speck glimmers at lip's edge.

"Pay?"

"Your tipped wage."

"It's the minimum, I think."

"So, no better here than at Ruby Tuesday's or Tim Horton's?"

"They might do a dollar better at Tim Horton's. My older sister worked here, so I work here now. The owner is nice. It's a good crowd around here."

"A *godly* crowd."

"It is. The Lord does shine down here. And he blesses even the cream cheese."

"Oh, I bet, that's why I'm looking forward to it. Harvest Oven never fails. You're lucky to be here. In times like these, this is what keeps communities together. You graduated from Ithaca High?"

"Two years ago. I was at Mid, and now I'm working. I'm figuring out what I might do next."

"College is great, but college isn't everything. I never went there. People are surprised when they hear that. But it's easy to learn to talk like someone who went to college. You tuck a few adjectives and adverbs in your back pocket. You peruse a newspaper here and there. A percentage of it, somewhat sizable, is a question of manners—or the appearance of manners."

"Acting, performing. They always say, *fake it 'til you make it.*"

"The secret . . ." and I see her silver name tag, glinting ". . .*Kyla*, is to already believe you've made it. There's no faking. You tell yourself, right now, you've made it. You affirm it. You act, and you create that reality."

"Create that reality . . . like manifesting? I listened to a podcast about that."

"Something like it, only less hokum. If you're going to get anywhere, you have to get out of the new age, the woo-woo, anything astrology-afflicted. It is the devil's work. This, I'm talking about, is belief. You should see yourself as God sees you."

"As God, yes, I do go to church. I can do that."

"I preach at Trinity of Pine Haven. There are many young people like yourself, Kyla. It's a strong cohort." Suddenly, the conversation tires me, and an odd nostalgia for the inside of my air-conditioned Chevy takes hold. "I assume that cream cheese roll has been heated?"

"Oh yes, right away, sir."

In the time it takes Kyla to retrieve my roll and set it down in front of me on a thick white plate, a familiar figure cuts into my periphery. His movement accompanies the jingling of a bell, overhead at the entrance, and he emits a guttural sound; how ludicrously out of place he is, slinking and skulking like he's possessed of something zoonotic, his inner organs fetidly black. He doesn't see me.

But then he does. A stool is open next to mine and, clearly, I did not think any of this through—the likelihood he would be seated next to me, breathing in, breathing out, his dark beard ever-thickening.

"Reuvain," he says quietly. "Please, let's talk."

"Get out of here, now."

"Please. I promise, I only want to tell you—"

"I want to hear nothing from you. You are stalking me and I will call the police." I am talking, like a sitcom hustler, through gritted teeth. "You are going to be arrested and thrown in jail."

"Reuvain, Reuvain—it is *you*, if anyone, who might go there. If the facts are lined up a certain way, if a jury is presented—"

I stand up and bull myself through the double doors, bell tinkling, and out of Harvest Oven altogether. The raspberry cream cheese roll is left behind, a small casualty. At the Chevy door, to my horror, is his reflection.

"I just want to talk."

"You want to talk? Get in my car then."

He complies, opening the passenger door as soon as it's unlocked.

I turn the key and the engine grumbles to life.

"My brother. It's been some time."

My brother, my brother. Oh, what is this, what invasion, what pestilence, what insistence? . . . Imagine Daniella now, what she would say, another man calling the *only child* Theodore Starr a brother. Imagine, really, what Daniella would say if she knew it all, even this afternoon with Genevieve, if whatever she suspects matches up against vertiginous reality, if she can even produce a notion. But few can. Few can fathom what waits behind the curtain. Curtains are thick, after all, and it's a greater feat than it looks to pull one back, to *force* one back. And what if only disease and rot are behind them? What if, by closing the curtain, you escaped it all, as any individual with a modicum of intellect and ambition would? This is the pioneer spirit, the American Mundus, reinvention to stave off perdition, to work your way *closer* to God. The true God. And my brother, and his people, knew nothing of that.

He dares to come here, to assert *himself*, to intrude on what he could never imagine if I handed him ten additional lifetimes.

He demands to be seen. I turn to face him, which is more than he deserves.

"Eighteen years. You never could count, Yoel."

We careen out of town. I switch from St. John to 114 and bolt north on the country road, slashing through the cornfields and silent windmill blades. He smells like Triscuits or some warmed-up snack, and his skin is wretched; ruddy, splotchy, with the constitution of deli meat. I glance at him, glance away, and take us up to a higher speed. I'm weaving into a nonexistent passing lane to get around the used Honda plodding at sixty-five ahead of me. He breathes, this one, and breathes loudly, and I've decided to take him into my car and drive.

All I can do is drive.

"I've dreamed of this day."

"What do you want, Yoel?"

"I wanted to see my brother. Is that so hard to imagine? That family might seek out family."

"I have nothing for you."

"I don't come asking for money or any favor. I have paid my way. I manage a nice portfolio now, including South 4th Street. I am doing quite fine. As you might have."

"I am doing quite fine."

"You are, Teddy. Teddy Starr. I like that. It sounds like, what, a circus performer, a news anchor, a star center fielder for *the* New York Yankees. . . ."

"You get this afternoon and then you get the hell away." It's the first time I've sworn, out loud, in at least five years. "You get the courtesy of this car ride and nothing else."

"Aren't you curious?"

"Not about you."

"About how I am here?"

"You stalked and skulked your way to the middle of the country, the middle of the mitten, where you are not wanted."

"I thought I would be treated better."

"If I wanted anything to do with you . . ."

"You wouldn't be, what, *schtupping* the wife of that friend of yours? Or the wife of the other friend? Who can keep track?"

Yoel is fouler than I remember, but what I remember is a chrysalis. He was seventeen then, lithe with watery eyes and the trace of a stammer he has apparently conquered, little like the man, marooned in fat, that grins from my passenger seat. He has sat himself like a grand old pasha, nearly in repose, the afternoon light falling across his lumpen face. I feel a cold, hard dagger coming up in me, and the question is whether to deploy it now or later.

"How long have you been skulking around Pine Haven?"

"Barely a month. Not time at all. Two months ago, three months ago, I might have come. I considered, really, in the last six months. I wanted to act at some point. I will say, if there was no internet, I wouldn't have been here."

"Yoel discovers the World Wide Web."

"Father taught me. I only improved when you left. I had to stand on my own then."

We're deep into the country, humming on an empty two-lane road toward a nature preserve up north. It's the only place, really, I can think to go. So much of this isn't tenable—not now, and not ever. And I have appointments.

"I don't care."

"Of course you don't. Out here," and he gestures, wildly, toward the corn, "why would you? Such a nice, trim goy, with your trailer park, your church, and your sprawling house bumping up against a golf course. I can imagine waking up and hearing that *thwack thwack thwack* of club against ball. What a feeling! Reuvain, my, you have come so far."

"When we get to the nature preserve, we can take a walk."

"A preserve! You know, I've been all over the world. Paris, Rome, Berlin, Istanbul, Osaka. But never here. You, dear brother, have brought me *here*. To where America begins—not a hill in sight. Ample parking. Front yards *and* backyards. Hunting season and Jesus Christ. I feel almost blessed to have come. I have nice little suite now up in Mt. Pleasant, I've been running up a bill, I have to say, but I take such a nice morning walks by the river. And you've got the pleasure of driving me now, and I get to see so much."

"This is the last you will see of me. I don't care why you've come, why you've come now, or what you're interested in. You're not wanted. You will never be wanted. I am here and you are *there* and you will stay *there*."

"Reuvain, why—"

"I'm not Reuvain. I will never be Reuvain. Do a public records search. I am Theodore Starr."

"I know who you are. Fifteen years ago, you petitioned the court. I do my research, just as you do—just as you taught me, and father taught me."

"You've come to irk me, then. Like a little gnat. What else? What do you have to offer me, when I want nothing to do with you, with Mother—"

"Mother is *dead*, Reuvain. Two years gone. That was almost a trigger for me to go, to seek you earnestly, to troll the archives and databases and see where you might have gone. A young man on the run, a young man *wanted*, or almost wanted, I should say. I've done so much for you. I don't expect any gratitude, of course. You aren't capable."

He's still smiling.

"How did she—"

"*Die?* She was never well. It was miraculous she went as long as she did. If you have to know, stage four lymphoma. All those aches, all those pains, and she was gone in five months. I sent her somewhere nice; I wasn't going to let her rot in Maimonides."

"I'm sorry to hear."

"Of course you aren't. Sorry for what? You're sorry I found you. You're sorry for your vanity. Who knew a pastor could have such a digital presence? You've been photographed quite a bit. You've what, done a few speeches or the invocation for the Luce County Republicans? They've got high-res photos of you. So do church conferences in Ohio and Indiana. So does your real estate website. Teddy Starr must be photographed, it seems, again and again. And you thought, with a clean shave, I wouldn't have noticed. You thought this would go on in perpetuity."

"I hope, when you manage your properties, you're giving the Yitzhak Gantz touch. Mold, rat droppings, clogged toilets, asbestos, polyurethane peeling off the floors. You've got to make your buck, Yoel."

"Your trailer park is worth a one-bedroom apartment on Flushing Avenue, and it smells much worse."

We're fifteen minutes from the preserve, two more turns on the grid, and the Chevy is approaching ninety miles an hour. I don't feel the speed. It's almost fiction or, at least, an affect imposed on the tunneled reality of this vehicle, Yoel somehow still here. I'm waiting for him to dematerialize, little dandelion spores of Yoel floating off into the afternoon sky. My options dwindle. I didn't think it would come to this.

If I'm going to get anywhere, I can't shout.

"Let's try get down to it. You're here. You've found me. You don't want money. What is it? Get out with it. I'm not going to New York."

"I would never ask you to do that. The community certainly doesn't want someone choking on treif, worshipping false idols, making a mockery of his marriage. I don't want you in New York. I'm content with you here, just as you're content. What I might be less content with is the construct."

"You've learned such big words, Yoel."

"For many years, I imagined this moment. I would ask you, with quivering lips, *why*—why did you do it? Why do it like this? Why not face up to what you've done? Why abandon those who still loved you? Why come here, of all places, why decide you must be Pastor Teddy Starr? And then I knew asking those questions would be a stupid thing. It would be, perhaps, the stupidest thing. Because I knew all the answers. I knew them, implicitly, at seventeen, more than a decade before I would discover the Starrs of Pine Haven, your muscular Christianity. I knew you had to run because our father was dead and you were standing there, at the top of the stairs, and you had to get away as far as possible. And far as possible, it turned out, was here."

"A magnificent speech. Netflix-worthy."

"And beneath this new veneer, the same old rot—my brother, beloved brother, rotten brother. Let's go for a walk. I'll feel better when we have air."

"You'll be at the right place."

The Remus Nature Preserve is just one sharp left off 131. The service road is uneven macadam, a rumbling ride until we're through a cream-colored gate and into a lot that is still, even with the pleasant weather, mostly empty, owing to the yawning distance between Remus and the next populous township. It's 109,000 acres, largely undeveloped and sprawling north, red pines and meandering rivers and a waterfowl refuge. I've come here twice, once with Theodore and once alone, and the trails are alien enough to me.

I cut the engine and let a silence settle between us.

"I could see, at least, how you got used to the air out here."

In my trunk are a range of useful knickknacks and oddities. There are, helpfully, hiking knapsacks and bottled water. I see a deflated basketball, a deflated football, an empty cooler, two lawn chairs, and a miniature stuffed owl bought or won at the

Flapjack Jubilee last year. Buried below the two lawn chairs is the twelve-inch Pelican V100 vault case in desert tan, foam interior included. Stainless steel, an O-ring seal, and easy open double throw latches—watertight, crushproof, and dustproof. I bought it two years ago and, unlike other fathers, keep it here, not in the house. I've never been keen to have a Glock 44 where I sleep. This might be the bleeding-heart lib inside of me or just a consideration of probabilities. Odds of death increase; out here, they decrease. And the case is here, right where I need it.

"Do you want any water?" I call out to Yoel from the trunk, my hands now busy, unlatching the case as quietly as I can.

"Oh, I'm just fine."

"I'll put two in my knapsack, just in case. I get thirsty when I walk."

The Glock 44 passes, with two Aquafina water bottles, into my knapsack, fitting snugly with the crushed-up T-shirt and Clif Bar that has been left down there. I zip, grin, and slam the trunk, coming back my brother's way.

"We'll walk and we'll talk. And then you'll go back."

"A half hour will do. It has been so long. Despite everything, I am deeply glad to see you."

"I almost feel the same way."

There are deep trails and shallow trails. I want something intermediate, isolated enough without losing my way. The woods, since childhood, have made me uneasy, and it's understandable why they've always attracted occultists, Wiccans, and other deviants. Inhumanity lurks out here; death stalks close. Creatures do not comfort me, nor do leaves exploding underfoot. God intended man to clear what he could, to extract and leave.

He left us here to conquer.

"Out of respect," Yoel says, "I will call you Teddy."

"If you wanted to respect me, you'd call me Pastor Starr."

"*Pastor*, then. I do appreciate your time, even if given reluctantly. When I go back, I will tell little Aron, Rebecca, and Mendy I found their uncle."

I try to imagine what Yoel's children might be like; nothing is conjured. There is Yoel and Yoel's reflection in the stream we pass, over a plank bridge and into the deeper wood. He walks quickly, like he might be on a city street, and I consider how, exactly, this will all have to go, what can lead me out of here and back home, alone.

"You found me on the internet, then. Old story."

"I wouldn't have otherwise. And it was challenging, regardless. You did a fine job. For a long time, all I dreamed of was *this*—to walk alongside you. Then I dreamed of big speeches. I dreamed of revelations. I dreamed of a denouement. You know what it's like to run, Pastor, but you don't know what it is to long for something for so long, of *this* world. We all know longing for God, for Hashem, eternity. But this was not that. This was a flesh-and-blood event, conceivable yet unattainable until I saw you, finally. Your face flashing across my computer screen. Your invented name, linked back to what you were. What kismet it was. God's blessing truly."

"I still don't know what you want."

"What I want? Is this not enough? Or almost enough? I'd ask questions but I know the answers. I know the why. That's an old story, and deeply American. You're like Father, in that way. The Gantz clan was one great churn, from one identity to the next, one scheme to another, straight out of the pogroms and to the shores of the new world where we were hardly wanted. Pale of Settlement urchins, across the sea, and to think, their great great-grandchildren have surged to such a position. You have quite the portfolio, Pastor Starr. I didn't mean to demean your trailer park at all."

"I don't care what you think about that or anything really. I'm running out the clock here. We're going to be driving back once we make a little circuit on this trail."

"I've expanded Father's portfolio. You might be happy to know that, as a man of commerce. I'm up to twenty-three hundred units. It's an income blend, too, I've got a condo tower in the mix, finished two years ago. It's not healthy to only sniff around for the vouchers, the subsidies, the families who stiff you, even if they mean well. It's not a way to live. Father never understood that."

"He never understood many things."

"The day after, I remember it so well—there was a light rain, and it was an unusually warm January day. I woke up in my bedroom and you were gone and Mother, as usual, was sleeping through the morning. It took her to the real underbelly of the afternoon to appreciate what had happened. I didn't worry too much the first day. I thought you'd be gone the weekend. Then I understood. Mother, to her credit—once she was fully awake, *really* awake—she knew right away."

"Another yarn from Yoel."

"You have this very infantile notion of the past, I have to say. I didn't come to insult you. I came, in one sense, merely to commune, to be face-to-face. There is nothing to replace blood. Nothing. To say it's thicker than water is an understatement. *This*, whether you care or not, is where we were always headed—this is meaning, made."

"What do I get wrong about the past?"

"Everything. Your lifestyle is evidence enough. A name change, a wife, children, property—do you think it's really anything against the past? What has made you? You're like that boy sticking his finger in the dike. You have such utter belief. You can snap your fingers, get a train ticket, hitchhike, do whatever it is you did to make your way here. A man, reborn. You're like a little

Buddhist. *Only the present matters! Only the now!* You really think nothing else matters."

"It matters to the degree that I'll tolerate a walk through the woods with you."

Yoel is lighter on his feet than I would have imagined, given his size and age. He is a dancing bear running through his midday calisthenics, or whatever it is a dancing bear would do. His feet thud a half pace ahead of my own and his head bobs forward as if he knows exactly where he's going. The question now is how I'll complete the transfer out of the knapsack without him noticing or noticing too soon. It's good, at least, he's pushing deeper into the brush, further isolating us from prying eyes. My chest is tighter than I'd like, my heartbeat's skittering, and there's a foghorn throb at the front of my skull. A filmic web creeps up on my vision, just enough to blur at the point of focus.

I can hear Yoel breathing.

"Did you ever get baptized?"

"Not your concern."

"I imagine you told them you were baptized as a child. Adult baptism would not be convenient for, what is it, your narrative—no, you were a man, to them, born as you were supposed to. *Of this place*, I imagine. A Michigan man. You've done such fine work. Not a hint, a trace, of your old speech. No Yiddish pollution. Nothing Hebraic at all. A wondrous Protestant specimen."

"You still sound polluted enough."

"And what of you, dear brother? Are you calling them *suckers*, now? And *pop*, for soda? My little Midwestern goy. Such a blessing."

Yoel did always know how to talk. Like me, a motormouth, if less practiced, less disciplined. He liked to bleat and blurt, hunt out words to give shape to his more protean impulses. It is impressive, in a way, that he's here. If I felt better about it, I would say something sweeping about *farness*, a closing of distance, from one world to the other, even if his transmogrification hasn't been on the scale of mine. Here, he's on the outside, and revels in it; I half imagine he went stomping up and down the Arby's, asking for kosher beef.

"I'm almost curious about how we are here, together again."

"Everyone leaves a trail, whether they try to or not. You were photographed, for one. Shaving a beard doesn't erase an identity. They love you on the Christian internet."

"The internet is godless."

"You're photographed at Republican Party fundraisers. You know, they like the Jews now. You didn't have to accept Christ as your savior to do that."

"You spotted a photograph and thought, 'I know that man.'"

"Something like that. But I do want to ask—*have* you accepted him?"

"Jesus?"

"Of course, brother."

"I'm an ordained pastor."

"A political answer."

"Jesus undergirds all I do. He is the light, the reason, the pulse. Blood and air and water."

"If that was true, you wouldn't be doing what you're about to do."

Should I be impressed? I have to be. He is my blood. What he is doing, I could have done, and vice versa; Yoel may look upon me, despite his disgust, with some tinge of awe. We are not seers, but we are deducers: we can register currents, weigh contingencies, comfort ourselves in the cloudburst of eventualities that will doom or justify any given plan. Look at him now, coming through the brush, with canine ambition. He hasn't left me yet.

I swing the knapsack around and unzip the top compartment. Yoel turns, just fast enough to see my hand shoot through for the

Glock 44. It's been fourteen months, maybe more, since I went to a shooting range, and the heft of the weapon is, for that first moment, striking. Yoel's lips crumple closed. He is up against a tree trunk now, his breath hot and low, his eyes naturally wheeling to the barrel of my pointed gun.

"You're going to do this," he says.

"You must have known. I can't have you here, like this."

"What you did to Father—what rage you must have felt. I think often about that."

"I don't care, Yoel, what you believe or what you know."

"This is intention. You've been waiting for this. You've aged into it. Whatever wickedness was a nub in your soul then, it's taken root now. But you're trembling."

"This is not what I want. This is simply what has to be done."

"Your right hand shakes. You won't miss, though, because you've got me right up against here. You can't miss."

"You understand."

"I won't share any secrets. How about that? I'll disappear tonight. I'll be in the ether, then nothing. Gone, gone gone."

"I don't *trust* you, Yoel. I don't fucking trust you."

"I came for a reunion, and I can leave."

"You came for disorder, disunion. You came because you couldn't handle what I've done. You couldn't compute why Brooklyn wasn't good enough, why Hashem didn't satiate, why a man would need to *ascend*. Yoel, I love you. You're a violation. You're sin. I love you, and that's why I have to do this."

I pull the trigger and wait for the songbirds, perched just above me, to erupt into the sky.

PART II

6

On the morning of my nineteenth birthday, I woke up late and alone. It was a chilled Wednesday in January and I gazed out on our yard, a whirl of brackish cement and mutant trash-cans, and considered what it was, that day, I could do.

Consider New York, but consider this—there are not only cities within cities, but galaxies upon galaxies, whole universes thrown together yet screaming apart, as parallel as any interdimensional realm of the greater imagination. I knew this then, and still do. What I had there, on East 15th Street, was one existence, and I had to decide soon whether I'd strike out, melding into another existence or vaulting out altogether, into the depths I was warned against since I was small and all was that savage binary, treif against non-treif.

My father, it must be said now, had nothing to do with Mackinaw City. If he wasn't going west of New Jersey, he also wasn't making aliyah. He hated airports, airplanes, the concept of suspension above what he could no longer touch. A fear of flying wouldn't explain what Yizhak Gantz believed and did not believe.

My theory was that he did not like getting so close to God. Fly high enough, and you might graze Him.

That day, I was alone. My mother wasn't in the house with me. Yoel was at school, Yeshiva of Flatbush, and I was theoretically due at my father's office in forty-five minutes. But I wasn't going to be there in forty-five minutes because I wasn't going to make my train. I was still in bed, wound tight under the covers, my head wrenched toward weak morning light. The city inhaled at this hour, just before the rush, and I preferred to miss as much of this early morning as I could.

At high noon, perhaps, I'd step out.

My room was the second grandest in the house, the second bedroom, gifted to the first son. This was the only advantage I held. It sprawled, octagonal, like the great flooring of a fin de siècle ocean liner, varnished cherrywood glinting in the milky light. There was a bookcase of unread books, a Torah hardly touched, a Schottenstein edition of the Talmud, and a series of painted race cars I had once considered hobby-worthy but didn't any longer.

Mother, I remembered, had gone to the doctor. We were within walking distance of Dr. Fishman's office, and this was a blessing for her because she needed, always, to investigate her ailments. If Yitzhak Gantz was a man too beset by his neuroses to visit a doctor, lest he be told mortality was encroaching, Libby Gantz needed reconfirmation, each month, of her mortality. She wanted it forestalled, like all of us, and she was able to spend mornings, afternoons, and nights fixating on stomach gurglings, mucus agglomerations, and faint rashes. She was, I think, a beautiful woman, and I can see this more clearly now than then, when she wasn't yet a reflection in a tidal pool of memory.

I got up and got dressed, though there was no reason to. My father's office certainly wasn't a reason. I still dressed in the clothes they wanted me to—dark blue slacks, a white starched button-down, and black leather shoes purchased, on sale, at Avenue M Men's Shoes. I trudged to the bathroom, let out a burp, and began brushing my teeth, running the Crest Whitening madly over my front and bottom rows, aiming only there because that's what people could see. The smoking had already stained my teeth the dullest of yellows, like yolk blended with dishwater, and I knew this was no way to face a day not if I was going to care this much about my smile.

And I'd care because *she* was going to see it.

No, not my mother. Not anyone who had set foot in this house.

A large house, as you can imagine, is far vaster when it's empty, when all human activity has migrated outward. It is quiet enough for you to believe, wholeheartedly, everyone who inhabited it died long ago, their spirits left to dully float over the banisters or through the dumbwaiter, too weary to properly haunt anyone. The house was too large to feel lonely, too antique. When I tramped over the floors, I could hear the echoes three hundred years behind and imagined what it might sound like in the distant future, when critters mated in the kitchen and serpents laid their eggs in the bathroom sink.

The dining room table sat twelve. My father had believed, once he was rich, he was going to have a very large family. He would be blessed, forever and ever, because Hashem was shining down upon him. Hashem blessed his acquisitions, his financing, his movements across the cityscape, the meticulous scouting and sifting of land. What had his father, my grandfather, owned? Absolutely nothing. They were, short of apostate Jews, the very worst kind of people my father believed existed in this city: tenants. When he uttered this word between his full and briny lips, it conjured something insectoid and entirely lost. Do not become, he told me, a tenant. Do not rent. *Own.* It was like a pharaoh berating his son about not becoming a slave. Land, next to God, was the greatest currency, and might have outflanked Him if Yitzhak was honest enough with himself.

By this morning when I was eating breakfast, he owned nineteen apartment buildings with three hundred and sixteen units. This I knew not from digging through any papers or public records but from his own pronouncements. My father quoted his progress, out loud, to all of us. "I have a made a new deal, dear boy," he would say, taking me in with the sweep of his arm, "and I feel this is a winner." And in New York, they were: my father was making acquisitions exactly when you wanted to, when land values could only rocket upward. It was the 1980s, the 1990s, the new millennium. The city was not only an investment again, but the investments could not long be waved away as speculation, a bid for a hazy future. My father was getting rich. *We* were getting rich, shuttling from a two-bedroom co-op to a two-bedroom house to here, this six-bedroom Victorian battleship thrown up originally for a Bowery Bank executive in 1906 who wanted to live in the country which meant, then, Brooklyn.

The frum hadn't yet made their way.

Breakfast was an egg I fried myself. I had decided, last year, to eat less, and this meant, when I found myself in the mirror now, I was razor-boned, angular, sharpened edges everywhere below my skin. If I was gaunt, I wasn't pale, since I raced so much outside now, done with yeshiva, usually done with working, hunting for whatever wasn't in the house, wasn't anywhere near here.

A great black throat, opening up, opening wide, taking me.

The egg was lousy because I was lousy at frying it. The phone began to ring and I ignored it; it was, without any doubt, my father making his first call from the office. He wanted me there sitting up front, theoretically learning about what it took to regularly extract cash from 316 units. If every unit had, on average, two people, there were 632 human beings who, each month, owed my father money. I wasn't against this at all—the owing, the extraction, the so-called power dynamic—but it exhausted me to imagine Yizhak Gantz as a self-styled, if not licensed, overlord. I wasn't going to pick up the phone, now on its third ring, and become what I had always been, a tenant in his house, a tenant he happened to create.

I lied. I wouldn't be out at high noon. I was out now.

Arctic air had blown in from the north or the east, but this was the day it had fled. The sidewalks shimmered with melted snow. Mothers were shoving strollers again. A handball was cracking against the wall of the playground. I still wore my kippah and a dark overcoat, my armor nearly sound. I had stopped wearing my tasseled fringes, my tzitzit, I had kept my beard light. There were plenty of frum who were clean-shaven, but my father wanted the weight of hair, reveling in how it hung like a cloud fattened with rain over his jowls, gray muddying an otherwise rich shade of brown. My own brown. When I ate more and he ate less, we looked alike, more than Yoel ever would.

The bodega on Coney Island Avenue sold me a packet of cigarettes and a *Post*, which I paged through quickly and tossed out. I read, like anyone else, for the headlines, the manic declarations and siren calls, the froth and the fury. My father hated the paper, even if it matched his politics, because a tenant with a rat infestation had managed to make one of his buildings into the subject of a lively story, dragged out over two days, my father forced to issue, through the firm he hired, a neutered promise to speedily rectify the problem. I do not know if it was ever rectified, but I do know, in a small corner box, my father's headshot was printed and he never forgot it.

"Rank anti-Semitism!" he bellowed the day after the story ran. "Do you think they do this about the Greeks? Do they care? These parasite journalists?"

"What about the Greeks?" I asked, immediately regretting it.

"The *Greeks*," he began, and here was the danger, that he would keep going, deep into the gloaming of his own mind, boring the rest of us into a stupor, "I will tell you about the Greeks. Libby!"

My mother had been baking a challah, which she did then and rarely bothered with now. "Yes?"

"Do you know who owns the majority of residential real estate in this borough, if not this city?"

"I would guess the Greeks."

"Tremendous, stupendous guess. Absolutely correct. The Greeks. The Greeks, oily and reeking, feta flaking out of their rotting teeth. They think the Jews are greedy, the Jews money hungry. No, no, it's like telling the fox he eats too much when there's a boa constrictor right there, halfway through his meal of deer. My buildings are a bounty, a wonder, next to the slum your run-of-the-mill Bay Ridge Greek will throw you into. Water that ranges between Antarctic chill and refrigerator runoff. Heat that hisses in once a year, only when the temperature dips below fifteen. Rats the size of schnauzers haunting your Third Avenue walkup, right over the Irish bar that doesn't turn down the eighties rock until three a.m. My tenants live in Versailles compared to that. And yet the *Post* targets me. It takes the complaint of *one* tenant, *one* family, and it besmirches the Gantz name. I might sue."

"You should sue," Yoel said, likely not knowing, then, what it meant to sue someone.

"I am talking to my attorney tomorrow. Hatred is everywhere—never forget this. The more success the Jew has, the more he will be hated. We are a striving people, a fighting people. The Greeks have always been a predator people, a snake people, it wouldn't surprise me if the snake in the garden was a Greek. That, perhaps, a Torah scholar smarter than me can prove. What do *you* think, Reuvain?"

I was always shocked to hear my name out of my father's mouth, even if he said it every day, not hesitating to deploy it when it wasn't necessary, like in moments when there were only two of us and the only witnesses to any conversation were the furniture. In his mouth, my name became an accusation. It was a spear aimed for the stomach, to disembowel but not necessarily kill.

"I think the snake probably wasn't a Greek, but I don't have any Greek friends."

This was true. No Greeks, for reasons pertaining entirely to where we lived—among Jews, and in the periphery of Asians and Hispanics—had befriended me.

"I will call my attorney."

My father called his attorney, but nothing came of it. The stories stood and were forgotten about, except by him. If I had the interest, I would have explained a daily newspaper is designed around ephemera and what stirred outrage on one day could be deeply irrelevant on the next. Only two- or three-week stories mattered, or stories involving depraved sex acts or outrageously violent death. Not ordinary death—New York was a city larded with it, awash in blood. This did not mean it wasn't safe to go outside. I was always outside, and I had only been mugged once, at knifepoint, and the Mexican who did it was tubby and glassy-eyed in his oversized FUBU sweatshirt and no threat to anyone, really, I almost paid him a courtesy by giving him the twenty-two dollars I was carrying then. He had put in the effort.

What it meant was that no one would care about the rats crashing through one apartment in a six-story prewar building on Ocean Avenue. My father's rotten luck had been that it was a slow news day and the *Post* needed filler, four hundred words to pad out the local section. I eyed my copy in the trash and considered whether I should have paged through it more closely, just to see if my father reappeared. He was due.

On this day, my birthday, I wanted to see someone special. I had still not had sex yet. This wasn't an embarrassment because I wasn't married. I first learned this was something I *could* be embarrassed about when I started skipping out of yeshiva and floating through early afternoons at the Avenue J playground, my kippah jammed into my pocket. No frum went to the playground. It was for the Asian, Hispanics, and whatever white Catholics might have wandered through, a full block for a cement softball diamond, basketball courts, handball courts, and a rusticated play area that was supposed to be for small children and usually attracted a dedicated band of weed-smoking skater kids. I decided, in the time I had liberated myself from yeshiva, to figure out handball: it seemed like a sport anyone, with enough effort, could conquer.

I bought a blue Sky Bounce at a bodega and started practicing. Practice was taking an open court and trying to smack the ball off the wall and back, repeating the process until the ball was knocked wildly out of the court or didn't reach the wall at all. When a ferocious game broke out between players who were far better than me, I watched. Chinese would play Chinese while the Mexicans and Puerto Ricans clung together, each claiming their own courts. Occasionally, interracial doubles would break out and I, reedy and runny-nosed, would lean up against the fence and try to keep score in my head. Since I never wore my kippah, I was never Jew boy. I was just the white kid who always seemed be around at one o'clock.

"Quit fucking staring," an Asian kid said to me one afternoon. "You gonna play or not play?"

It was simple. Of course I would play. It was doubles, three Asians and me, and they were all my age or slightly younger, lank and fierce, two of them wearing frosted tips. They volleyed and killed with knife-blade precision, the ball striking the very bottom of the wall, every time. One of the players smoked as he played, the cigarette loose but never dislodging from his lips. To avoid using his left hand, his weakest, he slashed at balls hit to his left side with his right arm across his body, a backhand that seemed ill-advised but always delivered. He was the best of the three, and he happened to be on my team.

A sleeve of wildflowers wound down his left arm, which he kept exposed as much as possible. Whenever he hit a kill or a crippling crosscourt shot, someone would cry out, "Ey yo, fuck you, Teddy." He flexed his tattoos, as a way of showing off.

Teddy, I would come to learn, ran this little playground.

In the beginning, I'd find myself on Teddy's team because Teddy wanted a challenge. He was suspended somewhere between eighteen and twenty-one, plainly too evolved for high school, his rage on the court a blunt instrument.

It was fury, and it was a dance. With balletic rage, he rearranged the geometry of the courts, his ball cracking low against the wall, unreachable every time.

Teddy preferred me to playing one-on-two. He preferred this playground to Coney Island, where the best players went, though everyone insisted he was better than all of them, too. My mistakes, my fear, my beginner's tremble—it made Teddy, in doubles, work all the harder, because every player was coming for me.

And targeting me was worth money. The games went at fifty dollars apiece. "You get half," he told me quietly, "so don't fuck it up." Strange to cut me in so early, but that was one of Teddy's mysteries. We won because he won; I gladly allowed him to take every shot hit in the middle or even on my side, as long as it was a reachable. It was a parlor trick, Teddy in one corner with his cigarette, me with my felt kippah jammed in my pocket, sweating radically, and trying not to mess it up for him. Watching him was an education. He ran to the spot where he believed the ball would be, microseconds ahead, always. It was understood he'd continue to be my partner because that was the only way these doubles games, to him at least, would be a challenge.

We hardly spoke, other when I'd call out "good shot" and he'd grunt back. Occasionally, he'd toss in another warning about not "fucking" things up.

I knew Teddy was good because the Mexicans and Puerto Ricans deferred to him. In the racial hierarchy of the playground, they were above, though their hold was always tenuous. There were more Asians. The Mexicans liked to smoke weed and play, while the Asians like Teddy preferred cigarettes. Cigarettes, Kools or Marlboros, whatever I came across, were also my preference.

The more I played, with Teddy and others, the more competent I became. The more my reputation evolved: from alien liability and familiar novice to dependable, tight-lipped white boy. I said little because I had no frame of reference, really, for what they offered; I was equally not Mexican or Puerto Rican or Chinese or Korean. I did not attend a public school. I could not come to the park on Saturday. I was not eating from the hot dog cart milling at the corner, its seductive treif hotdogs soaking in filthy water. I did not know anything about the television shows they watched. I did not, most importantly, know anything about fucking.

They all, including Teddy, knew something.

"How many girls you been with?" could be the question to begin one conversation between Teddy's friends or someone else in the crew, a periphery player who dropped in on the weekend.

"Man, I lost count."

"Yo, I'm not talking about cuddling or some shit. Like who have you deep-dicked?"

"Too many to count, like I said."

"You're full of shit."

"Your mom is full of shit."

"Don't talk about my mom."

"Your mom talks about me. When I'm fucking your mom."

"Your mom makes me milk and cookies after I fuck her."

"Your mom takes me to Taco Bell after I fuck her."

"So does your sister."

"I don't have a sister."

"Yeah you do, I made her with your mom. I'm your dad."

"Fuck you."

Girls—physical girls—drifted into the playground rarely. Some watched, one or two played, and the rest were channeled through anecdote or memory or imagined altogether. Kai said he sixty-nined with a girl who went to Midwood. Eric said *he* sixty-nined with a girl who went to Baruch College. Rob claimed, after seeing *8 Mile* with his bros, he had a three-way with three chicks at one of the chicks' mom's apartments over in Sheepshead Bay. He told the story with practiced restraint, like he was reading off a CVS receipt, all to convey he had done this many times and would continue to, as long as he liked. It was a matter of when, not if, they'd have sex tomorrow.

For a long time, I believed all of it. No one talked openly about sex at yeshiva. There were girls we liked or didn't like, but fucking was for the privacy of your own thoughts, for whatever you hoped to hide from Hashem. No sex, of course, until marriage, and no pleasuring yourself. The boys at the playground didn't brag about jacking off, as they called it, but it seemed to be an ordinary part of their lives, especially if they weren't destined, on that particular day, for three-ways and sixty-nines. It was like practicing your dribbling.

Teddy didn't talk about sex. When the boys slung shit, called each other *retarded* or *fag*, Teddy held himself at a remove. It wasn't that he disapproved; he could use the words himself, and he never told any of them to stop talking about their allegedly gargantuan cocks, so big they could fuck through a concrete wall, and balls as large as the sphere at Flushing Meadows. It was, rather, a power in absence, a lesson I struggled to learn as I aged: the less you talked, the better. Let others fill the gaps, the lacunae. Let them babble. With words come trouble, opportunities for failure, and in silence there is always possibility. The less Teddy talked, the more his mythos could be burnished, not that he was one to care.

He smoked, he played handball, and he left, to points unknown. The neighborhood was enough. No one ever went with him.

On this day, I saw him playing alone. He was rhythmically smacking a small, hard blue ball against the wall, the types that the top amateurs used. My hands would never be properly calloused to handle its impact and I watched, silently, as Teddy wound geometric patterns in the cold air, striking at deep and unsettling angles. I had gotten better, but whatever I did, however long I lived, I wouldn't be anywhere near Teddy.

He didn't see me. He was rallying with himself, playing through points at a furious pace, his eyes burning at the wall. I leaned against a parcel of fence near the entryway, clawing at my jacket pocket for a pack of cigarettes.

The first smoke on a winter's day, at that time, was like little else I had experienced. It was as close to ecstasy as I could come, since, back then, my virginity was still very much intact. The nicotine was hunger and thirst sated simultaneously in such a pure fashion—*pure* in the sense of what is unvarnished and pours most directly into the soul, not what is carcinogenic—that I could, for moments, pray to these cigarettes, not just thanking Hashem for authoring a world where they may be smoked but treating these Marlboro Reds as deities themselves. I exhaled, as best as I could, and let the smoke hang in front of me, suspended in the cold.

Teddy still hadn't seen me.

At this very moment, I would be expected at my father's office on Adams Street, overlooking the courthouses and the Brooklyn Bridge. If I had a cell phone, he would have been calling it, but it was not yet a popular concept to hand cell phones to teenagers, frum or not, and so I could only imagine his fury at a happy remove. I saw my father stamping and braying, as he often did, bits of spittle leaking out, his dour secretary unable to soothe him as my mother might have tried years ago before giving up. In a different family, he might have trained his ambition and wrath on his loyal younger son, but Yoel, at this time, was a student of the Torah. He was going to be a rabbi. This was, in every sense, a blessing, except my father could only celebrate this outwardly. What was a bounty for the community, yet another man committed to Torah study, was a disaster for the business. A rabbi was not going to help him manage a budding real estate empire. A rabbi was not going to be his successor.

Hence, as I leaned against the fence and smoked my Marlboro Red, I felt his wrath most acutely; I felt it literally, and in the abstract, removed from it by many miles, at my distance. It still, despite my posture, *bothered* me. I defied him, but I was bothered by it—did that make sense?

Did it have to?

I preferred not to go. In that sense, as my father would tell me, I was just unintentionally echoing an invented character from a nineteenth-century work of literature, only I didn't enter the office in the first place. I understood, for my father, this was all deeply convenient. If one son was going to be studious, the *shtarker*, the other had to at least be the hustler, the boy willing to muck himself up in the secular world. And well, wasn't I halfway there? Reuvain Gantz was at the courts, lapping up his street knowledge, puffing delicious Marlboro Reds. Without my kippah, I could be any Irish or Italian ruffian, maybe Irish, ruddy-cheeked when the temperature fell. The trouble was none of this was business. It was not real estate; it could not be transacted.

I was as worthless to him as Teddy was worthless to him, unless Teddy or his family rented in one of my father's buildings. It was possible. His portfolio sprawled impressively across Brooklyn, Queens, and the Bronx, since he had been something of an indiscriminate buyer, beyond following the principle, always sound, to buy low and later sell high. He owned buildings crammed with Jews, buildings crammed with Asians, buildings crammed with Puerto Ricans, and even a complex that had become, for some reason, a hub for Senegalese and Liberians. I didn't even have to play my cards all that correctly for these buildings, one day, to be mine: I was firstborn, and Yoel cared too much about Talmudic riddles. Ancient rebbes weren't cashing rent checks.

But again, this preference—to not be where I was supposed to be. Watching Teddy, I knew there was no enumeration here, no opportunity. It was, by any objective measure, active stagnation, action with no greater end than action itself. Handball didn't even have a professional circuit. Teddy was not training to play for the Knicks or the Yankees. He, as far as I knew, wasn't heading to college or wasn't in it, since he was old enough and never seemed to have anywhere to be.

He was here, his wrists whipping, his sneakers sharp on the concrete.

I decided to speak.

"Teddy," I said. I let his name hang in front of me, the sound heavy in the cold. The playground, I saw, was otherwise bare, the children at school.

He kept playing. There was a point against himself that had to be finished, two low missiles into the left corner that needed to be retrieved and shot back into the middle. The only player who could beat Teddy was Teddy. It occurred to me that I had never seen him lose.

He let the ball snap off the ball once more and caught it in his right hand.

"Yeah," he replied, slowly turning to face me.

"Any of the guys coming out today?"

"Later, probably, when school is done."

"That makes sense."

"You don't have any school, do you? I thought you would."

"I graduated."

"College?"

"Taking time off. I'll see. I'm supposed to be working right now."

"You have a job you're not at?"

He didn't ask to accuse, and he wasn't probing, at least not in the way most people would, hunting for information to be filed away for later revenge or to be blasted right back with prejudice. He was not asking just to ask, either. He spoke gently, unlike anyone else who not only played handball but attended the Yeshiva of Flatbush; he spoke, at best, like my mother, as person who would not injure anyone, not even to save her own life. My mother, now off on one of her errands, doctor's appointment or disappearing into a supermarket, her feet light on the chilled linoleum. My mother, her bones seeming hollow, like she could float away.

"I'm supposed to be somewhere, and I'm not."

"If you're here, you're supposed to be here. That's how it is. If it was a place you were actually supposed to be, you'd be there."

He clenched the ball tight in his gloved hand. "I can tell. You look at ease. You look like someone who just wants to hit a ball against a wall."

"Well, yes." And I decided to push onward, because when else would I say this much to Teddy? "My father's office isn't a place I want to be right now."

"You work for your dad?"

"Sometimes. He wants me there."

"What, he's a lawyer or something? I know a lot of you Jews are lawyers."

I had never said I was Jewish, and I had always kept my kippah studiously hidden. I never had payos because my father simply wasn't observant enough. Here, I was simply white, ambiguously and gloriously so, and I wanted to keep it that way. I could be anyone, anything, any of the Brooklyn light-skinned polyglot. Why not a pale Arab? But here, no, Teddy had found me. Maybe he knew my name was Jewish, and if so, I had failed to arrive with a proper pseudonym. There was no malice in his voice. No accusation, no savagery, it was a fact peddled from a stereotype derived from blunt reality: *we were really lawyers.* We banked too. We owned apartments that were rented to poorer people.

And we could be, certainly, poor. I just was not one of those poor Jews. I liked, at the time, the theory of being poor or struggling, how it might have forged character or made me whole. Perhaps I could play handball like Teddy—not that Teddy was poor, I knew nothing of his family, even on that day—or accomplish some other physical or psychic feat my upbringing had made nigh impossible. Perhaps I was only railing, internally, against my Jewishness, that cocoon—how we all clung together, huddled on our great swaths of concrete, shuls marking the territory as piss might, only these were holy, sprung from Hashem.

I had never felt holy.

"Not lawyer. Real estate. He owns stuff."

"Commercial? Residential?"

"More residential. He's talked about getting in on the commercial side, office space, but he said he didn't trust business tenants. Businesses come and go. Renters keep renting. It's an inexhaustible resource."

Teddy cracked the ball down and hard, getting to the wall's unreachable bottom. It rolled away from us both.

"You've gotta get your piece," he finally said.

"What?"

"Your piece. His *piece*. My parents work in, but don't own, a restaurant. They don't have their piece. Not everyone gets it."

"Not everyone gets the opportunity."

"No, they don't. And those that get it and take it, they don't let go. They have no reason to, no incentive. Why give it up?"

"I don't know."

"It's easy to call it a have-and-have-not thing, but it goes a lot deeper, I think. What I learned, at least, was that nothing was going to disrupt this, not really."

I had never heard Teddy talk like this. It was the two of us, in that playground, and he was walking slowly to the bench where his ball had stopped rolling.

"Nothing, yeah."

"We watched the end of the world, except it didn't end. Here we are, you know? I was in school that day and the teachers didn't know what to do or say. Did they with you? Two towers, burning in the sky, and then they're gone. Collapsing into dust, dust that, for a time, swallowed us up. I was at Stuy, I was down there. I felt like I saw the future. I felt like I saw what was coming."

"Death and destruction."

"I saw the end, and the never-end. I saw it clearly. Anything could happen, and the order could only be displaced so much. I see people like your dad and I understand. Your *piece*—no one is going to take it from you. Your stake, your land. Terrorists can keep flying planes into buildings and there will always be enough buildings left that someone owns. Maybe a nuclear weapon changes that."

"A blast radius big enough so no one owns anything."

"Except I don't think it'll ever come."

Teddy was back to rallying with himself. He didn't look at me.

"You should go into work after all, I think."

"Why?"

"Because the world won't end. Nothing ends. We're still here, playing handball, after the towers fell. Whatever ending does come, it's long after we're dead. We're in the early innings, the first quarter."

"I should work because I can't count on the apocalypse."

"Something like that."

"You want to play?"

"I'll play you lefty."

This was what Teddy did to make it fair. I had both arms and he'd throw his right arm behind his back. It wasn't an insult; it was the only way we could compete. I was a child; he was a demigod. I took first serve and it hit my hardest into his right corner, forcing him to run around and smack a left-handed forehand. My serve was great and it didn't matter. He pivoted and smashed the ball down the line, far away from my flailing arm.

Once he had serve, it was done.

"We should play longer so I have an excuse to be here," I said.

"You can stay here no matter how badly you're losing."

I didn't know this was the day my life would forever change. I didn't know this was the pivot point of my own history. Or, more accurately, I didn't know it was the fissure, yawning wider, and I would have to make the leap into an unknowable tomorrow. Then, I wanted to keep playing with Teddy, and hunt up the only girl I had ever liked, who came to the park here with the Midwood High kids. She was around my age, that I knew, and her name was Talia. I thought of her as I played, casually at first, and then with an intensity that was astonishing, even at the time. I imagined her standing against the fence watching me, and I turning back, after smacking a winner, to offer the thumbs-up of a deranged action star. I was losing by twelve points and suddenly, after an unexpected surge of shot-making, I was down eight, relentlessly pounding Teddy's right side. He had to hit cross-armed, his left flying across his chest and jabbing outward, a flapping that looked unnatural, even for him. I was testing him. His expression didn't change, even as points kept accruing to me. I was down seven, then six, then five.

Talia, I saw, was with me this whole time.

A man can live with apparitions. He can do it when he is intensely lonely and when he isn't; his mind can warp shadows into people and people into ideas, and there can be an architecture for all of it, a cathedral rising out of astral sand. I could see Talia here if I wanted. I could play harder, and she would appear. The reality was my hand striking the ball and this pulsing, this pinwheel of pain, bringing me closer to her.

It was plausible because I wanted it to be plausible.

"You're on point, man," Teddy said. "You're got it today."

"You've got it every day."

"I do, usually, but there's a magic when *you* get it. When it's not likely, and then it is—you discover something about yourself."

We were both breathing heavily. I was still serving.

"I'm discovering that if you used two arms, you'd beat me."

"I haven't lost a one-armed game in a year."

"I believe that."

"It's a disadvantage, sure, but it's also clarifying. You can learn the best and worst about yourself. You don't know anything until you're inhibited, and you don't really know anything until you're broken. Deeply broken. A shivering, naked being, and then you begin to learn. You begin to pull closer."

"I think I've felt that way."

"No," he said to me. "But you might someday."

I served him deep and raced close to the wall for the return, guessing he'd go left and smashing right and putting him away. I had to let myself believe I could win. Years from then, such intentionality would come into vogue—the manifesting craze, the online influencers convincing a fragile generation that all their hopes and dreams were a matter of mere will—and I could understand that sort of seduction, the religious zeal to invest in the unseen, whether Hashem or something pagan. The *seen* world, in part, was simply too rotten. Judaism, Christianity, Islam, the Greco-Roman worship . . . All of it came back, in some form, to that blunt fact. What you couldn't see, what lived in shadow, always offered more promise. What was inside me, in this match against Teddy, was oceanic.

What you would have seen, had you been there, was a thin, pale boy with a kippah jammed in his pocket, a navy Reebok sweatshirt clinging to skin slickened with warm sweat. You would have seen him yelping like a little dog or a savvier, if fogged, mammal. You would have seen another boy, a young man, swatting at a blue rubber ball with one arm, his weak arm, and still guiding it exactly where he needed it go.

The game was to twenty-one. I had tied Teddy, at last, at eighteen. He was serving. I saw Talia again, bearing witness.

"I was tied in a game seven months ago," Teddy said. "This is good. I like where this is."

"I'm glad I'm challenging you."

"More than that. It's the unlikeliest challenge. It's what I never would have imagined, waking up this morning, if you gave me a thousand chances to dream it. *Tied* with Reuvain? No. And that excites me. You have to be excited by what you never expected."

"Most people would dread it."

"Most people don't know how to live."

Teddy's serve was a fake-out; his left arm swung back to whip the ball crosscourt before it straightened out, at the very last microsecond, breaking the feint and hitting the ball on a missile trajectory straight down the line. I broke the wrong way, and corrected myself just in time to wave at the ball with the fingers of my left hand, making limp contact. The ball, somehow, was heading in the direction of the wall on a fly and it was apparent, as a ribbon of drool fell off my bottom lip, I would live at least to see this next point.

Teddy sprinted forward, caught the ball on the fly, and lightly tapped it into the corner. It brushed the very bottom of the wall, unreturnable. He had a lead and he would not relinquish a lead.

"Shit," I said quietly.

"The fact that you got that serve is enough of a wonder."

"Listen, I watch you. I get better by watching you."

"You're the best Jew I've seen, at least."

"You're the best Asian."

And he began to smile. "Naw, that is definitely not true. You need to get out more."

If I stayed here, in this game—if I found a way, somehow, to transpose the values of this game to what was coming next, the depths of the approaching night—I might have reached a very different place in my life. I might not have found myself, years later, holding a gun pointed at Yoel in rural Michigan. I might have been, as a multiverse would dictate, in New York City, nudging along a minor real estate empire or, better yet, taking up a quiet two-bedroom somewhere out of the reach of a subway, coming down to the park on Sundays, kippah affixed, to play my quick games against an aged Teddy. Why would I, in this multiverse, be wearing a kippah, when I couldn't bear it on my nineteenth birthday—or any day, really—when I entered the playground?

I'd like to think, one way or the other, I would have grown comfortable with God.

Here, too, consider the bluff—as I played, I offered a silent prayer for victory. *Let me win, Hashem.* I who kept Shabbos only begrudgingly, snuck pork, and couldn't study, with any seriousness, halachic texts. I who had no regard for the *density* of Judaism, the millennia of suffering and reckoning suffocating you like a maniacal serpent, its fangs dripping with the history you never learned. I still prayed. I prayed often. I believed when it mattered to me.

And this, I learned, was one secret of religion. Religion outlasted civilizations because it managed the trick of personalization while inculcating the hive mind. Temple, church, mosque, it did not matter, and it did not matter if you worshipped angels or devils or something more liminal or ancient, like a thunderbolt-tossing sex addict. Prayer was for when your flesh failed, when you needed the aid of the unseen to make a crumb of your dream real, to validate the inordinate suffering of a life lived on a blood planet, blood Earth, more than a hundred billion humans come and gone. I reviled the rituals, even as I prayed; I wanted life ordered but ordered on my terms, my imagination, my ambition.

I didn't know what it was, what I was reaching toward, flailing at, what I needed out of the formless dark. I knew I wanted to play handball and I wanted to win. And I knew I did not want to work for my father.

Teddy quickly won his twentieth point.

"Match point," I offered, before he could say it.

"Indeed. Let's make it a fierce one."

Teddy feinted down the line but I knew it was feint and broke to my right for the crosscourt, which came at a dastardly angle that, with enough effort, I was able to cut off with a strong forehand. Teddy immediately charged, ready to kill the ball on a fly off the wall, and I followed his body, deciding that he was going to hit the ball into the left corner, a sort of inside-out stroke that only he could execute.

I guessed right and he heard me grunt, our shoulders smacking briefly as I dove past him and reached the corner, my knees cutting concrete. The ball was touched, just enough, to get back to wall and graze it, a kiss that was more luck than anything practiced, anything learned. Teddy was too late.

"That's what I'm talking about," he said, smiling at me now. "Make it work. Make it last."

"We can't have the game end so quickly, I suppose."

"Most guys who come out here, they want to dominate, they want to kill. An evolutionary imperative, I suppose. They think in those terms, which can be a real poison. *Survival of the fittest.* And then? What do you do once you survive?"

"Enjoy it, I suppose."

"But how? That's the trouble. All they imagine is survival, victory, and then the future gets murky. *Once you've won, what will you do?* They sputter. They want to hurry on and hurry on and then they're confused, and then they're angry, and then it's immiseration—the state of play, who we are. Here, between points, you know what I think?"

"I think we can enjoy it."

"I think we can suspend death. Right here. It won't last, it's the fragility of the moment, it will break—but *wait*. One more moment. One more beat. One exhale. Death can't take us."

I could only understand Teddy so much then, but if those words had resonated with me then, were made real in that moment, it's not implausible my life snakes elsewhere. I, who had always been and would continue to be a victim of the hydra-headed past and future, falling backward or scheming forward, unable to appreciate the chasm in between, that vast state of being we call the present. One reality was power—at nineteen, I didn't know what it was, but I knew I had to grasp toward it, in my own way, that it would only be acquired on the terms I could eventually devise, the terms of my own imagination.

Teddy was someone who did not take any interest in this, and never would. I did not know what his parents imposed on him, but it was not like what my father held over me, his budding slum empire, and the promise of a ledger of ever-accumulating zeroes. I would have to go into the office to get my future. As defiant as I was, I still believed, on that day, that I would, at some point, have to return.

It was not about getting right with God. It was about getting right with Yitzhak Gantz. Yoel would never have such a burden. He was born to study, and that was enough.

"There's no place I'd rather be," I said to him.

"For the glory of this, huh?" He held up the ball and bounced it to me. "Attack my right. Attack where I can't reach."

"You'll get it. Maybe I'll surprise you."

"No, that's overthinking. I've overthought some of these points. You need to attack. That's the phase now. If you're going to win, you'll have to attack."

"I might want to confuse you."

"That's your fear talking. That's trembling on the precipice, letting the height get to you, letting your heart ride high, up and hard, in the back of your throat. You need to attack, now."

"You'll be expecting it on your weak side."

"But it's weaker. If you hit it well enough, I won't return it the way I'm supposed to—and if you do what you're supposed to do, you'll defeat me."

"I—"

"Now, Reuvain."

On his command, I cracked the serve to his right again, as hard as I possibly could. It flew out, past the baseline, and I got one more.

"Don't be afraid," he said. "Don't let it catch you, constrict you. Blast your way through it."

A player who didn't know Teddy would think he was trying to undermine me. They would tell him to shut the fuck up, *to let me play*, and whine later on that his constant jabber interrupted their flow, that ineffable ability to lock in and ball. They would accuse, in their pettier moments, Teddy of waging psychological warfare, his encouragements calibrated to cause a kind of physical rot, his advice a Trojan Horse. The player, observing us, would consider this assessment correct and total, and judge my impending loss that way.

But the player would be wrong, as most people are wrong, as *I* would be wrong, again and again, as I vaulted away from this life and into a new existence I was sure, until the day I aimed my gun, would be superior to this one. Well, the flight was done on my own terms; my choice to scurry to the Port Authority, to buy a ticket, and to rumble onward into the Midwest, points unknown. Michigan wasn't New York, and really anything wasn't New York; in that way, every trite observation, recorded and stashed away from warmer days, was true. The kaiju destroys the city, but the City is the kaiju, New York more sublime and monstrous than any nuclear-poisoned lizard or space dragon, more dominant, more totalizing. The Bible never fathomed a city like New York. No ancient could. Teddy might have understood—if I pressed him. I saw how Islamic terrorists, driven to madness and rapture by their hatred for America and lust for Allah, outraced the visions of Blake and Kant when they seized two commercial airliners in the heart of the empire and committed the most spectacular act of symbol annihilation a civilization has ever known. No one had dreamed of it and yet it was done, the towers crumbling in clouds of ash and blood. New York remained. New York was a city on September 12 and 13 and 14. Atta, if they knew, must have been livid.

Here we were, playing handball. Atta hadn't taken that from us, either.

"All right, enjoy this one, Teddy."

It was the best second serve I had ever hit, as powerful as any first, and Teddy couldn't run around it to hit a forehand. He had to backhand, his left flailing, and the return was weak enough that I had a rare advantage. I took the ball on one bounce and smashed it to the right, forcing another backhand. His return, softer than he wanted, was back to the middle wall, and I decided to follow his advice and keep blasting to his right. It was his weakness, he only had one hand to use, so this was the only feasible option, the only option that was worth any effort if I was going to win.

My mistake, simply, was deciding to hit a drop shot. Teddy was too fast. He would always be too fast. By the time I tapped the ball and it was fading to the left-hand corner—I had stopped following his advice—he was pouncing, ready to kill it. He didn't do this with joy. I could see, in his passing gaze, a kind of sadness. And I realized what it meant: *he wanted me to play better.* He maybe, even, wanted to lose. This was a foreign feeling to me, as someone who always lost and badly wanted to win. I was sloughing about, rubbing my nose, blinking through the tears that came with my unending forehead sweat. Teddy didn't know what it was like. He hardly sweated at all.

"Match point," he said.

This time, I couldn't please him. He slashed the serve deep and I returned high and up the middle, right where Teddy would put me away. And he did. Despite his willingness to extend the game, he didn't hesitate. He had a job to do.

"Good game," I told him, and we shook. His right hand returned for the shake.

"You rose up. You nearly did it."

"Emphasis on nearly."

"You want to play again?"

I often think about what would have happened if I had said yes. The tendril of one reality would have flown outward and I would have grabbed it, letting it lead me through a long day of handball, twelve, thirteen, or fourteen games, all against Teddy, because he would have done it. I understood that. Whatever was out beyond the court, he didn't want to confront it. He wasn't rushing, and maybe never would. I felt, as soon as the game was over, a compulsion to go. This was the other tendril. This was the acute, overriding passage of time, and the awareness that as I stayed away from my father's office, I needed to make the most of it; such an American concept, really, the *most*, as if existence were gorging yourself at the hamburger stand and little more. Now, I'd know—go play handball, tire yourself, and head home. That way, you won't find yourself in the future forest with a gun.

Then, I had to keep going. The apparition was calling. Talia.

Teddy knew her too.

"I think I'm gonna roam around a bit."

"You're tired already?"

"No. And I want to keep going. But I think there's someone I'd like to see."

"She must be interesting if you're leaving here."

"Interesting, yeah. I'd say that. I'd definitely say that. Thought I didn't say she was a *she*."

"I know it is. I can tell by how you're starting to look around. The only question is whether it's someone I know."

"You know her, she comes down here."

"That describes more than one person."

"You've talked with her before."

"That describes more than one person."

"I'm not good with descriptions."

"Try a name."

"I should. That would be easy." I found it challenging, then, to say her name out loud. "Talia."

"Talia, of course."

"I felt like seeing her today, maybe, I don't know. It's a strange idea."

"You like her?"

"I like lots of people."

"You wouldn't abandon a game like this for lots of people."

"Maybe not."

"If you're serious," and he drew closer, his right hand bouncing the ball, "she works checkout at Doody's."

"Where?"

"That fucking hardware place, you know, down in Sheepshead Bay. It's actually pretty good, if you need special glue or mousetraps or those plastic storage bins. My mom goes there a lot."

"She's working there now?"

"I'm not her supervisor. Maybe. You never know. I know she's been working there since she graduated. When you go, you don't have to hide it, you know. She doesn't care."

"It?"

"Your yarmulke. I don't think she cares. You're always taking it off, jamming it away, then throwing it back on when you think no one's looking. I know Jews take a lot of shit and I've given it myself—and people have given me shit, I still get called a slanty-eyed fuck—but you're never going to get anywhere skulking around like that."

"I wouldn't say I'm skulking"

Teddy stopped bouncing the ball. He seemed suddenly weary, as if I had said this to him in several past lives and he was the only one now who could recall each conversation.

"That's exactly what you're doing."

"I'm fine with being a Jew."

"Then wear it."

"I don't always want to."

"You think when you come to this handball court you become a different person? I used to think like that too. Cross the barrier, enjoy a temporary rebirth. It doesn't matter that you're stocking frozen foods or cleaning up piss off the floor of a bar if you're demolishing a dude on the court. I'd see Wall Street guys come down here and they'd feel the same way, like clearing three hundred grand a year was nothing if you were getting your ass handed to you by some Mexican who bussed tables down the block. And yeah, it's true. But nobody comes here to hide, either."

"I'm not hiding," I replied, unsure whether I believed what I was saying.

I took the subway down to Sheepshead Bay, at the southern end of Brooklyn. It was, once upon a time, a low-slung fishing village reeking of slain porgies. By the time I was barreling down on the train, riding the whole way aboveground, it was a post-Soviet outpost, Russians and Turks and Kazakhs and Chinese crashing together in one of those outer-borough tableaus that inevitably turns all of them Republican once their English gets good enough and the liberals start chipping away at tax time. There were Jews there too—most of the Russians and Ukrainians were Jews because the Soviet Union wanted nothing to do with them—but they weren't frum, not up for Shabbos or anything more than a slapped-together seder, maybe a fast on Yom Kippur if they were in the mood. My kippah was on again because I was thinking about what Teddy told me. I was thinking about it hard enough, particularly how he pronounced *blood*.

I bounded off the train and downstairs to a grumbling streetscape. Fruit stands, nail salons, a Russian candy store, and a tractor trailer defiantly blocking traffic in two directions greeted me. A homeless woman howled for change from a tall, princely crate. I had two quarters and flipped them to her outstretched coffee cup. She didn't look up and kept howling. Before I left, Teddy had told me Doody's was on Avenue Y and I proceeded vaguely in that direction.

I was feeling lighter, like I had accomplished something when, in fact, all I was doing was walking.

Was it the knowledge that I had escaped my father's office for another day? That he was, by now, fuming loudly or silently, his rage perhaps sanded down by the realization of my absence? It was afternoon, not morning. I wasn't coming and he knew that. Just as the dark backing of a mirror is needed to see your reflection—and the guarantee of death lends life meaning—my father's wrath informed my forward progress. That, even he almost understood, and it was why we never went more than a day without disagreement.

In that way, we were very much alike.

I lost time walking south instead of north, where I needed to go. I wandered among electronics outlets and a shuttered nightclub. Soon I was returned to where I needed to be, and then up to Avenue Z, which was a helpful reminder that Y wasn't far ahead. Talia and I, at that point, had spoken four times, all at the handball court, all brief interactions of "hey" and "what's up" that established nothing beyond an exchange of names, which we had made once. I wagered she did not remember mine. It was a strain on the tongue of anyone who wasn't Orthodox or acquainted with the obscurities of the Old Testament. *Roo-vain*. Are you vain? Where's your vein? A weathervane? Ruing in vain? It wasn't as obviously Jewish as Shlomo or Chaim, and for that I was mildly grateful. It meant little on the handball courts. At times, I had considered other R names, like Robert or Ricky or Ross. I didn't know if Teddy was a Theodore. I never got the chance to ask.

After hustling past a Waldbaum's and a Catholic church, I saw the hardware store, a squat single-story structure with rare parking out front. The awning was a carnival yellow, the lettering in a pleasantly bulbous swoop, and there was a bald man with an artichoke complexion trying to ram two pieces of plywood into the backseat of his station wagon. He was sweating, working as hard at this as I had at handball, and I was grateful he was successful by the time I approached. The parking lot was full but there was little chance, in the afternoon on a weekday, a hardware store was this popular. Most people probably parked here and walked somewhere else.

I moved along with a hitch. It was nerves, and maybe soreness from the game just played. As I neared the store, I felt weaker, a clutching and then a burning of the muscles, my breath choppy. I wasn't sure, exactly, what I was doing. This was a gift of youth, to drift along unencumbered, and I suddenly had no words, no idea really where to go. The gift had left me bereft. It started with a thought on the handball court and here I was. I knew, a thousand times over, I'd choose Doody's and the chance at Talia over my father's office and I would keep making that choice. Or, I assumed I would *keep* making it—that other days would resemble this one, my floating around Brooklyn, my father raging from afar. There could be days I went to the office to placate him and maybe, one particular day, I'd do my job well, well enough to hunt up the leeway for more escapes.

I assumed so much.

Doody's smelled faintly of rubber. I walked in straight ahead, not looking at the cashiers, attempting to gather myself in an aisle out of view. I stood against a row of Tupperware and decided to count in Hebrew. *Echad, sh'nayeem . . .* It was a language that I never came close to mastering, despite my years at yeshiva. The Hasids spoke Yiddish and I was no less at a loss there, struggling with the German conversions, the way the language, like thick chunks of tuna, stuck on your tongue and jammed up your teeth. I only wanted English. It was the language of commerce and the language of the street, and it was, certainly, my father's language. He felt the same way, even if he never said it out loud. Our conversations were always in English; he was not like the Satmar landlords who couldn't read letters or emails and always had to bark out half-formed sentences on the phone.

But I was counting in Hebrew. Perhaps the struggle was a comfort. I still hadn't looked toward the cashiers. I was pretending to browse for containers to hold my leftover sandwiches. If I waited longer, I could summon whatever it was that needed to be summoned—the appearance, the words, the ease of an approach I had never known. When you speak with someone less, they gained a greater purchase on you; Talia did not fade, she only bloomed. What was her life really like? It was physical, this pull, but it was also something greater because I had never cared so much about anyone else.

Instead of glancing toward the cashiers, I plunged deeper into the store.

It was larger than I had thought, a sprawl that went on for another fifty yards; if I was skilled enough, I could scramble together the materials to build my own little cottage. The underside of my excitement was fear, and I couldn't mask it, even to myself. I could increasingly feel the ludicrous nature of my presence, the rank absurdity of what I had become, someone's sly joke in Aisle 6, dipping past the potting soil and outdoor plant foods. My kippah, of course, was tucked away. I was All-American, hiding out.

"Do you need help?" a red-vested employee asked me, as he wandered into my aisle. I looked like someone who either needed help or was going to steal from them.

"No, just looking around."

"You sure you don't need something in particular? You looking to plant? You need something for Mom or Dad?"

"You have, uh," and I searched around for what could be plausible or what I could at least see, "rakes?"

"Yeah we have rakes. What kind of rake?"

"Any rake would do, really. I, uh, my dad wants a new rake to rake the leaves. You know how it is."

"Can't be too prepared for fall in the dead of winter."

"Something like that. He likes to get ahead of things."

"Aisle eight."

"Aisle eight, okay."

I only had a few minutes. I wasn't a doddering retiree or someone plainly laid off. There was no reason for a nineteen-year-old to wander a large hardware and home appliances outlet in the middle of a workday. I was stealing, in their view, or I was possibly mentally ill. No teen wanted to be here unless he was plotting something else. And I was a plotter—my motive had nothing to do with rakes, and the employee knew this. Still, I had to hold a rake. Weigh a rake. Show I was considering a rake. The longer I did this, the more unhinged I might appear. The best I could do, with my limited cash, was buy the rake.

I finally saw, at the very front of the store, Talia was working checkout. Teddy had steered me right. He knew. I held the rake and eased forward, my heart thrumming, globs of sweat inching down. I was the only man, the last man, the rake man, I had everything and nothing to say, the only offering myself. It was an act of unvarnished arrogance and it was, in retrospect, where my selves would diverge, one into the unknowable future, the other buried behind, aggressively forgotten. If not *the* birth of Teddy Starr, it was *a* birth. I felt a curious surge in belief I had never known before. Then, and still now, I believed in God far less than I let on. It coursed through me as I entered the checkout line, keeping several feet away from a stooped, gray-haired woman nudging packaged trash bags along the conveyor belt where Talia, in her own store-issued red vest stood. I held my rake, rigidly and stupidly, like it was my scepter and I had come to the medieval fair. I would slay nothing and no one; I could only hold it and stare.

The old woman thanked Talia, took her plastic bags, and shuffled onward. I was next. I placed the rake on the conveyor belt, smiled at it, and stepped forward.

There's a common complaint among men who've been spurned or men who have never tried to be spurned, that women hold the advantage in most ad hoc social interactions. Young men, in particular, believe this, and they view their plight as both singular and unfair—women, it seems, have troves of men they can seduce at any given time while men are forced to thrash about like trout suffocating in air. This is the male as *victim*; how dare this or that befall *me?* Here's an obvious secret about belief: if you think it enough, it will be true.

So, if I believed myself the victim, the half-wit, the boy stuttering into the presence of the girl I wanted, more than anyone else, to take a walk with and perhaps do something more, I would become this. If I believed something else—if I willed another person in the stead of who I might be—another outcome would be produced. Personhood is not fixed. I wasn't sure then and I am sure now, my gun in hand, that this is the correct way to understand the period of time between birth and death. It can never and will never be fixed. Flux is the state of play, the only state. I was arriving where I needed to be. I was standing in front of Talia.

"I can't believe I'm buying a rake," I found myself saying, looking up to meet her copper-tinged eyes. She smiled at me.

"You're going to rake snow."

"Yeah, for my father—well, he wants a rake. Or might need one. You never know. He wants to plan ahead."

"I know you from somewhere."

"Actually, I was about to say, me too, from the Avenue J courts. I play down there. You know, with Teddy and the rest of them."

"Teddy! Of course. He was at Hudde with my brother. I don't play much but I like to hang around at the courts."

"You should play. I'm terrible, pretty much, and I get in there. . . . Not that you'd be terrible, you're probably better than me already. I just played with Teddy—"

"Then you must be good."

"No, he played left hand only. That was the only way I could compete."

"Did you compete?"

"I, yeah, I did. I came close. But again, left hand against two hands."

"My brother said Teddy is the best player he had ever seen. He used to play a lot. Now he's in North Carolina. Basic training."

"He's brave, to be in the military right now."

"It's what he always wanted. He's ready for whatever desert we invade. He likes organized violence."

"As opposed to disorganized."

"You could say that. To go into the army, you need a mind like that. I don't know." She stopped herself and glanced down at my rake. "You really want to buy this?"

"I suppose I do. I made it this far."

"Well, it's your $9.98, not mine. You tell your dad to enjoy that rake."

She scanned it and handed it back to me. "And I'll assume you don't want me to bag it for you."

"Unless you have rake-shaped plastic bags."

"I'll check in with my manager. We keep those in the back, the long noodle plastic bags for real psychopaths."

I only laughed when it became clear to me, from her threadbare and soon-spreading smile, she was not serious.

"I'll take two, at least."

No one was behind me. No supervisor seemed to hover either, ordering Talia back to work. This little bit of kismet allowed us to keep talking.

"Two nonexistent noodle bags for you, coming right up. It's good you asked for two."

"Why?"

"You'll have to double bag your rake. You don't want it to rip through."

"I didn't think of that when I asked. I just liked the idea of two nonexistent noodle bags. Why not three? Five? Eight?"

"We have it all here. All brands of bags, rakes. Sorry, remind me again, what's your name?"

"Reuvain. Reuvain Gantz. It's not a name you hear around all that much, in certain places at least."

"Talia. You are lucky Vitaly, my boss, is out sick today. He doesn't want us talking to customers like this, even on a slow day. He's got metrics in his head about how it costs us business."

"I am lucky. Better to be here then, I don't know, walking to the subway with my rake."

"Yeah you are. But you know, a customer will sneak up behind you one of these days. I'll have to ring them up and you'll be out of luck."

I decided to attempt my gambit. It had, until I approached Talia, only been a gauzy notion, something in the distance to stumble, half-blind, toward. I go to the store, find her, and then—well, it was this. It was a meeting that was cinematic or even novelistic in form and construction, fundamentally *easy*, given the counters of my life until that point. In that moment, I accepted that ease. What I imagined, up ahead, was nothing like what actually awaited me. I only saw more Brooklyn, more New York, more Yoel, more Yitzhak, more days, perhaps, like these, where the tension and gravity of a life was derived from what my father wanted and what I wanted and the manner these desires, in some crackling form, resolved themselves. Tomorrow, maybe, I'd go into work. But not today. Never today.

"When do you get off work?" I asked her.

"Five. Why?"

"I'm in the neighborhood for a bit. If you want to keep talking, get food, I don't know, it was a thought. . . ."

"Every guy wants to get food or a drink, take pills or something. You need to, what, imbibe or absorb or take stuff in just be around someone else. It's like, people can't walk? That's impossible, I know."

"I'd definitely like to take a walk."

"Yeah, me too. I need to stretch my legs. You'll be around at five, five fifteen?"

"I will be."

"You're going to be hanging out with your stupid rake?"

"I assume. The stupid rake will have to come with me."

"Maybe we'll throw it in the bay. Meet me then over by the water, on Emmons. Near that park all the way on the corner. I forget which other street it is. It doesn't matter. You'll figure it out."

"I will."

"Good, Reuvain. Now I do have to get back to work. But I'll be seeing you."

I left the store and walked in the direction of the bay, which I knew to be south. I had one hour. It was, to that point, the most miraculous moment of my life. I was going for a walk with Talia. I, me, Reuvain Gantz, kippah stashed away, in my track pants and knockoff Nike hoodie, in a color that was somewhere on the spectrum between navy and sludge. I did, in this sense, look like anyone else—another kid passing through—and this might have helped me. I couldn't threaten Talia because it was everything she knew. My beard, a forgettable dark brown, comfortably hugged my face and never grew unruly enough to suggest I was someone who wasn't where I was supposed to be. It hardly suggested frum.

Without my kippah, I could be an Irish or Italian kid with a beard, and what of it? Nothing to think about.

I passed through the streets in a gleeful fugue. The traffic lights, errant pigeons, lonely homeless, and malformed pushcarts couldn't register. I came upon a swaggering catering hall, Baku, near the water, and imagined a distant wedding there, to someone who might have looked like Talia or was, in fact, her, with hundreds of guests, including my father, streaming through, paying their respects, celebrating what we had done. Unlike other frum fathers, my own father had never instilled a pressure to marry. He didn't fret, like neighbors, that a nineteen-year-old lacked any immediate prospects. He had married at twenty to my mother and I don't think he believed it was an accomplishment.

The fugue held all the way to the bay, where fishing trawlers and party boats had clustered, each waiting for an influx of human beings who were, as the sky dimmed to a watery gamboge, nowhere to be seen. Several fishermen, on land, teetered at the bay's railing and gazed dreamily into the murk. The fugue broke when I began to wonder whether Talia would actually show up. I knew little about her and what she would do. She gave him her word but what was her word worth? Why would she, really, bother with me? What could I offer her?

I didn't have the money I would one day have. I didn't have the grounding in community, and the might one could derive from that. I was a dissident, an outlier, and whatever I could claim, on that day, was my father's. I worked at his business, I took home what he deigned, and I lived in his house. I was, at most, an appendage. Talia would tire of that if she wanted any part of it at all. Whatever boys she dealt with, they weren't me and I felt that was their advantage.

I sat, deflated, on a wooden bench, dried bird shit beneath me, and considered how I would spend the next hour, still clutching this stupid fucking rake.

At some point, I would meander home. I didn't have the courage to flee because such courage would have to be manufactured; events, ultimately, would force me to do what I, sitting at Sheepshead Bay with a hardware store rake, never could. They would force new dreams into me. I anticipated, always, my father's rage. I was like a mariner reading the clouds for a rainstorm. I had chosen the handball courts over him and I would pay.

I had a watch, a battered Timex, that told me there were still thirty minutes to go. I walked toward our meeting point and whatever the evening held. With the sun fast vanishing, the chill could finally press into me and I could remember that this was winter. The high of my game with Teddy had long passed. That, I realized, had kept me warm for hours, along with the anticipation of meeting Talia. I blew on my reddened hands, slung my hood over my head, and kept walking, faster to get some sort of heat into my body.

I had left the rake on the bench. It had served its purpose, but it was too cold now to hold it, my hands running into my pockets and pressing against my thighs, like they were, on their own, two small skittering animals. I sneezed and a wad of mucus dripped down off the ridge of my upper lip to the pavement below. This was who Talia would see, the shivering little boy, and my nails dug against the felt of my kippah, deeper and deeper.

I could not see then what came after youth. I could not know the armaments I would acquire with time. I knew nothing, certainly, of Jesus Christ, and what it would mean, in a town I had never heard of, to learn his teachings and command others. Not to learn *to* command others, though that would be a happy by-product, one of many reasons for being.

Here, I only had the cold and my hope. I finally sat on a bench and watched the sky darken. Seagulls huddled like old men, drawing inward into their feathery coats. I had fifteen minutes to go, then ten, then six. I tried not to look at my watch. Two boys came upon my discarded rake and one claimed it, waving it giddily at the other. A frail man in a polyester parka arrived with a plastic bag filled with bread and began throwing crumbs to the seagulls. They swarmed, first ten and then fifty, white hungry streaks against the dark. The man rained more bread, enough that the battles grew less ferocious, each seagull content to corner and pick at their own crumb. I had heard, somewhere, this was all very bad for the seagulls, some sort of ecosystem destabilizer, but I couldn't recall why. Would their stomachs explode? They seemed gleeful pecking at the crumbs. The man, in his parka, was content to see them struggle and get fed.

I, too, sat and watched, crossing my arms to keep out the cold as my breath hung smoky over my flaking lips.

The boy with the rake was now marching, his friend trailing behind, the two of them enacting their military dream. The boy without the rake begged for the rake. The boy with the rake swung hard as the other boy jumped back. They both looked Russian to me, but I couldn't hear them, the wind burning in my ears. After catching his breath, the boy without the rake lunged and seized the rake, becoming the new boy with the rake. His friend cried out and I heard the echoing of a *fuck*. He was just playing around; he was angry. Who could tell where the breach happened, amusement dribbling into rage, the rake meaning nothing to them and now everything? If I hadn't bought it, they wouldn't be here battling, and I considered whether I should be guilty. I could have chosen, at least, to still hold the rake.

But I simply didn't want to.

I turned right and left, and then spun around to see if anyone—only one person, really—was approaching. She wasn't. There was an absence of Talia in every quadrant. I told myself to not be surprised, that this was to be expected. I spoke with her, and what else could I expect? She owed me nothing else. The day was already better than what I could have hoped for when I set out for the handball courts and decided I wasn't going into work. I hadn't sat at a desk and answered telephone calls for my father. I had charted this day. In my own way, I had dreamed it into being.

One boy, the boy who had originally taken the rake, had it back. The other boy seemed to recognize his own defeat. They were talking again, not shouting, walking away from me and toward the four-way intersection. I saw, in the distance, a car wash owned by a player for the Knicks. I eyed my Timex and looked elsewhere, not liking what I saw.

The boys were gone and I stood up.

How many minutes late could Talia be? She was sixteen minutes at least. I decided I could wait at least thirty, maybe forty minutes. My father would be home before eight. Beating him home held logic; his rage was radial, to be managed in swelling increments, and I could hold my ground if I was waiting in the kitchen when he returned. Perhaps I'd pretend to be studying. My mother and Yoel would undoubtedly be there and their presence could blunt him further, force him into . . . what, exactly? Yitzhak Gantz didn't surrender to anyone, let alone his shirking son, and I could only resist and keep resisting and hope, someday, to let him understand I was not going to be managing his apartment buildings. I didn't know what I would do instead and that was part of the leverage he held over me, my inability to produce an acceptable counterlife. I was not going to study Torah, not when Yeshiva of Flatbush barely graduated me and my Hebrew, on most occasions, coagulated on my tongue and went nowhere else. I was too restless to be a scholar. My father would have respected me if, sometime after graduating, I could have imagined a business proposition. He had a reverence for numbers, even when they were half-baked. I had not dreamt up any ideas for him. I wasn't sure I ever would.

What I longed for, perhaps, was a dream. Today, it was Talia. Yesterday, it was Talia too, and she had swallowed me up, I realized, for the better part of six months, from summer to fall to this January nightfall. This was, of course, not something I could ever present to my father. It wasn't even that Talia, undoubtedly, was not Jewish—she was Italian—it was that women, on their own, were not worthy of aspiration. Women were not appreciating assets like a six-story, 104-unit apartment building. They were, like family, to adorn a life but to not be your waking-hour investment. My father saw us at most for one and a half hours a day. After my mother served dinner, he retired to their room in every sense of what the word *retired* meant. He was finished for the day and wouldn't reemerge. What reason could he possibly have? He had earned his money at work and he had eaten his dinner. Sleep was the only other worthwhile endeavor left.

"You're gonna get cold sitting there, you know? You need to stand up and get the blood pumping. Especially in a raggedy hoodie like that."

Her voice broke open the frosted silence and I turned to see her standing behind me, in a black down jacket and a hood pulled tight over her head. "I like cold walks, you know. Because I actually dress for them."

"I wasn't sure if you'd make it."

"I sometimes get bogged down past my shift. Always shit percolating. That's what a hardware store is. I got here when I could. Home is boring."

"Home is boring for me too."

"Well, let's walk around the bay. You'll get frostbite otherwise."

We swung through a Holocaust memorial park that I should have reflected upon more, given how much my community still operated in its shadow. We, unlike other families on the block, were not descended from Holocaust survivors and my father never had an overriding concern about Jewry. His brothers, my uncles, were liable to bemoan anti-Semitism at family gatherings, the Palestinians who attack Israel, the everyday *schvartzes* lurking in the midst, while he shrugged at them and kept working. Part of him believed, undoubtedly, they were all making excuses. He had gotten rich, hadn't he, so how anti-Semitic could New York be, or America for that matter? Hitler hadn't anything to do with my father. And it wasn't as if the machinations of any particular Israeli government were going to matter to his rent rolls. I understood my father's perspective, as someone fast receding from his own Judaism, and why even Nazi slaughter would become, after a while, an abstraction. There were anti-Semites in Brooklyn, but no Nazis. Neither my father nor I could take anti-Semites all that seriously, since nothing of ours was being expropriated.

"You walk around here a lot?" I asked.

"My dad's apartment is, like, just down that way." She pointed at a dull white brick building. "I stay with him on weekends. I won't have to in the next few months but I might anyway since my mom is such a pain in the ass."

"They live separately."

"Yeah, big deal. Half the kids I know have divorced parents. Honestly, it's better that way. I see all these stupid Disney Channel shows or whatever about how hard it is for divorced kids, how traumatic, splitting up, Mommy and Daddy don't love each other. I was happy when my parents divorced."

It occurred to me I knew no parents who were divorced. Frum did not divorce. I, of course, knew *of* divorce, just as I knew of pornography or the concept of partying at a club on a Friday night. But Talia was right—every conception of divorce I had, from both my own community and the broader culture, was one of tragedy and failure. My father might not talk to my mother for a week but he would not divorce her. It would be like slicing off his right arm and tossing it in the gutter. Or, perhaps, some other appendage.

"That's—that's something I haven't heard before," was all I managed.

"Well, get around a bit, Reuvain. Sorry. If people are miserable, should they stay together?"

"If they're miserable, no, though marriage is a commitment. Or it's supposed to be."

"A commitment in front of God, right. I believe in God well enough. I'm not sure he wanted a man to choke out a woman or a slap a woman or call her, I don't know, a sick and twisted bitch. And I don't think he wanted a woman, driven insane by all of this, to slash his tires and hold a kitchen knife to his neck. Or if he did, well, I don't think I want to meet him."

"My mother and father don't like each other all that much either. My father is definitely the yeller. He's never hit. He yells and leaves, or he'll go quiet for hours. He'll refuse to answer."

"They should get divorced too, then. You're old enough to deal with it. Everyone will be better off."

"They would never, ever do it."

"Well, it's a win for me. They say divorced dads' apartments are terrible but that one over there, see it? It's the third floor one. He's got a little balcony and there's bird shit everywhere but it's not a bad place to sit and waste an afternoon. I'll smoke out there sometimes, he doesn't care."

"I can't imagine what my father would do in an apartment, or what they would be—maybe, yeah, he'd be better off and we'd all be. But he wouldn't do it, no. I know why."

"He doesn't want to go through with it, probably. He'd have to split everything in half. Or it's about religion. Some people don't want to go against God like that."

"It's less religion maybe than embarrassment. He'd see it as embarrassing. And he'd see living in an apartment as especially embarrassing."

Talia turned to me, her eyes boring directly into mine. "What's so embarrassing about apartments? I've only ever lived in one. Have you ever been around Brooklyn?"

"I, yes, I didn't mean it that way. It was . . ." I was sputtering, wounded, straining somehow to not lose her while communicating exactly what my father did and how he felt about the world of real estate. "He owns apartments, that's all. He has a management company."

"Oh, a landlord. So he sees it as like the slave master going out and living in the stables with the slaves?"

"I'm not sure I'd put it that way. But I don't agree with him. When I move out, I'll probably live in an apartment. I'm trying to quit my job, working for him."

"What's *trying* to quit? Either you fucking do it or you don't."

"It's hard when your father is the boss, when there's an expectation built in. My brother, he expects him to study, he doesn't expect him to manage apartment buildings."

"I stood up to my dad plenty of times and he's the type, you stand up twice or three times, he doesn't know what to do and he'll backhand you. But I did. And it worked out. I'll be staying there tonight. He doesn't bother me. You know, he even made out a second bedroom, had drywall put up where the dining room used to be. Dear old Dad sure is learning."

"Where do you think you want to go when you move out?"

"I'll probably never leave Brooklyn. Though I should leave Brooklyn. Everyone should leave where they're from. You won't learn anything staying put. You'll just become the smallest, ugliest version of yourself, a little frightened toad."

"I haven't thought about it like that."

"That's why you're here, maybe. To think about things you wouldn't have otherwise."

"We should all be doing that, everywhere, maybe."

We were on the side of the bungalows and mansions, gazing out across the bay back at the array of Russian, Turkish, and seafood restaurants. The fishermen were packing up, hustling away their buckets and poles, and pearly bulbs of light had come on over us. Up ahead, a small half-moon broke through the sky, a spectral finger reaching toward us. Swans and seagulls skimmed the water. I had never quite felt this way, bound unalterably to the present; future and past were signifiers of dead time, what never was and never would be, and all that would ever take place was my walk with Talia, our bodies inches apart.

"I don't know if I'll leave the city, but I think, now that you mention it, I'd like to."

"Well, if your dad is a landlord, you'll always have a place to live here. Maybe rent-free."

"He'd never do that."

"You'd be digging into his profit margin, I suppose."

"I would. You said your dad lives over there. Where does your mom live?"

"By all the Jews on Ocean Parkway. But we aren't Jewish."

"I figured."

"You can tell? Nothing wrong with Jews. We're Catholic. Irish and Italian, who cares? Dime a dozen, like my dad says. You Jewish?"

Unlike Teddy, she didn't know or hadn't guessed. "I, yeah, I am."

"Look, like I said, nothing against them. A lot of people hate Jews. But you know why? Really? They're just making excuses for their own shit lives. They can't get a good job, their apartment is full of roaches, ceiling leaks, their boyfriend is a cocksucker, their girlfriend is a bitch, whatever. Rent got jacked up *again* because there's no discount for your life absolutely sucking. You're twenty and going nowhere, thirty and going nowhere, forty and halfway to death and for what? For a one-bedroom with a mold problem, plaster walls, the guy next door blasting his stereo alone at one in the morning for no actual reason? You lived this long for *this?* It can feel good to hate someone, blame someone. My dad did it plenty."

"Blame the Jews. Some blame the Chinese."

"Blame them all. I think my dad, though half his building is Russian and Jews now, thinks the Jews are always a step ahead of him. He's old Irish. He wanted to name me Shannon or something but my mom stepped up thankfully and they went with Talia. He'd warn me when I was a kid about the Jews. He hated Blacks more but he didn't feel the Blacks were taking from him. They were too far away, too poor. The Jews were in your face. They owned things."

"My father doesn't necessarily like the goys or anyone else but he'll do business. That's his thing. I know he was complaining about Greek landlords for a while."

"Everyone complains about the Greeks. My dad thought they were a step ahead of him too. And you know what? They fucking were. Everyone is a step ahead of my dad. I've got to take extra steps just because he could never get anything together. He'd have all these little plans and dreams and schemes—open a bar, run a food truck, invest in car lots—and they came to nothing."

I could tell, for all the ways she resented her father, she wished he had been a success, whereas I was confronted with a successful father and was no happier. In fact, I often wondered if I would have been better off with a father who had less, one who barely managed anything and was content to turn a small profit at a butcher shop or candy store. Thwarted ambition was a terror, but so was *realized* ambition, particularly when it did not quiet any of the inner rabble. My father grasped at a greater empire, but it wasn't as if there was some particular wealth pantheon or fame quotient he wanted to reach—he hated when he appeared in the tabloids—and he had no desire to inhabit an even larger house. He churned onward like a shark, night and day, heading deeper into an ocean of his own making.

"My father has gotten what he wanted, and he seems no less miserable. He should be glad his own schemes have all worked out. But he's not. He won't be. He'll never be."

"Dads are like that. They're the sadder ones, I think. Moms put up with a lot of shit but dads try for a time to live their own myth until they can't anymore."

"Myth?"

"Well," and she swung athletically to meet my eyes, "maybe it's a man thing. Maybe you're different, Reuvain, but I don't know. I'd bet you *aren't*. Men have all these hero journeys in their heads. They're the stars of their own stories; they keep a commentary going of, like, their exploits, and life is about slowly stripping it all away, showing them how *not* special they are. Sad, huh? My brother is a little like this. My dad definitely. They'll think, against all evidence, there's a destiny waiting for him."

"I don't know if I think this."

"But I can tell you do."

We were near the gate of a community college, at the very end of where the sidewalk took us. The neighborhood, Manhattan Beach, had dripped past, an amalgam of chest-thumping wealth and the faded middle-class, one-story clamshell-colored shacks jammed up against a young oligarch's summer hideaway. Talia stopped first, leaning against a railing, a bay gust tossing her hair across her face. She wore, I noticed, light makeup around her eyes, and in the halogen glare her skin took on a painterly glow. She turned to look at the dim whitecaps and the boats skimming harmlessly around them.

"Then if I do, I don't know what it is."

"But you feel that pull, no? That yearning? You're out here in the world, making your way, and you think the world just might bend toward you."

"That might be a hope more than anything."

"It's why you came into Doody's. It's why you were able to talk to me."

Talia was the most beautiful person I had ever seen. Even now, there's a catch in my throat if I try to describe her to myself. What struck me was how much she seemed to know what fonts of awareness lay hidden from me. I didn't underestimate people but I could never be guilty of overestimating them either. And in Talia and Teddy, I found two people, right in Brooklyn, who had advanced far ahead of me.

"I came because I wanted to."

"You had ambition. You had belief. You had confidence. To approach me, you had to think I'd give you the time of day. You had to think, somehow, you'd end up out here."

"I didn't know where it'd go. I only wanted to talk. Teddy told me you'd be there."

"Teddy is one of the few people I've met who doesn't think like that—who doesn't assume a world bending toward him. He hasn't made himself the hero. He might never. And it's a shame because, if he did, he could be the rare person who made all his delusions real, you know? If he had them."

I placed both hands on the railing and leaned out toward the water. The breeze was a cold palm against my cheek.

"I still need to figure out what my delusions might be. I know I don't want to work for my father. I know I can't, no matter how long I live. I know, unlike my brother, I'm not going to study the Torah all day. I know I'm someone who can't wear my yarmulke half the time."

"What, you want to be a Christian now? I believe in Jesus but it hasn't gotten me anywhere. I'm still at the hardware store. With the Jews, at least, you guys don't think doing Hanukkah and eating matzoh balls is going to grant you riches and fame. You aren't worshipping to *expect* anything. That's what my dad never got. The Jews don't feel entitled. The Jews don't think God is just going to reach down and take care of all your little problems. I read the Old Testament, I sat through enough Mass, we even went once to one of these churches that did it in Latin, as if my dad knew what the fuck they were saying." She snorted and waved at the bay. "My dad doesn't know anything, but he'll keep pretending he does. That's what you do when you're scared and alone."

"You think your dad is scared?"

"Well, sure. Isn't everyone to some degree? It's all about levels, truthfully. You get scared of death in the dead of night or you're scared in the middle of the day. The night is supposed to be better because it's more logical."

"I'll get scared in the middle of the day, definitely."

"You admit that. I do too. The fear will sneak right up on you."

"You know, it's so cold, I might put my yarmulke back on."

"It's stupid you even took it off."

I reached into my pocket and fingered the felt edges, pinching it between two fingers and lifting gingerly, as if I had forged it myself in glass. I didn't feel anything when I put it back on but I didn't feel worse; there was no associated shame, no apology, no implicit hunch. I had my hood drawn up as well because it was that cold and getting colder. The sun was long gone and we were the only two people on this stretch of promenade, leaning into a sharp wind.

"Shit, it is getting cold," she added, now turning to face me. "Let's get a slice before I go home. There's a decent place a few blocks down, on Oriental Boulevard."

"I'd really like that."

We cut down one of the quiet side streets, bungalows bunched on each side of us. Talia strode quickly, two to three paces ahead of me at all times, despite my best efforts. We didn't talk as we walked, our hands each balled in our pockets, our heads aimed at the lost, pale lights of the boulevard. Cars passed but no people; the sidewalk, in this city, fully belonged to us for once.

I watched Talia hit the corner and swing right. I followed, grateful that I was expected to be there when she turned around.

We were on a block with a closed college bookstore, a closed Subway, and a pizzeria like a great white fizzy mouth opened wide in the dark. Warm, garlic-scented air blasted us as we slipped inside, and I felt around for the handful of dollars I had left.

"I'm getting pepperoni," she said to me. "What do you want?"

"I can get my own. Probably plain cheese."

This wasn't a kosher pizzeria and I didn't care.

"Nah, I'll buy for you. Guys are always buying things for girls. Nice for me to exploit, but a stupid expectation. Besides, it's cheap here. They're still charging a buck."

"One plain then, thank you."

"One. How about two? You afraid to eat? I'm getting knots as well."

"Two is better than one. That's true."

The pizzeria had several narrow orange booths made of hard plastic and I sat in one as Talia waited on our order. We were the only people here. Usually, even in the evening, pizza places could crowd up in New York, but this one was out of the way, on the edge of a neighborhood only accessible by a long walk from the subway or a bus. On the wall were posters from various movies and television shows. I recognized Kramer from *Seinfeld*, whom I knew about through pop culture osmosis—we did not watch sitcoms at home—and the bludgeoned face of the actor who played Rocky, whom I now know—but didn't know then—was Sylvester Stallone. Unseen speakers piped in pop music I knew well but couldn't name, dance music overlaid with a female vocal and a drum machine. Only one man, as far as I could see, was still working at the pizzeria, heating up the slices and the garlic knots.

"They do a good slice here," Talia said, halfway between me and the man behind the counter, who had hooded eyes, a soft beard, and might have been Syrian or Albanian.

"Oh yeah."

It occurred to me, at that moment, there was no place in the world I'd rather be. I felt this, in a fleeting form, at the handball court, and it returned with far greater force as I waited for Talia. What I didn't know then was how rare, in life, this intensity would be.

Talia returned with our slices, one for her and two for me, along with four garlic knots.

"You didn't want two slices?" I asked.

"I'm claiming three knots instead. You try one. They're good here. Big, a bit gooey. A lot of places fuck up knots. Not Antonio's. They always come through."

"Ah, this is Antonio's. I didn't even notice."

"The guy who owns it lives in Mill Basin, nice place on the water. My dad thought, at one point, he could open a pizza place, own it, operate it. One of his little dreams. It never came to anything."

"He couldn't get some investors together?"

Talia took a small bite of her garlic knot. "He never knew how to talk to people. Either the normal way or strategically. There are people who know how to get things from other people and people who *want* to get things from other people but don't know, really, how to do it. They're malformed in some way."

"Your dad tried to take advantage of people and failed?"

"Yeah. He'd love to wheel and deal if he could. All his wheels break."

My slice was scalding, the cheese runny, and I tried to eat slowly. I was hungrier than I realized and I was burning the top of my mouth as I tried to take off a larger chunk. I was thirsty too.

"I'll get a soda," I said.

"Let me get it."

"I can get the drinks, at least. You want a can of something?"

"If they have orange soda, yeah."

I walked over to a Coca-Cola-themed cooler that was, to my surprise, mostly empty. There were no orange sodas, no Fantas, nothing of the like. I reluctantly reached for a Diet Pepsi.

"No orange soda," I called back to Talia. "You want anything else?"

"Sprite, maybe."

There were 7Ups but no Sprites. I decided this would be good enough and paid for one.

"Soda options are limited," I told her, sliding over the 7Up.

"They get cleaned out by end of day. 7Up has a diseased taste but I'll do it. It'll mix with the pizza."

We ate and I tried not to talk with the cheese, sauce, and bread sloshing around my mouth. Talia ate with far more precision than me, and I noticed how she kept dabbing the corners of her mouth with a napkin. Her light brown hair, which usually tumbled just past her shoulders, was now tied in a ponytail. She sat up straight, like her spine had been lightly electrified, and I felt, in turn, my own inattention to my physique, how I melted into the booth.

I couldn't look away from her.

"This has been fun," I said.

"I haven't had a day like this in a while. It's been good. You're all right, Reuvain from the handball courts."

"You're Talia from the handball courts."

"You play, so you get to be from there."

"You should play too. Girls play."

"Of course they play. I like watching. It's more interesting that way. I like to see how the games unfold."

"You pick people to root for?"

"I will. I'll switch it up. Somedays I'll pull for the Mexicans, others the Chinese. Teddy I pull for, but he wins so much, you want an upset too. He doesn't realize sometimes how much he wins."

"I thought of you watching when I played today."

"Yeah? And what I was I doing."

"Just leaning against the fence, watching. It made me play better. I wanted to show you I could."

"For the idea of me in your head."

"Something like that."

"I like how you talk, Reuvain."

A boxy Panasonic hung in the corner, tuned to a soundless soccer game in a distant European nation. The spectral figures weaved through static, blotches of flickering red and green, the ball little more than a white spore. I thought, for a moment, how nice it would be to sit with Talia there, in a sun-blasted stadium in a country foreign and free. If we were there, would I have to go home? Would I have to face my father?

I had never been on an airplane.

"Talia, have you ever been on a plane?"

"Yeah, why? We took a family vacation to Disney World."

"I was thinking about how I've never flown on one."

"The best part is getting above the clouds. I always made sure to have the window seat. You remember you're seeing something that no one for thousands of years could ever see."

"Are you scared? I know people get scared."

"My mom doesn't like flying. But no, I love it. I love arriving at airports. I love the anticipation, the people in motion, not being here and not being there. Some people don't like that, being the passenger, existing in between. Sometimes you're most free there."

"I know what you mean." We were standing now, throwing our paper plates in the garbage. "Or, I think I do. I always liked the idea of going somewhere else, being in transport, broken out of the city. Right now, I wouldn't mind flying right out of here."

"You're not looking forward to going home, huh?"

"No, not at all."

The night was colder. Either the temperature had dropped or I was failing to adjust to the gelid air, what the pizzeria had kept at bay. I pushed my hands back into my pockets and watched a dark cloud of breath take shape from my lips.

"I can walk you back," I said.

"Lucky for you, I'm straight ahead, and then a bit right. Your best bet heading home is the subway from Brighton Beach."

"After I drop you off, I'll take my time getting back."

"We should swap dads for a day. I wouldn't mind someone with ambition, even if he's an asshole. And my dad is an asshole anyway. So why not someone who's done something with this life?"

"It'd be easier, I think, if my father did nothing."

"You say it and you might even think it's true. But until your dad is three months late on rent and your mom is screaming at him and the landlord is sending very strange and ugly men to knock on the door, you don't know what any of it means. It's not your fault. Your dad *owns*. He's got a big stake jammed into the earth and he's not going to be moved. That's all I wanted when I was a kid."

"Do you want that, when you're older? To have a house? Family? Kids?"

"A house, sure. I don't want anyone to bother me, to be able to tell me to leave. I want five or six big rooms and I want to tell my mom and dad, well, you're *not* welcome, not if I'm not feeling like it. I don't hold any grudge. It's not about power, either. It'll be about my own peace. You haven't found it yet either."

"Maybe not."

"Definitely not. I don't know many people who have. Teddy might be closest."

We continued down the wide boulevard, hugging the empty sidewalk. To our left, across the way, was the beach and the blackness of ocean. I couldn't see it but knew it was there. If I had stayed, I could take her to the beach. All I would have had to do was ask.

We spoke less as we drew closer to her father's apartment building. The wind had picked up and spongy clouds were cloaking the moon. She had slowed and I paced her on the side of the gutter. I had heard, somewhere, this was where men were supposed to walk. We reached another avenue, passing a second pizzeria and a Greek restaurant, and transitioned from the single-family castles to the medley of brick-skinned apartment buildings and glassy condos. As far as I could remember, my father didn't own buildings over here, but it was conceivable he was always adding to his portfolio. His records were barely computerized and the facts I gleaned from his budding empire were mostly confined to file cabinets he asked me to trawl through and organize. It was not impossible he was the landlord for Talia's father's building; he operated under several different LLCs and never attached his name to a property.

"You didn't have to walk me all the way back. But I do appreciate it, Reuvain . . . Reuvain *what?* You told me, and now I've stupidly forgotten."."

"Gantz. Like pants, with a g."

"Well, mine is Cosgrove. I don't mind it, to be honest. It's the one good thing my dad gave me. It always reminded me of a meadow or a field or somewhere cool and secret, dappled in a bit of a shade. Come to the *Cosgrove*."

"I'd go there. It's better than getting stuck in a Gantz. The less I say my name, the better. It's always stuck like peanut butter on my tongue."

"You know, I don't mind it at all. You should own it. That's more attractive. Say it out loud, three times."

"Really?"

"Yes, I command you."

"Reuvain Gantz, Reuvain Gantz, Reuvain Gantz."

"Congratulations. And now you get this."

Talia dipped forward and kissed me on the cheek. Her lips were warm, despite the chill around us, and I almost fell backward onto the gum-smattered pavement. I had never been kissed before by someone who wasn't my mother.

"You have a good night, Reuvain," she said to me. She flicked her head upward. "This is my stop."

"Let's walk again, soon."

"You know where to find me."

I watched her disappear, a gorgeous wisp in the lobby's buttery light, and I gently touched the spot of skin where her lips had been. I waited in front of her building, as if there was more for me to do.

And then, a great ball of light inside of me, I walked toward the subway station.

Whatever fear I had of my father had leaked away. It was past nine o'clock; he was undoubtedly home and dinner was long consumed. Yoel was always in bed. If my mother was in bed, my father was in his study to avoid her. And if she felt compelled to stay awake in the living room, he would be in the bedroom, reading in silence.

None of it could touch me because of Talia. She was armor and shield. I made it to the subway station, waited another fifteen minutes, and boarded a Q train groaning to Midwood. The car was mostly empty, save for a small gang of teenagers and a homeless man turtled up in an oversized down jacket. I stared straight ahead, out the window and to the whirring dark.

I dashed out at Avenue J and down the stairs at a rocking gait. I wasn't hurrying to meet my father. I wanted, simply, the rest of the night to be done because it was dead time, time without Talia. Soon enough, it would be tomorrow, and I could imagine again how I'd see her. What was the purpose of this quiet walk back home, alone? My father would be awake or he wouldn't. My mother would be awake or she wouldn't. Yoel, likely, would be in bed by now because he never, under any circumstances, stayed up late. It seemed cruelly wasteful to be here, when the possibilities, with enough waiting, would be far grander.

My home was on the corner, in possession of lush front and side yards. Flecks of ice clung to the grass like white hairs. I stood outside and waited. Most of the window lights were off. The house surged up through the dark to meet me. I let the coolness of the doorknob's brass linger on my skin. It was time to go inside.

The foyer and living room were empty, the Steinway piano waiting, against the corner, like a sleeping animal. No one in our household played but my father, at some point when I was young, decided he liked the physicality of a piano. I ambled, taking my time through the dining room, where plates and silverware had long been removed and washed, and to a small table through our galley kitchen where my father sat, his eyes floating over a notebook and several stacks of paper. He was squinting through spectacles and scrawling small numbers with a ballpoint pen. He didn't look up.

"Reuvain."

"Hello."

I came closer. He hadn't yet dressed for bed. He wore an eggshell-white dress shirt with a starched collar and black pants, a silver watch glinting in the crescent of light a nearby lamp had left behind. In his chair, his back balletically straight, he was like a centurion in the hours before his deadly work.

"You didn't come today."

"I didn't."

He was still writing in the notebook. He hadn't yet looked up at me.

"Where were you?"

"I was out. I meant to tell you. I had a few things to do."

"*Things*." It was a word, so lacking in precision, that he could chew on with particular derision. "I'd ask what they were, but I'm not sure you'd tell me."

"I played handball for a bit and then I saw a girl I knew. We walked around, ate pizza, and I took the train home."

My forthrightness surprised me. I had no intention of being honest with my father. I thought, when pressed, I'd weave together a story of ill-health or a need to formulate a new, ill-defined business scheme that could meet his approval if it sounded grand enough. I wanted to stall slightly, spin my wheels, and go to bed. I wanted this day to be over. A simple lie could have placated my father, or at least done more to avert what was to come in the next half hour. I'm surprised, still, I was so direct with him.

"Instead of coming to work, you hung out in a park? This is what you do, Reuvain?"

"It's what I did."

Now he was staring up at me, his ballpoint pen rested.

"I don't quite know what to do with you."

"I should have told you. I wanted, today, to do this instead. I didn't want to go into the office."

"I would call this disappointing, but that would convey, I suppose, my expectations remain raised. They're diminishing. They were raised, once raised quite high."

"I don't know. I suppose I don't like going into the office."

"You'd *prefer not to*. Do you know where that's from? Probably not. They don't teach those books at Yeshiva of Flatbush. *I would prefer not to*, the scrivener said."

Now, unlike then, I know my father was referring to a canonical Melville short story that he learned about in the early years of his life that would exist, forever, in a sort of penumbra, inaccessible even to those he, in theory, loved most. My father, in the worst but most intriguing ways, could always surprise me, and he was as pregnant with as many selves as me, maybe more.

"I don't want to go anymore, at all, I don't think. I enjoyed today. I enjoyed the park. I don't think—I don't think I can keep going into your office."

My father stood. His features were quiet, betraying little, and his grayish eyes met my own. I listened for my mother and brother and heard nothing.

"Would you like to work elsewhere?"

"I don't know where I want to work."

"There are a few different types of people in the world. There are those that don't know what they want or what they want to do—but they *hope* to find it. They seek. They're like little lost ships at sea. But you, Reuvain. You're of a different sort. I always knew this, even as I saw your talent. You were going to build an empire, a real one, or you were going to turn to dust. Not literal dust—you'll live a long life. But you were going to, slowly perhaps, be like dust. Just like your day today. Drifting and drifting—for what? For entertainment? For a crush?"

"You'll never understand it."

I began walking toward the staircase. The conversation was like a serpent, already engorged, and slowly crushing me; I was not the primary prey, maybe, but I was hunted enough and I needed now to be alone. My head burned, my vision was rheumy, and whatever rejoinder I could muster had withered and died in the back of my throat. I walked slowly, staring at the floorboards, noticing how they shined. An Albanian woman came every week to clean the house and she was very good at her job.

"You shouldn't be afraid of empires. You shouldn't run from them."

I stopped on the second stair and turned to him, the muscles in my neck throbbing.

"If I want an empire, I'll build my own."

"You'll build your own like the boys at the handball court and that girl you follow around? You'll do it at a hardware store and a stroll around the bay with a little goy? Don't get me wrong, Reuvain—unlike other fathers, I don't care nearly as much if you find yourself, from time to time, tumbling with goyim. It's New York City; it's going to happen. What I am more interested in is that you believe this meandering path is getting you somewhere. Yoel, blessed Yoel, is sleeping now and he has half your brains and twice your convictions. In the end, with that combination, he will have an empire and you'll be swimming in the gutter."

I grabbed the railing, my fingers hot and strange, like they didn't belong to me at all. My father *knew*. I had never mentioned Sheepshead Bay. I had never mentioned a hardware store. Someone who worked for him had tailed me or someone he knew had seen me and relayed the information. This city was not mine, and never would be; he had, like a gluttonous prophet, claimed every cubit of psychological and physical terrain. Go to his office or not, it didn't matter. I kept walking up the stairs and he began to follow me.

"Your empire doesn't impress me."

"Then what does impress you? What moves you?"

"Whatever it is, it isn't here."

"I remember when you were born, you hardly cried at all. Others saw it as a certain contentedness or even stoicism. Behold this baby, they said. Does nothing bother him at all? Do you know what I saw, Reuvain?"

I was near the top of the steps. I assumed it was a rhetorical question and declined to answer. But the silence that hung between us told me something else. My father wanted my answer. He wanted it very much. And I wanted, just as urgently, to not give it to him.

"I'll tell you what I saw when I looked at you. I saw a great and terrible sadness, a sadness that would not lift, no matter how much we held you and kissed you. Hashem had made you this way. With Yoel, it was different. He was a baby of the world, and his happiness and sadness corresponded to the forces in front of him. Yoel had a calculus. You, Reuvain—you were a void."

"You're a void."

It was an impish reply and all, at the very top of the steps, I could manage. I was staring straight ahead at a garish nineteenth-century grandfather clock my father had kept on the second floor. It was due to groan in three minutes. My father reached me, his bulk sweeping past mine, and leaned against the wallpaper. He was not breathing hard at all.

"I only hear sadness, not anger. And that, in its own way, makes me sad. I love you and you cannot properly rage. You don't know what to rage for. You're a husk, waiting and wanting, and that isn't going to change. What will change, eventually, is the decisions you make. I have no doubts that, after a few years of showing up and observing, you can succeed me and build a better company."

He cleared his throat and began to unbutton his sleeves, gently rolling them upward like he was preparing to till the soil outside. A single bead of sweat glimmered off his temple and his skin, normally pale, was flushed lightly rouge. I had expected the phlegm-soaked bellowing, the simian gesticulations, but he was no more ruffled than an undertaker. I could only wait for him to continue.

"You can build that company because of your mind. Ambition is better than a mind, but your mind will make up for what you terminally lack. It can, with proper direction, make cathedrals here. Or at least rental apartments. I know, at least, you have no ethical quandaries about extracting income from the income of others, often those who have little. I know you don't care."

"Just tell me how you knew where I was today."

His smile was a glittering scythe flicked outward, shown to me as a warning. I had to respect it. However long I had lived, he had lived much longer, and no amount of indignity—or mere wrath—could change this.

"You'll understand if you think about it. When you get to my age, you have friends everywhere. They look out for your interests, if you treat them the right way. I worry this is another lesson you'll never learn."

"A hardware store friend, a pizzeria friend."

"You're like your mother in that way; you conceal nothing, despite your best efforts. You wear your secrets on your face. You've subdivided your selves and they all hang like little monkeys from your flesh. One day, if you live long enough, you might apprehend the hidden nature of this country. We are Jews, and we are Americans. If you forget the latter, you're off the cliff. You are nothing to history."

"I should worship pizza and hamburgers, then. And play handball. Lots of it."

"You've found the flakes of America, the dandruff and the bits of garbage. You've gone there first. You've gone, more stereotypically, to goyim flesh. I love you, Reuvain, but you are one of millions, and I observe you every day, just as I observe your brother. I will never lie to you, no matter how much you lie to me. I will tell you exactly what you can and can't do, and how you're failing."

"You run a gutter empire."

It was all I could say to him, my syllables papery on my teeth. We were facing each other at the very top of the staircase. He had finished rolling up his sleeves and crossing his arms, the bands of muscle, like little harpsichord strings, pressing against his skin. He was still smiling.

"When you speak, I hear sadness and desperation, and I want to help. That's why you'll have a job with my company, always, and that's why, if you begin to engage with your future, it will be yours. But if you continue onward down this path, I know that you'll be a more curdled version of who you are now."

I waited for Yoel or my mother to race out of their rooms but I knew, at this point, they were fast asleep. They were not coming out to intervene. Yoel, then, was too meek to say anything, and my mother, struggling through periodic headaches, preferred to avoid any and all commotion. With each passing breath, I wanted to slink away. I longed for sleep. He was close to me, and I could smell the trace of lamb on his lips. My mother had cooked a good dinner.

"You run a gutter empire," I said again.

I still turn this line over in my head, all these years later. The *gutter* empire. A dagger clutched tight, thrust at the throat.

There was a tremor in my father's grin. It was decaying into something familiar, a smile that couldn't hold—here, I thought, was the goblin father. I only needed to keep saying the magic words.

"You run a gutter empire."

He was soundless now. We were opposite each other, his back to the staircase. He was rangy, my father, and he wore his girth well, like he had been preparing his whole life to inherit another fifteen pounds. His beard was like mine, only thicker; his eyes were like mine, only gently wrinkled at the lids, and they shone beautifully with rage. In another life, I could hug him. Beneath the fat that time had stuck his bones, there was the purity of muscle, contemporary action. I only saw some of it then. I was new to the world, and new to mistakes.

"You close your mouth now, Reuvain."

He had rarely hit me in childhood and never hit Yoel, who gave him no reason to be hit. There were men in the community who hit their wives and my father was not one of those men. He had no interest in petty violence. If he was going to change, it would be here, his body beginning to clench. I was going to change him. I was the gateway.

"Gutter empires for gutter men."

He grabbed me first. The record, known only to me and those I might tell, will reflect that. His right hand, with its thick digits, burrowed into the bone of my shoulder, and he found my gaze again. I could see, in the shudder of his lips, a broken emotion approximating grief and the greater effluvia of rage, all of it crashing together at the center of who he was. I didn't want to be grabbed. I didn't like it; no, I *loathed* it, and in his action I unearthed a far darker and more immediate realization, one shot through me like dragon fire: I would do anything to get his hand off.

Anything, anything.

"You don't know what you're saying," he told me, his voice hushed.

I took his own hand and ripped it away, using my left shoulder to shove him hard, hard enough to remember what he had done. He stumbled back, with far more force and desperation than I ever could have imagined then. I didn't know I had strength; I didn't know I had power. I didn't consider he was at the precipice of the stairway and his back loafer would catch on our carpeting and he would continue his fall, one step and two and three and four, down and away like he had been blown into orbit and was grasping at the memory of the marbled Earth, his eyes wet with terror, his mouth exploding open. His spine thudded and his neck cracked and he was, against the cherry wood stairs, like a great and terrible figurine, his limbs wrenched catastrophically outward, blood pouring from where his skull had been broken.

He cried out, but I could hardly hear it.

"Father," I said.

I met his body at the foot of the staircase, where his legs were draped and his head, swung sideways, aimed blankly at the kitchen. He had tumbled and slammed into hardwood. "Father," I said again. "Father, wake up." The blood continued to roll in thick, miraculous streams from his skull; I didn't believe such a quantity was possible.

My own tears, comparatively, were feeble.

"Father, wake up."

I waited and waited for his breaths to return. I bent over him, my thin shadow mingling with his own. I wanted to cry out to Yoel and my mother to call an ambulance, to save him, even if I knew that would have been futile.

I wanted to cry out even as I ran, crashing through the kitchen to grab my coat off the chair I had slung it over less than an hour ago. I took a wool cap and I ruffled up the only scarf I could find. It was Yoel's and it would now be mine. I burst through the front door and charged headlong into the night. My chest burned with a fear unlike any I had ever known. Anything behind me, I decided, was abyssal—the house, the lawn, the trees, even the street lamplights I passed. Nothing was more impossible than a backward glance. I heaved, saliva and stray bile slipping through my teeth, and kept running. I had to keep running.

Down the avenue, a straight shot, a death shot, to the sickly glow of the train station and its cold machine air. Twelve minutes, twelve gargantuan minutes, and I was in another Q, hurtling toward Manhattan's core. The ride was a misery, my eyes bloodshot and thrown earthward, bodies thrashing in and out of the car, none of them aware of what had happened or what I had done. I saw the sign for Times Square and jumped out, wafting through the station's chaos until I caught a set of stairs and then another set of stairs, more enormous this time, and the scorched nighttime above. The neon burned me, the signs screaming for money, the bulbs of light glittering like raised scimitars. I wandered into and out of the street, dodging the men dressed as Disney characters and the filthy men caterwauling for change. I walked, for no reason at all, to Bryant Park, and drifted back over the steps of the library to the mouth of 42nd, which would take me to the buses.

I had enough cash for a ticket, several nights of cheap motels, and one square meal each day until early next week, or whenever I decided vending machine potato chips would suffice.

A Greyhound for the Detroit bus station would leave in twenty-six minutes.

As I sat on the Port Authority bench, dazed and alien to everything around me, I saw a bright sign for a convenience store. It was closed but the sign was still lit in a calm, chemical red, not so different than the neon of Times Square, not so different than anything I had seen. Yet it was, right there, all I could look at. I almost felt its warmth, if it had any to give.

STARR & CO. DELI.

I closed my eyes. My father was dead and I was going out into the country.

PART III

7

The bullet erupts against the tree trunk, spraying shards of bark over Yoel's shaking head.

He is staring up at me like the little brother he is when I take his collar in my left hand and wave the pistol in my right. He says nothing when I slam the pistol against his jaw and blood, in long bright spurts, dapples the bent grass.

"Get out of here," I say to him. "I never want to see you again. Tell no one you were here."

And then, like a cockeyed, death-bloated gargoyle, he begins to laugh. Blood is leaking down his chin.

"I lied to you, dear brother."

"What?"

"It's too late."

"I won't miss next time. The first was a warning."

"I suppose it would be in my best interests if I kept lying to you, but I can only be like you for so long, shimmying from one lie to the next, inhabiting whole worlds of make-believe. It starts to *hurt*, Reuvain."

I swing the pistol on the backhand and crash it against the other side of his face. He yelps and stares back up at me, more blood rushing down.

"The envelopes are in the mail," he says. "They're all in the mail."

I lower the gun. His eyes are locked on mine.

"What are you talking about?"

"I explain everything. I have photographs. It's an informational packet, really. The tracking information tells me one has already arrived at your house. Assuming your wife is home, which she is, she is reading it. It's addressed to *her,* after all. Another went to your friend Landry. And another to that nice woman, Gertrude Breckinridge. There are others, you lose count really when you send so many."

"I will put a bullet through your head."

"You will. Or you won't. It doesn't matter anymore anyway—that is really my point. I set this all in motion. They are all learning about Reuvain Gantz. They are learning about the Jewish boy who killed his father and fled to a new town to take on a new identity and lie and lie and lie and lie—maybe they will see you like Christ reborn, Gantz into Starr. What a flourish! I'll always admire you, my brother. No matter how wretched you are."

"No one will believe any of this."

"I spent enough time following you to know that one person will believe all of it. And she is the only one that really matters. She is home, with your children. She is reading attentively."

I raise the pistol and he shudders like an electrified, waterlogged little toy, his eyes swinging away from my own. For all his blather, he doesn't want to die. No one does—even the suicidal have their regrets. He fears the unknowable as much as I do.

"Mother saved you, you know," he says, more quietly this time. "Without her, your future wouldn't be possible."

"No one saved me."

"When we woke and the ambulance came, she said he had accidentally fallen down the stairs. She never mentioned you even though she knew exactly what happened. She understood. I wanted to believe, for a very long time, it was an accident. My father dead, my brother gone—some strange, terrible accident."

"I didn't mean to do it."

"Convince yourself of whatever you need to convince yourself of—like that name of yours. Wear it like a bloody mask. The truth will follow you into death."

"I didn't mean it, he grabbed me first—"

"You sound like you're nineteen again. Sniffling, whining, the world handed to you and you can't fathom what to do except wallow in your own wretchedness. I heard what you said to him. I was a light sleeper, Reuvain."

I inch backward, away from the tree where he is sitting and bleeding, still smiling up at me.

"Gutter empires for gutter men! Gutter empires for gutter men!"

Yoel's voice is cracking, bursts of saliva spraying off his bloodied lips. His eyes strain toward me, like I am his murderer or his salvation, his grin only hardening. I keep walking.

"Gutter empires, Reuvain, for gutter men!"

I aim my gun at his temple and, before firing, range it upward so the bullet explodes about fifty feet above him, against a branch. I fire again and fire again and fire again. He is staring at me from his tree, his torso lax and swollen, his finger pointing at me.

"I'm going to leave you here, Yoel. Never contact me again."

I'm easing away until I'm not, high-kneed dashing through the woods, leaping over branches and reaching for the clearest path to get back to my vehicle. My breath is hot and jagged and my lungs ache, but I don't stop until I'm back at the parking lot, jam the key into the ignition, and gun the Chevy back onto the empty local roads. I decide it's best to not think and just drive, clench the wheel at nine and two o'clock like I'm in driver's ed and the open road promises death and destruction if my attention wavers for even a microsecond. The long Michigan evening burns bright and I wish, for a quavering moment, I'm returned to New York, where the descent to dusk is rapid, final, and fatal if you're in the right mood. I reach ninety, not yet on the freeway, not looking out for the state troopers like on an ordinary day.

In Pine Haven, I swerve into a Shell station and pump gas into my tank, even though I'm more than half full. My hand is spongy, perspiration-soaked, and when I'm done, I charge into the convenience store and try to hunt up turkey jerky. I want a large packet that will set me back at least fifteen dollars and I find it up against the wall, among a parade of beef sticks, beef shreds, and cheese and beef combo packs. At the front is the clerk, Hulan Rocker Jr., the son of Hulan Rocker, who once bought a two-bed, one-bath starter home from me when the market was slack and interest rates preferred to not exist. Rocker Jr. is meaty and pea-eyed like his father, his tawny hair already thinning. He grins at me and offers a hello, how are you today, and I tell him just great, just great, love this turkey jerky.

"You got some good spice there," he says to me. "Extra kick."

"Always need the extra kick."

It's possible Yoel was lying to me. There might be no dossiers arriving in the mailboxes of those who I cherish most, the very pillars of this community that I've, in my own way, helped to build. Anything remains possible as I sit in the car and briefly, very briefly, rip through the turkey jerky, tasting the profound welter of salt. None of this, really, is good, and I finish after a few bites and drive straight to Hearst Road. The living room windows flash warm, welcoming light, and I settle the Chevy in the driveway. Yoel was lying to me. He can get eaten by a bear or hitchhike home. None of it is my problem.

Life is tidy, as long as you manage all the angles.

The door is unlocked, as always—this isn't New York—and I enter with a jazzy step, keeping it light. "Honey, I'm back!" I call out.

Our castle is quiet. No shouts, no laughter, no thumping, no pitched battles between Chloe and Austin, no bemused groans from Theodore. No one responds to my call. I try one more *honey* and hear, in the distant kitchen, the sound of dishes rattling together.

My wife, my bountiful Daniella, stooped over the dishwasher, loading up our silverware.

"I'm back. It was a whirlwind day at the office, you wouldn't believe it. How is everything, dear?"

She is in a sleeveless athletic top and running shorts, the Tiffany pendant I bought for her two Christmases ago still fastened around her neck. Her skin has a light and scintillating sheen of sweat.

"Your father never belonged to the Mackinaw City Players," she said, still looking at the dishwasher.

"Excuse me?"

"I can tolerate a great deal. When I made my commitment to you, in the *eyes of God*, I told myself this would be a journey, like one of those great, transnational steam-engine trips, something to be enjoyed but also endured. I chose you, Teddy, because you seemed to make sense. Did I know how you looked at other women? Yes. Did I know how you might sleep with other women—"

"I haven't *slept* with anyone."

"I told you, I can tolerate a great deal. I know what you do—I've known, let's put it that way—and I made my own arrangement with it, my own calculus, that must not have been very different than what you figured in your own head. If we have *this*," and she waved, grandly, at our polished nickel kitchen island, "why not let him have his occasional women? What does it matter to me, really? A fuck here, a fuck there. He brings home a paycheck, he reads to the children at night, he shows up, when he can, to the basketball games. This town is full of fucking men like you. At least, in your case, you're actually paying the mortgage."

"Daniella, really, if you'd let me explain for a minute, if you're talking about Gertrude, she's a dear friend, that's all. . . ."

"You don't have to spin your wheels for me. No matter what I say, you'll do what *you* want—you'll scurry about, from here to there, your penis enflamed and ready—and I'll be expected to smile at you. And I could. I really could. I thought, for a moment, of having my own affair. But then I remembered I was too busy raising our children. Where to find the time? Where to begin?"

"This is really ridiculous."

"Tell me where your father is from."

"I told you, we grew up in Mackinaw City."

"A good story. You were always so good at stories. I always wondered, why stay here, in Michigan? Now I know the truth."

"Whatever you got in the mail, it's a lie. All of it."

"Your poor mother. You kill her husband and she's left there to pretend her son isn't a murderer. What a saintly, stupid woman. If I were her, I would have tracked you down like one of the hounds of hell. I would have dragged you back to the pits."

She has finished loading the dishwasher and setting the timer. The churn is familiar and welcome; I wonder, somehow, if we can reset, if the night can be salvaged and we can grab dinner somewhere, maybe at a steakhouse in Mt. Pleasant.

"The letter is all lies."

"Nothing about you quite added up. Who were the Starrs? What theater troupe? Why was your accent so unplaceable? When, exactly, did you find Jesus? A Jew, though. I didn't peg you for a Jew. There aren't many of them around here."

"I am *not* a Jew."

"You converted. Or pretended to. So I suppose you are as close to telling the truth as you'll ever be. You aren't a Jew, but you certainly aren't a Christian or anything resembling a godly person here on this Earth."

"Where are the children?"

"The Hannons. A sleepover. They won't be coming home."

"And then?"

"I'd prefer you'd never see them again."

I lean back against the countertop, trying to imagine a medium-rare porterhouse and a cold glass of Coors, my wife on one side, my three children on the other, all of us in a ring at one of those broad, polished tables dropped thickly near the replica deer trophies. We can still make it before closing if we leave now, if we head to the Hannons and scoop up the children, it's a clean twenty-five minutes on the freeway. . . .

"You don't mean that."

"I don't even know who you are. Teddy, Reuvain. What are you even named?"

"All of it, you have to believe me, all of it was—it was for a reason, Yoel, my broth—the man who wrote the letter, he's mentally ill, let's start there."

"It was a beautiful package. I have it upstairs. Other wives would think it was the ravings of a maniac—a letter, photographs, and even if it was all assembled with such care, even if it was personally addressed to them, they would believe their husbands. They were taught to believe their husbands. God wants this. But God doesn't want liars and blasphemers. God doesn't want the wicked. God will understand when I don't listen. God will only judge you. A murderer from New York City, scuttling out here to do what—to make money? To make fools of us? Well, yes. And to hide. You hoped to hide in this family."

"Daniella, please, if you'd let him explain, I'll start with Yoel, *he's* the one, really, who you should be asking questions about."

"I won't let you hide. Your brother was industrious. Half the congregation received packages. He was following you, making sport of you, as you made sport of us. *Your husband, Teddy Starr, was born Reuvain Gantz in Brooklyn. He is, first and foremost, my brother, and he killed our father.* I've got the opening line burned into me now. I can recite it until I die."

The porterhouse steak is the emperor of steaks. Only one other steak offers the fusion of the butter-tender filet mignon and the classic beefy flavor of the Kansas City strip in a single package. The porterhouse is the big, burly brother to the T-bone: cooking it is a delicate art. Thaw at least twenty-four hours beforehand. Preheat your charcoal or gas grill on high. Place the steaks over the hottest part of the grill and sear for one to three minutes. For the perfect medium-rare, grill up to thirteen minutes for a one-inch steak and up to seven minutes for one-and-a-half-inch steak, turning about one minute before the halfway point. Your meat thermometer should reach one hundred and thirty degrees. Rest your steaks for five minutes before serving, covering them lightly with tinfoil. This is extremely important. The heat of cooking pulls the juices in the meat toward the surface. If you slice into the meat immediately after cooking, those flavorful juices will splash your plate, and not reside in your steak. Letting your steak rest will give the juices time to sink back in and throughout the meat, keeping it moist and flavorful. "We should go out for steaks. Let's grab the kids. Lucy's Prime or, if we have to, the Outback. We can do porterhouses and mashed potatoes."

Daniella is nibbling at her thumbnail, an unseemly habit I've told her to ditch. Her eyes flick toward me and a smile drags, loosely, across her face.

"If you ever want to see me or the children again, you will go up in front of the church on Sunday and tell everyone the truth. You will tell them who you are. You will spare nothing."

"Daniella, really, I—"

"No court will side with you. I will clean you out. You will be a disgraced, poor, *fake* pastor in a town that will want you dead. You don't understand. I am from here, not you. You were always an outsider, strike one. But you had two strikes to give and property and God will take you a long way. I will make sure, Teddy, Reuvain, whoever you might be, that you will never see Theodore,

Chloe, or Austin again. I have half a mind to drag Theodore to court and rename *him*."

The longing for the steakhouse dinner with my family, which had become so distinct to have already been hardened into a future memory, begins to fizzle. Any way I'm playing this, it's not getting me there.

"It doesn't have to be this way."

"I married a lie."

"I'm here. I'm me. I'm always me. I care about you, Daniella."

"I see nothing in your eyes. Nothing. Like two cold marbles. How *did* you kill your father?"

"It was an accident."

"Yoel wrote otherwise."

"He didn't see it. He was in his room. I saw it. I fucking saw it. I was there. It was an argument, he—my father—put his hand on me. I pushed, harder than I thought. He tripped on a staircase."

"Vile."

"That's what happened."

"I don't believe you."

I'm still slack against the kitchen counter when Daniella reaches for the marbled paper towel holder, the one I ordered, on a whim, from an Italian manufacturer. Her hand, as she begins to raise it, is shaking. Teardrops glitter tenderly on her cheek's half-moon curve.

"I want you gone." She is screaming now, like a television wife, like a prime-time banshee. "I want you gone!"

"If you want me to go for now, yes, we can cool off. I'll take a drive. We can get breakfast tomorrow."

"Tomorrow is Saturday. I don't want to see you on Saturday. I want to see you at church on Sunday. I want to see you, in front of everyone, telling them who you are."

"That's a very hard thing to do. Maybe, first, we can work it out privately, keep this in the family, as family things should be."

"You will never see your children again."

"Daniella, please."

"I will tell Gertrude Breckenridge's husband, too. I will go right to him and he will be at this house with a shotgun. He will blow your skull to bits and find a sympathetic judge and walk in less than a decade because it will be a crime of passion and no one likes a lying, philandering, blasphemous, fraudulent fucking pastor poisoning their town. A rotten, sick outsider—imagine the jury that judges you, all these nice folk from around here, Luce County-born and raised. They'd show more mercy to a roach crawling around their daughter's bed."

"Let's just talk about this, we don't have to go out to dinner, let's just sit down and *talk*."

"If you think Harry Breckenridge is going to rot in prison for sending you to hell, well, you don't know much about the world, for all the scheming you've done."

"If I go to the bed-and-breakfast, they'll wonder why I'm there. The owner, Icky Hoy, bought a rental house from me last year. He's trying out landlording on the side."

"I don't care. Go up north. Go crawl in a ditch. Do everything but die, because I want you alive on Sunday morning. That's the last favor you'll do for me."

The Holliday Inn, eighteen minutes north on 127, takes me for two nights and gratefully doesn't know me from Adam. I pass over my credit card, grin and bear it at the wan thirtysomething behind the counter, and take my room, 204, at the ill-lit corner of a T-shaped hallway. This was, at one time, a Holiday Inn Express until the franchise, for reasons unclear, was abandoned, and new independent ownership rebranded with the same color scheme and an additional L. Locals don't seem to notice the difference. My room has a queen-size bed and a view of the parking lot.

I flip around the television until I land on a Tom Hanks movie, one that means nothing to me and exists in my mind without a definitive title. Hanks has always been, for me, one of the very worst and most overrated actors, a man who conned millions into believing dorm room–quality impressions of the mentally handicapped and spiritually stunted could define generations. My eyelids are heavy and I sleep fully clothed on top of the bed.

When I open them again, I've dreamed nothing. Plum-blue light is making its way behind my curtains. It is, my cell phone tells me, Saturday morning. The television is still playing and the Tom Hanks movie is long over.

What to do? There is no one to call. Everyone I might call has been compromised. I am teetering on destruction, if not outright destroyed already. Yoel made a real study of my life. He had watched me. Everyone of relevance has a care package. I understand this, now, because my phone, barely charged, begins to ring.

It's Big Landry.

I ignore him, as I do the call from Adrian Mueller. The morning passes this way, phone calls unreturned. They're undoubtedly conferring with Daniella. I can fathom, from my hotel walls, all of it—the insectoid murmuring and whispering in Pine Haven over my fate. *Have you heard about Pastor Teddy Starr? Do you think it's true?* Daniella wasn't wrong: small-town folk are hungry for prey, always. I wonder what she's told Theodore. She is someone who could, with ease, tell him. Surely, it must begin to dawn on her that she won't be salvaged if she follows her heart and her rage. She is righteous now, will hope to *stay* righteous—that's one of her talents—but she'll bend at the muddier reality ahead. She is taking the word of a nobody over me, someone who could be, if read correctly, an actual lunatic. Who sends anything in the mail? Yoel is one tick off from penning a manifesto, bomb attached.

I don't take any more calls. None are from Daniella. If she asked for forgiveness now, I would grant it to her. Of course, she might say *I* should ask for forgiveness—for my deviancies, for my lies. I should prostrate myself.

But she wouldn't have the Heart Road home, *her* dream, the very little manor she drove by as a child and tapped on the window and told her papa, one day, she'd live there. She wouldn't have Theodore, Chloe, and Austin. She could have had children with another man, of course, but they'd be wretched, ugly, and poor. They'd be imbeciles. What kind of stock does she think she's finding in Luce County?

I almost fling open the Holliday Inn windows, which are fastened shut by custom or law.

As the day slinks onward, warm and sunny from my window, Talia comes to me. Talia who would be forty now, perhaps with a family of her own, Talia Queen of Brooklyn or Talia Queen of nowhere, Talia who kissed me that night and taught me more than I might ever know that to grasp on to certain moments, if they are brilliant enough, is the purpose to life, to sink your fingers in bloody and never let go.

Talia doesn't know what became of me. She never will.

Let this town burn. Let all towns burn.

Let Yoel try to get himself home, bloody, from that nature preserve. Let his unctuous sausage fingers quaver over his cell phone and try to summon an Uber *there.* This isn't New York Fucking City, Yoel. Let him explain to the town cop who he is and what he is doing there; let him understand there is no such thing as shomer Shabbos here, that no God-fearing Christian wants anything to do with a heaving, kosher mess.

Nothing! Nothing! Nothing!

I can bull-rush the church tomorrow, my metaphorical or literal guns in the air, and tell them all what they think. That they don't deserve *me.* That my wife, in particular, would believe a letter from a stranger over her own husband, that she had failed to follow me and do her duty and now all of the congregation, all of Pine Haven of

Trinity—this glorious church, which I willed to its peak—is doubting its shepherd. I've imbibed the Bible; they've pecked at it like children after refrigerated bread scraps.

No one studies the Bible harder than a Jew who wants to forget.

No one studies harder than a man who needs to forget all he has done.

"Daniella, what would you have done?" I ask the full-length mirror, where I'm supposed to pose after arraying myself with my Saturday best. "What would you have done if you saw your father fall like that? If you were me?"

She can't imagine it. None of them can. They are stunted, static, deranged by routine. They don't know what it is to become what you want to become—a birth is bloody, a rebirth is fiery, metamorphosis is apotheosis, and none of it is as straightforward as grilling a porterhouse. It was hard work to become Teddy Starr. It was colossal work. If I handed Daniella or Big Landry or Brendan Hannon a hundred lifetimes, they could never arrive here—or not here, at the Holliday Inn, but where I was, circa yesterday morning.

I would like to see Daniella beg for change at rest stops on the Ohio Turnpike. I would like her to see her hawk scrap metal in Maumee, swab the floors of a Taco Bell in Detroit, or clean portable toilets at a construction site in Grand Rapids. I would like her to speak to no one, save her boss or the Mexicans in snatches of half-English, for nine consecutive months. I would like to see her scrunched like a fetus and shivering in a lightless and heatless basement apartment on her twenty-first birthday; I would like to see her, two days later, when she decided a new life must be had, one without cold or hunger or death, one where the light would burn brightly.

Teddy Starr—the name was a thunderclap. I wrote it once and twice and thrice and seventy more times on scraps of notebook paper, underlining each time, joggling between print and cursive, Teddy Starr and Teddy Starr and Teddy Starr.

The Holliday Inn is somnolent and dust-struck; I pass through the halls, nod gallantly to another clerk, and take my Chevy out of the parking lot and onto the local road back to 127. I want to drive home and tell my wife she can't destroy me. I want to find Yoel and destroy him. I want to do what I couldn't do yesterday and empty every last bullet into Yoel's shuddering body.

I want to drive straight into the nearest lake and feel the heavy, gray-green water pour deep and true into my lungs.

Instead of south, to Pine Haven, I swing farther north, the towns shrinking and becoming, through their namesakes, more Indian. This is the way to Mackinac Island, where I had taken Daniella and the children for several vacations, ferrying out and riding the horses and lapping up vanilla ice cream under a winking sun. There's no reason we can't go there again. Nothing *has* changed; I'm the same person I've always been.

A strange thought wheedles in: what if I had always been honest with Daniella? What if, when I was courting her, I told her I was not a merely a young pastor and real estate agent—soon to branch into owning and managing properties—but a New York native who converted from Judaism? What if I told her about my father?

What if she *knew*, when we first went out to dinner, I was born Reuvain Gantz?

I know what she would have done. I know what they all would have done. Daniella. Big Landry. Even Gertrude.

They all wouldn't have given me the time of day.

Life, for the Pine Havenites, is an orderly affair. Picnics and barbeques and homecoming dances and Sunday services and men's groups and flapjack festivals and fireworks and voting come November. Life is an arrowshot into the future, into the happy maw of death, and all should be as it is—as it is expected to be. Men like me aren't supposed to blow into town. They aren't supposed to find their footing, seize it, and rise—to triumph, to swagger, to eat up lucre and keep eating. I was *hungry*, Daniella. I *am* hungry.

I am greedy, but I am greedy for all of you.

Humming in the passing lane, nearing one hundred on a rocking stretch of 127, I glance down at my ringing phone. It's the first person I'd choose to speak to.

"Gertrude."

"Where are you?"

"It doesn't matter."

"You've really done it now."

"I haven't done anything. I've merely been myself, always."

"Harry was home when the package came. He thinks you're a deviant headed to hell."

"I'll see him there. Cerberus can gnaw off his scrotum while tearing at my arm."

"What are you going to do?"

"I'm preaching tomorrow, as always."

"I'm hearing the church council wants to call a vote. They'll want you gone."

"Not before tomorrow."

"You know them. They'll dither for the week and then stab you."

"Will you be there tomorrow?"

"I'll be there. I want to hear what you have to say."

"Your voice sounds light, Gertrude. Are you alone?"

"I'm in my car. I'm driving. You do amaze me in your own way, Teddy Starr."

"If the church votes me out, you'll never see me again. No one will."

"That's it, then? You're going to disappear and reappear in a new town with a new identity? This isn't the nineteenth century. Appleton, Minnesota, or wherever else is not going to have you. Teddy Starr's your last move."

"You don't know me, Gertrude."

"On the contrary. I never could have dreamed this, but it doesn't surprise me. Even the murder. You killed your father in cold blood. Have you read the letter? It's quite a letter."

"It's not true."

"Which part?"

The freeway forks and I continue north, weaving between two semis, one carrying products for Amazon, the other a Bugs Bunny–themed moving company you usually see closer to overcrowded, irony-drenched cities.

"I didn't kill my father in cold blood."

"You pushed him."

"It was an accident. It was not intended."

"Yet you pushed him hard enough. You were angry. And you fled."

"I needed to."

"I won't judge you. I don't judge you. In fact, I think you've reached the most interesting part of a life anyone can reach."

"I'm glad I can interest you."

"You're bitter because this all came to a head much sooner than you planned. But you're smart enough to know longing on this kind of scale can't be planned. Not only that, but can't be absent consequence."

"Longing?"

"To be new. To be you. To be the sniveling boy who did or didn't kill his father—to be standing wherever you were, in that rotten city—and be thrown into the future, into the new life. Your brother is weak. Your brother couldn't do this."

"Gertrude . . ."

"If you understand America, and understand yourself, you'll know what to do tomorrow."

She hangs up. I drive until I'm at the precipice of the Upper Peninsula, the Mackinac Bridge—inviolate and harp-like—strung over the silver-blue strait. I kill the engine and walk out. Fat bugs hang over me, black and gleeful, and I let them nibble my skin. Sitting in the grass, I watch the tankers divide the waves, so large and strange the more I squint, the more I try to discern the tired paradigm, man against nature, and how he flails up against it again and again and is thrown back like the sick little container of petty neuroses and frail bone he truly is, back into the cyclonic void where he belongs.

When the sky darkens, I drive to the hotel.

8

Trinity of Pine Haven is my own. I enter alone, and I'm draped in its silence. In one hour, the flock will begin to arrive, first for the Bible study I won't conduct and the Sunday school that Brendan Hannon's wife will presumably lead, as she always does. She hasn't been instructed otherwise, at least. I slip into my office and shut the door. I'll wait here for the first sounds outside.

Daniella hasn't called me. I don't know where she or my children might be. I don't know if she's bringing them to church. I don't know what the church is saying about me, other than that Big Landry called again and I didn't pick up. Sunlight inches across my desk. A strange bird raps on my window and flies away. There is only waiting, waiting, the putty of time stretched out to its dreary limits.

The plan will be to speak to my church. After that, I don't know.

Gertrude isn't wrong. There will be no third act; the reborn still die, and there's no other life I'd rather forge again. I close my eyes, recline, and wait for the rustle of life in my church. The putty of time, the soup of my brain, geologic shapes forming under my eyelids, beckoning to sleep . . .

And what's that sound? A ticktock knock that isn't subtle. My eyes open. The knock comes again, along with a guttural, phlegmy, and roaring voice that belongs to a man I know well. I shamble upward, peek out the window as if answers are offered me there, make my way to the door and open it up.

"Pastor, I thought you might be behind that door."

"Well, come on in and have a seat. No coffee here. I'm just pondering today's sermon."

"Have I come at a bad time?"

"Landry, for you, there's never a bad time."

Big Landry looms in my office, his thick thumbs in his belt-loops, a corkscrew smile on his face. He is early, the first to church, and I motion at him to close the door. There's a second chair, a black plastic pullout, and he settles his bulk in to face me, the smile beginning its slow fade.

"I hope you're doing all right," he says with a blend of earnestness and something else, perhaps acid-tipped curiosity. "I imagine it's been a difficult few days."

"Oh, not really. I've been here and there. I got a good night's rest."

"We've been having conversations, me and the board, you know—we value greatly all the work you've done for us here, at Pine Haven. You've built us into a real powerhouse and don't think I haven't noticed. There are people, and I won't name names, who want your hide now, who are on the warpath. People who've even spoken with Daniella, who has seemed to offer support for these allegations, or at least a lack of surprise. Though I was quite surprised, and they are allegations. A man is innocent until he is proven guilty. That is the American way."

"Tell me what you'd like to tell me, Landry."

"Well listen here," and he bends in real close, enough that I pick up the sprightly scent of his nicotine gum, "I don't want anything bad to happen. All a man has is his reputation."

"And his property."

"Of course, of course." Big Landry is sweating, his mottled skin gone peachy. His moustache shines extra white. "I want to make you an offer, all right. Man-to-man."

"Make it."

"You know this will get real ugly, real fast. I know Daniella's family. They're going to drain you for all you're worth. Del Justice has a vengeful streak. You've got quite a portfolio, some real prime properties and others that are ripe for growth. You were smart to get in on the trailer parks. As the college expands, there's conversion value there—five or ten years, those can be, with the right developer, little condos. Or starter homes. It would be a shame, really, if she ripped that all away. She's a lovely woman, but she doesn't have a sense of *value* like you and me, partner, like men who get it."

"I'm not selling to you, Landry."

I imagine, as he fights to keep his smile, his veins erupt with hot blood.

"It would be a fair deal, Pastor. And I didn't *finish*. I happen to know a church up in Alger County that could use some leadership. The pastor, he's a friend of my late mother-in-law, he's pushing eighty. He's bound to retire in a few years. It's a small church, you know, but there's room for growth. I can put in a recommendation for you. You work there, keep your head down, all of this won't matter. Jew, Christian, whatever's in your past—it's about hard work, up there."

"I'm not going to the Upper Peninsula."

"It's beautiful there! The UP! I've got a cabin, right near the Hiawatha. You'll fit right in. Plenty of winter sports and the summer, when the ice thaws, you should see it. Magical."

"I'm not going into exile in the forest."

Landry's smile, at last, gives way.

"Pastor—Teddy—I don't see what choice you have. I am being exceedingly generous. You have a connection here for a new church, to work under someone—"

"In a town of what—two hundred people?"

"A bird in hand, my friend, is worth more than two in the bush. And here, let me be honest with you, there are no fucking birds in the bush. Either your wife, soon-to-be-ex-wife, takes you for everything you're worth *and* you have no church to lead, or you make a square deal with me, walk away with a nice chunk of change and the opportunity to lead a new church one day. You don't want to go to the wilderness? Too much of a city boy? Well, tough shit."

"You can't make me run."

"You made yourself run, buddy. Do you know I almost believe you? *Almost*, that some psychopath came out of nowhere, mailed these letters and photos around, and made up a story to undercut a successful man like yourself. But naw—I can see it in your eyes. There's truth there. I know it. We all know it. You were always a little slick, Teddy. And I say this as someone who isn't so dry myself. I have no quarrels with the Jews, personally. I'll say that up front. Jews, they're a bit like blind mice trying to see. They're nearly where they've got to be. Not like a Muslim. Or, gosh, a Mormon."

"I'm a Christian. Now I'd like you to get out of my office."

Landry staggers upward. Behind him, through the door, I can hear the shuffling of feet, the low exhilaration of a Sunday crowd coming into being. It's my time, soon. Landry can't stop me from speaking to my own church.

"Last chance. We can talk numbers on your parcels. You sell to me, you'll lose much less than in court, fighting with Daniella. You're going to be dead broke, otherwise."

"Get out."

Landry says nothing else as he closes the door. I can still smell his nicotine gum. I lock the door, close my eyes, and wait for my time. It's coming.

Today, it's still my sermon to give.

Bind the unwinding of America to the dissolution of the Sunday morning, and see here how resurrection is possible. The pews are filling with waiting, hungry faces, their eyes bright with the sunlight of a new summer. They shimmer, my flock, even as they begin to bend my way, their wet lips crinkling, curiosity comingling with fury. Whatever has passed between them cannot be accessed by me; not now, anyway. I've been away from them a week, which amounts to a lifetime, and I haven't seen my wife and children for nearly two enormous and peculiar days, days that might determine everything from here until death. I've only spoken to Gertrude and Big Landry and I've learned enough.

I feel oxidized and ancient, like that statue bestriding the Rhodesian harbor, my brassy flesh collapsing into the brine. They gape at my crumbling. Among them, my wife, who has brought Chloe, Austin, and a simmering Theodore, who doesn't meet my eye. I amble to the pulpit, waving still, Adrian Mueller at the front reading off the announcements, his reminder that the men's group bowling outing is next Thursday. He is paler when he sees me and stumbles over a vowel. They might have believed I would turn into vapor and my willingness to make this all so incessantly *physical* unnerves them. Their little thoughts titter: *Why is he here? What is he doing?* I step up to the stage, where Adrian is handing me the microphone, and I take my usual position, behind the modest pulpit and in front of our modest projector, which beams up the lyrics to the hymns we sing before my sermon.

"Hello and welcome to another wonderful day here at Trinity of Pine Haven. And thank you, Adrian, for keeping us so well informed. What are we without community? What are we without each other?"

I watch the tightening of the lips, the hardening of the eyes. They do not want their pleasant Sunday roiled. They want me to speak quickly and leave. They want some version of what Big Landry wants: for the ickiness to subside, for order to be restored. Unlike Landry, most of them don't long for power for themselves. They have better angels, or *are* better angels. They simply, like me, want reality restored, want what they believed before Yoel intervened and violated all that they knew. I still don't know how many letters Yoel mailed. It's possible every single person sitting in the pews got one.

"I want to thank you all for coming again today. I want to thank everyone who has been so involved in this church, for making it strong, for making it a beacon of Jesus in this beautiful town. Before today's sermon, which I'm very excited about, I want to briefly address what you might have heard these last few days. I want to use this time to be honest with you, to help you understand what you might have heard or read."

I survey all the faces. Daniella, Theodore, Big Landry Shocker, Adrian Mueller, Brendan Hannon, Gertrude Breckinridge, Gregg Eggles, Titus Shimski, April Kleinschmidt, Bob Saddlebrook—they are all turned to me like expectant moons, heavy with the morning light pouring through the long windows. I straighten my shoulders, lean in, and consider what it is, exactly, I'm supposed to say.

"You have heard many things and none of them change who I am, how much I care about all of you, and how much I care about this church. None of them change my relationship with Jesus."

In New York, Jesus Christ is a swear word. *Jesus Christ*—not a far cry from damn, shit, fuck. It is better understood as Jeezus or Geezus. Chr-*eye*-st. Here, even now, when I say his name, the church hushes. The name will never lose its power. I will gild their ears.

"I am a disciple, like you all, of Jesus. Now and forever."

I am watching Landry. He has big, swollen, hunting eyes, mildly bloodshot, and he is not smiling. He is counting my properties, one by one, and how much he'll flip them for, in another year, after I slide them over to him at a crippling discount.

"But once, I was not. Once, I followed the wrong path. Once, in fact, I was bathed in darkness. I am sorry for not being honest with you about that. I am sorry for not being forthright. I felt great shame. Imagine the most shameful fact of your life, and multiply it fifty-fold. Imagine how much it might burn you inside.

"I was a Jew, yes! I was not baptized until adulthood. I spent years in sin. Once baptized, I decided to change my name, to reflect who I was, to reflect the Lord's light in my life, to reflect how I had, like all of you, accepted Jesus Chris as our Lord and savior. I sought redemption. In New York City, I was not living the life I wanted to live. I sometimes think, if everyone in New York City—all the deniers of Jesus, all the atheists, all the heathens—had a revelation like this, we would have a glorious kingdom right here, right now. And I think, too, of Israel, under attack, and how they have been God's people too since the days of Abraham. The Jewish return to Israel brings us closer to the return of Jesus Christ, closer to our last war. Where will Jesus set up his throne? In the kingdom of Jerusalem. As I was called away from my sin, I began to feel this, and when I learned it—when I studied the Bible with all my heart—it made perfect sense, in the way sunshine makes sense. It's in the scripture—those who bless Israel will be blessed. . . ."

They squirm, they blanch; Landry is grinning because he knows, perhaps, this won't work. My appeal is theological and they merely see a liar, someone who said they were one way and are in fact another. They merely count my lies. Regaining trust, maybe, isn't so different than regrowing a limb. It just doesn't happen, not really, not unless science becomes fiction.

If I have any hope, I'll have to reach past trust, even transcend it. I can almost hear my father.

"There is something else that you might have heard. A man claiming to be my brother said I, in New York, killed my father. This is not true. The man, indeed, is my brother. But he is the one who killed. It was an accident. He pushed my father down the stairs. He has long struggled with mental illness. He followed me here, to Pine Haven, and menaced me. I felt bad for him and didn't call the police. I'll be honest—that was a mistake. He confronted me and threatened me with my life. He is very ill. I do feel sorry for him. I should have been forthright about that, with all of you—many of us have experiences with family members who struggle with mental illness, addiction, or something they cannot control. The Lord can help them. I pray for my brother. He needs Jesus in his life. He needs guidance.

"But I will *thank* him—though he lied, he forced me to be more honest with all of you. I will tell you everything. I was named Reuvain Gantz. I was Jewish. I legally changed my name and converted. I was not born here, but I am raising my family here. Pine Haven is my home. It will always be my home, if you will have me. And this church will always be my church, if you will have me."

Landry is one barometer. Daniella is another. As they wilt, I know I am gaining ground. I know my church. I know when to keep pressing, keep charging.

"It's more important than ever we stick together, that we unite as a congregation. I've seen darkness. I've seen sin. I've seen what demonic forces do. I've stood athwart it all, rejected it, chosen Jesus over damnation. Today, in this country, we have a great evil. We have people, powerful people, who swim with the snakes. You are with God, or you are against God. America is a godly country. We are a godly people. But look around you today. Whether it's the glorification of the slaughtering of the unborn, the glorification of polyamory, adultery, avarice, deviant lifestyles, the eradication of gender—whether it's an entire political party aligned against *us*, that wants to take God out of American life and have us worship false idols, it's more important than ever that we are united, that we stand firm in our faith.

"We are just a little church here, on God's green and plentiful Earth," and I begin to pace, my chest rolling with heat, my flesh pulsing, "and we are besieged from all sides. We are besieged by godless elites, frothing on the coasts, who savage our way of life and lie to us—lie like any fork-tongued serpent might, to trick you into hating this country and hating who you are. They don't want you to live a Christian life. They don't want you to live *any* life. This is a war! I want you to understand this. War! War!"

I slam my hands and shake the pulpit.

"There are enemies who want to destroy me and destroy you. My brother—he, sadly, is one of them. He does not want me to walk with Jesus. Think of all those in your life who do everything they can to tempt you away, who idle like demons and long to trick you, to force you into sin. I wish it weren't so—I wish there weren't darkness gathering. I wish I could stand up here and preach peace and love, peace and love. I wish that's all it took. Imagine how easy it would be if we could save this country only that way. But we are holy warriors too—we are warriors for Jesus. We march out into the world, confronting the evil arrayed against us. We march out there, proud, proud to be worshippers, proud to live in God's light, proud to be of *this* wondrous church, Trinity of Pine Haven."

I slam my hands again.

"Tell me. Are you with me? Are you with God? Will you join me in this fight? I will lay down my life to fight evil—I am ready, and I am ready for Jesus to take his seat on the throne. The day is coming. Are you ready? Will you fight?"

"I'll, I'll fight."

It's the unsteady voice of Gregg Eggles.

"I'll fight, too," his wife adds.

"And me, I'll fight," says April Kleinschmidt.

They call and respond, call and respond, until the church is a great wave, *I'll fight I'll fight I'll fight I'll fight I'll fight I'll fight. I'll fight.*

And finally, trembling, there's Big Landry. He is suddenly loudest of all.

"I'll fight!"

"Yes," I cry back. "Let's fight!"

I behold my church, my church for all time. I beam at my flock of hundreds, soon to swell as word trickles out—we are the fighting church. We are the church that will *win* the culture war. We are the church that will, like Americans in 1945, do whatever it takes to secure our future. They are standing, cheering, even clapping. I slam the pulpit again.

I wait for Daniella to clap too.

It's taken time, but I've swam my way back to shore. I sleep in my marriage bed with my wife. She's coming around—I can note the slight upturning of her lips, the willingness to hold my gaze—and she'll be settled in once the town is settled in; we're already *in motu*, the wheels turning, the necessary arrangements coming into order. Big Landry, for example, has forgotten all about the UP. I've preached another sermon since, and all is nigh hunky-dory, save for the occasional quizzical stare from the pews. But uniformity is a challenge, and may not even be an ideal—I can make peace with the fact that, for a little while at least, a few congregants will have a few questions about Teddy Starr. I have time, at least, to knock back all the lies, especially since my rousing address to the flock righted so many ships. We're all in this fight, after all, against the enemies of the church.

I don't expect to see Yoel, that viper, again. He's smart enough to know when he's licked. He's met the army of Pine Haven, witnessed genuine loyalty, and will now beat it on back to New York. I have half a mind to hire my own private eye to tail *him* for a while, have my grizzled mercenary file sporadic updates from a smoke-filled Camaro on Avenue P, noting where Yoel has been and exactly when he's been there and amassing vulnerabilities for any potential counterstrikes on my part. I won't be surprised again.

It's a sun-spackled Friday, and I'm in a fair mood. In the office, they're still *processing*—to borrow a shred of psychobabble, which I really do despise—the recent revelations and what it means for our real estate enterprise. The answer: nothing! Money is being made. Sue Piffle, at least, gets this. She is as sunny as ever. I've made no accounting with her yet, and perhaps that's a mistake, as rumors tend to metastasize. But I've suffered no defections, and Sue is always on time, bright and ready to work. I tell her, around three, I'm heading home early, to see my family. What I don't mention is it's Theodore I'm after. He's not batting balls at one of his practices and won't be over at the Hannon household until the late afternoon.

We've got some business to settle, now that the noise around my so-called *narrative* is dying down. Chloe and Austin are young enough that all of this commotion will be like one jetliner overhead to them, lost in the deep clouds, and whatever explanation I proffer—*if* I ever do—will be plump with the residue of time's sweet passage. They may howl for a few minutes, ask a round of tedious questions, hustle (without my permission) to a school therapist, and spend the back half of adolescence piling up resentments, but that will be, mark my words, a very flimsy pile. He's a daddy's boy, she's a daddy's girl. We'll barrel through it.

Theodore is older, and susceptible to Daniella. I know my wife isn't fully sailing in my skiff yet. Time takes time, et cetera. I do fret Theodore. One, he's said very little to me since Yoel spewed his inanities, and two, he probably will have to answer for this among his friends, who are, at that age, going to motormouth their days away. If not celebrity gossip, then *my* gossip. And nothing beats a homegrown tale. I admit I've been slow to stamp it all out, to merely take enough satisfaction in the survival of my church and the thwarting of Landry's scheme while not playing offense, as I'm wont to do in other situations. But this is all *new*, after all, raw and still a tad bloody, and I've got to cut myself slack. Self-flagellators earn little but their own blood.

In the Chevy, I make haste to Hearst Road, blasting air-conditioning to mitigate against any undue sweat on my chest or back. I'm composed, but I need to look it, too. My son can't think of his father as someone who isn't as commanding as he's always been. If I lose my authority, what family is left?

I don't immediately see Daniella's car. I very much hope she hasn't taken Theodore and the kids on a shopping errand. If so, I don't know when I'll see them again. Meijer alone can be a vortex, and she may feel ambitious enough to work in a jaunt to Target. But behold, in our living room, my wife, safe and sound. She's watching television, Chloe and Austin to each side of her. It's one of those 2000s Disney movies we're supposed to feel nostalgic about but I can't muster much emotion for.

"The gang's all here!" I call out, embedding as much merriment in my voice as I can. Chloe and Austin squeal for their daddy and Daniella says absolutely nothing. It's one of those afternoons. She is unmoving when it comes to that blaring TV, and me.

"Is Theodore around?" I ask.

Daniella does not look up.

"He should be in his room."

"Very good."

I bid them a brief farewell and glide upstairs. I'm hit, temporarily, with the wave of another memory, my climbs to Gertrude's room. Those trips, for the time being, are on hiatus. Harry has returned, but I sense Gertrude is another one, like Daniella, who needs a moment or three to take a thorough accounting of the developments. I'm not too concerned. She'll bend back. We have an understanding, and understandings, in my experience, aren't readily extinguished. The future has plenty of greenery for us both and we'll stretch toward it, in due time; we'll amble back to each other and find ourselves, once more, in a pleasant enough tangle. Late afternoon was always my favorite time with Gertrude. But I'm here, in my own home, and though Daniella and I share a bed again, we haven't been intimate. I plan, soon, to change that state of affairs. Daniella can only resist for so long.

I shove that thought away, though, and reorient to the task at hand. I'm not here, on the threshold of my son's door, to simply make amends, to settle up and explain away. For one, I'm not sure *what* I should explicate, and how—he understands the sketch of it, my former name, my sojourn from New York, and a malevolent brother who attempted to end me. He knows his father would never intentionally kill anyone. I don't know how much I should spell out for him, what's necessary and what's needlessly incriminating. What is a child owed? I knock on the door lightly, wait, and announce myself. *It's Dad* sounds surprisingly choked in my throat.

"Yeah?" I hear from behind the door, my son's toneless reply.

"I'd like to come in."

"Door is open."

I nudge it open and see my son, in a Pistons jersey with a cotton T-shirt underneath, sprawled on his bed and staring into his phone. Like his mother, he doesn't look up at me.

"How's everything. Theodore?"

"Fine."

Oh, how I loathe monosyllabic replies.

"It must have been more than *fine*. Days are long, filled with all kinds of sensations."

"Mine was fine."

He still isn't looking at me.

"Did you do anything exciting?"

"Not really."

I decide, then, I'll run headlong, right at it. Sometimes the lancer's got to charge the armored car.

"There's something I'd like to discuss with you, Theodore."

The blue light fills my son's face, and he says absolutely nothing.

"It's important," I try again. "Very important."

"Okay."

"It's more than *okay*. Or, maybe it's not. Maybe it's actually not okay, at all. Why don't you look up from that phone? You can text Garrett later."

"I'm not texting Garrett."

"That's fine. It doesn't matter who it is. Would you—would you look up from your device? If you don't, I'm going to take it away and you won't get it back."

"You wouldn't do that," he says, eyes bearing down on his screen.

"Excuse me?"

"It would be social suicide. To not have a phone at school."

"Social suicide . . . I confess, that's not my priority when it comes to my family."

"Of *course* it is. I'm barely going to hang on, as it is, when I go back—not after what you did. Everyone's talking about it. Take the phone, do it. See what happens. See what it means to have me walk through school afterward. Give it your best shot."

I count off several beats in my head and let the froth recede; I cannot, at this point, let my temper get the best of me, especially with my son. Sprezzatura is underrated, especially in patriarchs. Around here, men think they have to be Big Old Dads, bellowing until they're halfway to heart attack land and their brood are cowering in a corner from all the swears and spittle. This is weakness, not strength, and I won't indulge. Children often desire, without knowing it, such a spectacle from their parents. They can crabwalk to a moral *higher* ground that way, and begin to justify their own behavior to themselves, all of it the fault of their braying Pa. I know better.

"Listen, Theodore, I know it's been hard for you lately."

"You don't know anything."

"I do know," and I decide, right there, I'll make my charge, "that friendship is very important. That you lean on friends to get through whatever might be a challenge. How is Garrett?"

My son doesn't answer. He is fully screen-gorged. Since he is turned from me, I can't make out what it is he's staring at.

"Garrett is an interesting boy," I continue. "When you were with him, at the jubilee, what was it you were doing? That TikTok challenge? Was that his idea?"

This time, my son's lips begin to move.

"What does it matter?"

"I want to know if you're originating these ideas or he's having an influence on you. I want to know if you're telling the truth."

"It doesn't—"

"No, it *does*. I need to know what's happening here, under my roof, with my son. How does Garrett feel about girls?"

"He feels what he feels."

"What about you, Theodore? What do you think? What do you feel?"

I wait and wait, and he is silent.

"You can tell me. What do you think of girls? Boys? Who do you like? I'd like to know if you and Garrett are friends, real friends, or this is something that should concern me."

For the first time, Theodore lowers his phone and breaks from his pose on the bed. He sits up and slowly turns toward me, the phone falling away. He is getting lanky, a quarter inch taller since the spring, and in two or three years, we will probably be eye to eye.

"I don't know," he replies, a strain of huskiness in his voice I don't particularly enjoy. "What do *you* think, Roo-vain?"

One beat, two beats, three beats—breaths are critical here, gulps of them, because I can't do to my son what should be done under the most just circumstances. A past-life version of myself, off on the prairie perhaps, could have stepped back and thrown a streetfighter's jab straight into my son's jaw, and gotten kudos from the town elders for keeping the home in order.

"You be quiet now, Theodore. Close that mouth of yours." He is standing now, his back ramrod straight, and there's the whisper of a smile on his lips.

"That's your name, isn't it?" he asks.

I close the distance between us. If I wanted to, I could pick the Rice Krispies crumbs out of his teeth.

"Homosexuality *is a sin*. Do you understand this? Does Garrett? I thought God was in that household."

"Lying is a sin. Murder is a sin."

"Homosexuality, Theodore—"

"Lying! Murder! Lying! Murder!"

He resembles me, Theodore, and he's got the punch-back instinct that can put a grown man into jeopardy if it isn't properly calibrated. He'll learn, soon enough. I can only do what I do now—grab him, hard, by the forearm and squeeze—and modulate myself so a point is merely made, not made permanent. I'm not here to incapacitate my son.

"Listen. You listen now. . . ." I'm even closer now, my head bent so my eyes lock completely with his own. "You are going to be quiet."

"You, you . . . you're—"

But the little boy returns, and he relents as I ease up the pressure on his arm. Small teardrops force their way out and dampen his cheeks.

"I don't know who you are," he says, very softly now. "I don't know . . ."

"I'm your father, Theodore. I'm your father and I love you. Even in sin—when you sin—I love you."

I wrap my arms around him and pull him into my chest. It's a light, pleasant crunch, and his tears begin to dry. I press tighter, stripping whatever rancor I may have out of my voice.

"I'm your father. That's all you need to know. That's all you'll ever need to know."

Behind me are familiar footsteps, popping off the landing and heading straight for us. I swivel to offer my greetings.

"What's going on?" Daniella asks, standing on the threshold of Theodore's room.

"Would you like to join us?"

I show Daniella what this is: a father and son, hugging it out. The tableau is all-American, and soon Theodore's eyes will be bone-dry.

"The modern world is a lot of flimflam, and we don't make time for each other—not like we should. That's the truth. Theodore was up here, we had a little talk, and we decided to hug. He's in high school now, a precarious time, and we've got to show him love. Come here, Daniella."

I beckon her to our two-man hug-huddle. I haven't let Theodore go. He's making, almost imperceptibly, a mewling sound, like a restless kitty.

"Are you okay, Theodore?" Daniella asks.

My boy knows what to do. He nods, right at his mother, and she draws closer. The three of us are together now, and I hook an arm around Daniella's thin shoulder.

"We are Starrs. We stick together," I say. "Never, ever forget that. No matter what happens, we are a family. If one of us breaks—if one of us wavers—we *all* break. That's the crucial thing, and the only thing."

I've got them both, my wife and my boy. Daniella won't look up at me now, but she will again. We'll graze each other and all will be as it's supposed to be.

The phone in my home office rings a handful of weeks later. Theodore is at his baseball practice and Daniella is watching the little ones in the backyard. I don't recognize the number and pick up.

"Pastor Starr," comes a voice that's suddenly familiar.

"Yes, speaking."

"This is Buck, Buck Shasta. How're you today?"

"Congressman! It's great to hear from you."

"Hey well, usually I'm calling people to ask them for money and then they're trying to gouge my eyes out through the wires until, well, finally I get my max check. But I'm not looking for any money today. How is everything with you, Pastor? Your name has been getting around a lot."

"Oh, it has?"

"One of my staff passed along that clip of your speech. Everything is uploaded to YouTube these days, huh?"

"We put up all of our sermons."

"This one, it seems, went a little viral. People like it. They like you. You're an interesting guy, aren't you? Vigor for miles."

"Thank you, congressman."

"Listen, I'll cut right to it and tell you why I'm calling. I'm not going to run for reelection, after all. DC is about as pleasant as a bucket of warm piss, as you can imagine. And an opportunity came up that pays me a bit more than nothing—PricewaterhouseCoopers wants me as a policy adviser, given I served on Ways and Means. Good payday, work out of Lansing, and I can stay the heck away from airplanes. I've been thinking on who should run for my seat and I was bouncing around names with my staff and, you know, I thought of you."

"You want me to run?"

"Don't sound bashful. You're not bashful. You're what, the Jewish pastor? You're probably full of shit. Or you *are* full of shit. I don't know. Hey, Trump is full of shit and I'm for Trump. I'm for Trump *hard*. No radicals are gonna impeach him again on my watch. But I saw what it was to be a bulldozer, to be a maniac, to bulldoze nonstop and well, damn it, *look* at you. I'll be honest too—the bench around here is thin. Real thin. Some loopy state senator will probably run but I want a man of God in the seat, I decided."

"I—that's great to hear. Incredible. Obviously, I have my church, my property management company—"

"Yeah yeah, you won't be the first full of shit, man of God, paper millionaire to go to Congress. You'll fit right in. I never could wheel and deal like that. I admire you, Pastor. I could see you slapping your name on a big golden hotel. Or, at least, I see you speechifying. My staff and I rewatch that clip. You sure gave them hell. Do you mind if I say that? Hell? You're a man of God, I know."

"Congressman, you can say whatever you want, don't worry about me."

"If I endorse you, it's a done deal. The loopy state senator can't raise the money anyway. Just raise a mill and that'll scare everyone off. You can raise a mill?"

"I think so, if I put my nose to the grindstone."

"Grindstone, right. You know people. You know how it goes. Ask for the max, right away, don't waste time with anyone who can't get you at least two grand a pop. I see something in you. Congressman Teddy Starr. Sounds good, doesn't it?"

"I think I can get used to it."

"And listen, you'll get richer once you leave. Quick question before I go. Do you mind if I ask something a bit intrusive?"

"Ask away, congressman."

"Did you kill your father?"

"No, I did not."

The sentence pours out of me with surprising ease. I hear Shasta clear phlegm through the landline.

"Well good. Do I believe you? Maybe. Do I believe Trump? Well, I better. It's his party until he's dead. You're a brawler too, Pastor. I saw the red in your eyes, oh boy, when you were on that pulpit."

"You'll endorse me, then."

"If you want in, it's yours. I'm with you. I want to see what you do. What did you say? *Let's fight, let's fight.* I love that. You see the barbarians at the gate, don't you?"

"I do."

"This country is changing fast, Pastor Starr. Before you know it, you won't even have a country. Sock your change away. In the meantime, it's fun to see your name, big and bright, on a storefront. And muck it up at a White House Christmas party."

"It's been a long time since I've been to Washington."

"The food's okay. Well, I should go. I gotta cut some ribbon somewhere. Think hard about it. Pastor Teddy Congressman Starr."

"I will, congressman. Thank you."

He hangs up. I lean back and sigh gratefully. His offer, with each passing second, grows more enticing. Once, I would have been dismissive. The temporal ways of politics, against the church, always seemed crude, or at least flighty. But I run over some logistics: I could still fly back to preach Sundays. I could skip once in a while and cultivate a junior pastor. My properties could be managed well enough; I wouldn't put the personal touch on rent collection anymore. Politics, really, is a natural next step, and it wouldn't be forever. I could see how I like it. Buck served ten years. And maybe other opportunities could arise—the governorship, the senate . . . and beyond that. Forty is the new thirty. In politics, it's practically twenty. After all the mishigas of earlier, I could use a fresh start.

Well, really, I *deserve* one.

I stroll to the backyard. There's Daniella, delicately sprawled in a chaise longue, her skin singed a mild rosé, her eyes shielded by the $850 Louis Vuitton sunglasses I bought for her last year. One finger is raised like a wand, tap-tapping her phone. Gwennie naps in the shade.

"Guess who I got off the phone with?"

"No idea," she says, not looking at me.

"Buck Shasta. It was Buck Shasta. He wants me to run for Congress."

She breathes and her expression shifts subtly, like sand.

"He's not running again?"

"He's leaving. A job in the private sector opened up. He wants me to run. He'll endorse me. It's practically a done deal."

Chloe is playing with two Barbies, one in each pudgy fist, and Austin nudges a red rubber ball with his foot. Daniella turns, as if she's about to call out to them. Her lips stay closed.

"It's done, Daniella. I think I'm going to do it."

Summer is here. The humidity is like a closing fist around my throat. Soon, we'll be up to the cabin, splashing poolside and then onto the lake, puttering around in a motorboat. If Daniella would kiss me again, all would be as it was; my ascension is assured and I want her with me, scraping the stars.

"I don't know," she begins, her voice low, her eyes still hidden from me, "what it is, exactly, you want me to say."

"A wife should support a husband, as a husband supports a wife."

"A wife . . ." Daniella is still gazing at our children, trying to see into them or past them, her wand finger retracting. ". . .I am that, I suppose. In church, that was my thought: *I am his wife.* My father always said it was a choice. I called him again and that's what he told me, with a caveat. To choose."

"Do tell what that caveat might be."

"Your success. As long as you keep the illusion alive. As long as you keep your waxen wings."

"You always had a way with metaphor."

Daniella still isn't looking at me. Her wand finger is down and her phone is resting blankly on her bare thigh. Within me, pin-pricks of rage begin to push forth.

"Run or don't run. None of it will change who you are. Not even if they elect you president. You will be exactly what you are."

"What am I? I love you, Daniella."

Daniella keeps her lips pursed. The pinpricks are grenades, each one ready to be pulled. I take a deep, heavy breath, and let the warm air rush out of my nostrils.

"You have nothing to say? You can't even turn your neck toward me?"

"You haven't even apologized to me."

"Apology? Fine. Yes. I'm sorry. There. Sorry. Sorry. Sorry."

A long, slow smile leaks across Daniella's face. Her shadow, at high noon, is tucked away, and she stretches her swanlike legs out, so her painted toenails hang like little cherries over the quivering edge of the lounge chair. I smile back. We're on a glide path—she can see what I see, the unfolding tomorrows, the victories and the sunshine, the inarguable power in our union, the power that won't be denied. She won't leave what I've given her, what I've shown her, what I can continue to give her as I rocket—with all of us—into the future.

"That's all?" she asks. Her smile is as bright as I've seen it in weeks.

"*All?* What else is there? You were there at church. You saw how they cheered. I told you, too, about Buck Shasta, what he's offering. Even Landry believes in me—Landry who wanted, for a hot minute, to bleed me of all I was worth, all *we* were worth. Daniella, this is bigger than all of us. We are a family. And we *are* this town. We're going to do so much more. You're not even forty. We have so much left to conquer."

"You'll never know," she says, still smiling, "what you've destroyed. You'll never know how I feel when I look at you. You'll never know what *they* think when they look at you. You'll never, ever, ever know. Oh, to be you—to be that vile."

I want to shout and bray, slam my chest, rip up a fistful of freshly cut grass and fling it on her like napalm. I want to do so much. But I can't, and I won't—we've come too far. She'll understand eventually. She always does. I'll just have to keep showing her. A $640 pair of flats can become a $3,640 pair. An overnight stay at a church retreat can become a White House Christmas party. A six-bedroom on Hearst Road can become a veritable manor in the country. If she wants us to build a tennis court with a swimming pool, we'll build that court. Laykold, GreenSet, or old-fashioned clay—her choice.

"I detect a little bitterness," I say, keeping my voice steady and clean, at a pulpit cadence. "Look, I could have handled this better. I wish I told you about my brother, my upbringing. I wish I told you about the other women. It was all very embarrassing to me. But here we are. Look around you." I spread my arms wide, taking in, as much as I can, our golden three quarters of an acre, the in-ground pool and vegetable garden and two children laughing in the trimmed grass. "Look at this—this is our life. What does the past matter? We have everything here. We have wealth, we have health, we have the town, the church, the people who love us, who look up to *you*—the first lady of Pine Haven. In the end, wasn't it worth it? In the end, we're here. We're here! It all worked out in the end."

Daniella crosses her legs and brushes the bridge of her nose, the sunglasses wobbling at her touch. She is staring straight into me, her eyes nearly visible through the glassy murk.

"In the end?"

She smiles as wide as I've ever seen her smile. There is, from her lips, the honeyed tinge of laughter. Her sunglasses slide off, her pupils large and shining and naked. I am all she sees.

"Nothing, Reuvain Gantz, ever ends."